A Taste For Hell

The Black Cat Series

Kendall McKenzie

For all of the grumpy, spooky, angry, morally gray girls out there. For the girls who were told to be softer, more polite, more accommodating, more submissive—and refused. You are more than enough. You are everything. You are seen. You are loved.

This one's for you.

AUTHOR'S NOTE

Hey, y'all. Let's talk content warnings for A Taste For Hell.

The Black Cat Series is intentionally inclusive, diverse, and loving towards BIPOC and LGBTQIA+ communities. I will never write anything otherwise and hope that readers find safety and comfort with that in mind.

A Taste For Hell features a lot of fun, laughs, and cozy moments to balance out the hard stuff, but please be aware of the following:

- One of the main overall themes is religious trauma, and the text is critical of Christianity as well as the institution of the church.
- Our FMC is a former Christian turned pagan and practices witchcraft.
- Our FMC faces discrimination based on her spiritual practice, as well as some bullying and bad treatment from her community.
- Anxiety, depression, intrusive thoughts, self-criticism, and panic attacks are featured.
- There is **no** sexual violence, but the story does feature loss of personal agency through spiritual attack, as well as lost time.
- Terminal illness is a main plotline (respiratory-related).
- These characters have filthy mouths—expect lots of swearing.
- Expect some gore, scares, and spooky, disturbing, and upsetting imagery. It's horror, after all.
- Expect monsters, ghosts, demons, possession, and talking to the dead.
- Our characters are chaotically horny and have dirty thoughts. Dirty thoughts are in many of the chapters.
- There is spice. The spice is graphic. For those who wish to skip (or locate—*wink*) that content, I will flag the chapters here: 37 and 38 have full spice; 27, 35, and 39 get pretty saucy.

CHECK OUT THE BLACK CAT PLAYLIST

These chapters have a vibe:

Chapter 1: "Black Magic" – Magic Wands
Chapter 3: "Resting B*tch Face: Part 2" – Julia Wolf
Chapter 4: "Spooky (Single Version)" – Dusty Springfield
Chapter 10: "Hot Blooded" – New Constellations
Chapter 12: "Hoops" – Julia Wolf
Chapter 15: "Autumn Tree" – Milo Greene
Chapter 17: "Where the Kids Are" -- Blondfire
Chapter 18: "A GOOD DAY TO D13" – Arankai
Chapter 19: "DEAD THRONE" – Arankai
Chapter 27: "Black Magic Woman" – VCTRYS
Chapter 31: "Demons" – Doja Cat
Chapter 32: "Nightride - Revisited" – A.L.I.S.O.N
Chapter 35: "Crush" – Cannons
Chapter 37: "Savages" – Kerli
Chapter 38: "Sick" – Donna Missal
Chapter 41: "Fall For Me" – Sleep Token
Chapter 42: "What It Cost" – Bad Omens
Chapter 43: "In the Air Tonight" – Natalie Taylor
Chapter 44: "Midnight" – Siobhan Sainte
Chapter 45: "Me and the Devil" – Gil Scott-Heron
Chapter 46: "Terrible Thing" – AG
Epilogue: "Deathproof" – Graveyard Club
Credits roll: "The Witching Hour" – Kerli

CHAPTER 1

The knife bit into Frankie Wolfe's finger as she squeezed blood drops onto the lines of her summoning circle. Right on top of the dandelion root. The drops hissed and floated up into black whisps.

"Is that supposed to happen? You didn't say anything about *blood sacrifices*," Juliette whisper-hissed the last words as if they were filthy.

Juliette. Client. Forties. Blonde bob. Insufferable. Her child needed help, which was the only reason Frankie was here. Frankie hated this woman and said a quick prayer to the goddess for this job to be worth the paycheck.

Frankie glared at her from the floor of her daughter's bedroom. "As I said, you don't need to be here for this." She thumped an animal skull in the center of the circle, which was entirely unnecessary for this particular working, but she hoped it would scare her client back downstairs.

It did not.

Eye twitching, Frankie pointed toward a window, and it blew open for her with a gust of October wind.

"What's that for?" Juliette butt in again.

For fuck's sake.

"An open, west-facing window gives the spirit a place to go after being cast out."

Before Juliette could totally ruin the mood, Frankie's eyes rolled back into

1

her head (also unnecessary but very effective at appearing dramatic), and she started whispering the words to her spell.

The candles flickered and stilled. Early dusk air also stilled. Street noise faded away.

"I'm telling you, it's just a little girl and I just need her to stop waking my daughter in the middle of the night," Juliette huffed. It was the fourth time she had said this, and it didn't make the statement true.

"Juliette, for fu—"

The stink hit first: sulfur and ash. Juliette gagged, and Frankie's eyes snapped to a dark corner of the room. Little feet in little shoes edged out from the shadow and into the circle, compelled to enter it by Frankie's spell. The rest of the shadows peeled back, revealing a young girl, maybe six. Shoulder-length black hair, overalls, and a pale blue shirt. White eyes, no pupils, no irises. Her skin smoked.

"See? I told you!" Juliette seethed over watering eyes, fanning the air in front of her.

Frankie barreled on through the working before Juliette could fully sabotage the cleansing. Before she'd have to come back to this horrible family's house.

"Evening. What's your name sweetie?" she asked the spirit with a saccharine smile, knowing the question would piss it off.

A low growl came from the child. Its voice was constructed of many whispers and a hollow echo. "I know who you are, and I will not leave."

"Totally get it," Frankie replied, cracking her knuckles. The child's face twisted at the noise. Frankie smirked. Juliette had finally stopped talking—thank fuck—and stood shaking in the doorway.

Frankie retrieved her bloody knife and pulled her bag closer. The child's face became enraged as it stepped closer to see what she was doing.

"Put away your herbs, *witch*," it hissed at her.

"No, I don't think I will." She thumbed over the vials of oil in her bag—wouldn't be needing those today. This was a fire-based situation. And the paycheck from this level of spirit would pay her electric bill, but not the rent for her store. No reason to use the good stuff. She pulled out a bundle of dried cedar. Her sight never leaving the child, she said, "Gotta pay the bills, you know how it is."

The child stepped to the innermost circle where Frankie was sitting. Its head tilted at Frankie before slamming a tiny child's fist into her cheekbone. A cheap shot. Hot, white stars exploded over her vision, and a burn ripped up her nostrils. She knew what would come next. Blood dripped out over her shirt and onto the wood floor. She wiped under her nose in vain, smearing the mess around. Her new black eye hadn't caused this—this was a supernatural nosebleed.

"This is why I wear black," Frankie said, mostly to herself. "But *you* didn't need to get all dressed up for me," she grinned, the blood running over her teeth. From her back pocket, she fisted a handful of salt and blew it in the child's face.

The child screeched, and its skin puffed into a plume of black smoke as its true form rose from the ground. It was about as tall as her. A humanoid shape, hunched over, with dark skin like a burning log. Between the cracks on its hide, fire flowed freely. Or was it lava?

Didn't matter. This was only a two-hundred-dollar gig.

Frankie grasped the cedar bundle and stood. "Your name, spirit?"

The spirit roared hot charcoal waves into her face. Its lanky, inhuman arm swung up, narrowly missing Frankie's already swollen cheekbone. She swore, gripping the side of her face, the black eye beginning to bloom in earnest. She shifted from annoyed to furious. "You're really going to make me do this, aren't you? Fine."

She snapped her fingers and the cedar burst into flame. She then blew on the cedar to extinguish the flame and direct the smoke at the spirit.

"Your *name*, spirit?" she tried again. The smoke settled on the spirit's bark-like hide, and it froze in place, now looking more like ashy, cooled magma than a burning log.

Its mouth opened with a crunch and a whisper slid out, "*Mulun.*"

"Thank you, Mulun." Finally. She had what she needed to make this quick. An easy two hundred dollars in her pocket.

Then again, the spirit looked pretty scary. She could charge more...

"Blessed by the cleansing power of the dark moon, I drive out the spirit named *Mulun*— guardian spirits, cast them out." Frankie dug a turkey's wishbone out of her other back pocket and held it in front of the spirit's face. "My sacred light fills this space and purifies it. I make room for goodness, abundance, and high vibrations. All unwelcome energies must now leave and never return—guardian spirits, cast them out. So it is said, so it shall be, so it is."

Frankie snapped the wishbone, the sound amplified by the ritual, the break soaking into every corner of the room. As the bone broke apart, Mulun collapsed into a pile of ashes, which then floated in a stream out of the open window.

Juliette cowered in the hall outside of the door, peeking around to see if it was over.

Frankie touched her cheek and winced. She needed to get some ice on this, stat. Using her sleeve to wipe the blood from her mouth, she turned to Juliette.

"Right, that'll be three hundred and fifty, or four hundred dollars if you want me to clean up the blood."

Half an hour later, just as the sun was starting to pitch over the hills, Frankie trotted down the front steps of the two-story Cape Cod-style house, a bag of organic green peas purchased from the bougie co-op pressed to her cheek. She was certain Juliette only offered it to get Frankie off the property as quickly as possible. She smirked as much as her swollen face would allow—this expensive bag of peas was going right in her freezer when she got home.

Frankie made her way back down the road toward the village square. Earlier in the day, she'd decided to walk to the client's house from her shop, which she now regretted as her Doc Martens nicked the back of her heels. Two years on her feet and barely broken in.

The town at dusk buzzed as tourists and citizens drifted out for their Thursday night dinner on the town. October had rushed in a few days ago, and with it, the leaf peepers. Frankie couldn't blame them—Sawtooth Bay was stunning in all seasons, but this time of the year, the town was obnoxiously charming. Perfectly autumnal: every shop featured displays of gourds, garlands of leaves frozen in wax, paper bats, and ghosts stuck to the glass panes. Some of the residents had started placing those little, tiny pumpkins on every fence post around their yard—a true testament to the way of life here, that no one knocked those right off.

4

Frankie loved living in Sawtooth, but it wasn't her hometown, and the people here were not always accepting of her services. Even when they needed them. Her shop, The Black Cat, was the only "metaphysical" store in her little town, fully stocked with all manner of herbs, tomes of occult knowledge, and packed with witchy goodness. And although she booked her house call services online through her website, the residents of Sawtooth tended to pop into the store and unload the full situation to her in person. To her extreme annoyance. Being the town's only witch living out of the broom closet, Frankie often found herself professionally somewhere between an exterminator, a healer, a mediator, and more often than she would like, a non-licensed therapist. It was astonishing how much emotional baggage people dragged into her life when she showed up for a job.

Most days had a similar schedule, especially in the fall when the shop was a lucrative draw for tourists. Breakfast in her ancient house with her ancient cat, then a walk into town to The Black Cat with her ancient cat. If no one had booked a house call overnight, she'd open the shop up and settle behind the counter with a new book and a massive cup of tea, or a latte from the café across the street. On the busier days, when house calls took up the entire day, Frankie would flip her shop sign to the side that said "The witch is out" before locking up for a few hours.

Today's gig had arrived in her inbox in the afternoon, and Frankie was thrilled to have the evening off. The autumn brought tourists, yes, but with a thinner veil in place, her spooky duties kept her autumn evenings busy. She walked downhill at a leisurely pace, gazing out over the tops of trees in burning color, muted by dusk settling in. Mist floated in from the Bay, hugging the town square's fairy lights and casting a fuzzy glow on the people strolling by.

By the time Frankie had reached the town square, her boots were killing her feet and she regretted not driving the truck today. She unlocked the shop's back door from the alley and used her phone's flashlight to retrieve her stuff and cat, Clementine, keeping the store's lights off. The last thing she wanted to deal with was a group of drunk Thursday-night girlies stumbling in to ask for tarot readings.

Clemmie stretched from the counter's cat bed and leaped onto her shoulder, nuzzling her face.

"Let's go home," she mumbled, exiting through the alley once more.

CHAPTER 2

Evan Lawson approached the familiar, dark, looming Victorian house, his steps crunching leaves and sounding way too loud for the quiet street.

He shouldn't have waited to do this until night. Or he should have brought someone with him. But he didn't want anyone to see him like this. And who would he bring?

Unlocking the front door and turning on the lights, Evan stepped fully inside with a deep breath in. His senses slammed with her smell—lavender, coffee, cashmere.

He could do this.

Evan felt his chest tighten as he stepped into the parlor and took another steadying breath, wiping his palms on his pants. The boxes were supposed to be stacked in the back sunroom. Which meant moving through three whole rooms of furniture covered in white sheets. A bunch of ghosts that had been waiting for him since he arrived in town a few days ago.

They called them hospital sheets, he realized.

The band around his chest tightened more and his vision grayed at the edges. His head roared. Evan stuttered through a few more breaths while stepping toward the back of the house before he tipped over the cliff.

He was outside the house. Facing the front door.

Had he even gone inside?

This must be some personal hell. He'd be doomed to repeat this pattern over and over until his ridiculous, anxious brain just pushed through. Why couldn't he just push through this?

He hated the way his heart was galloping, hated the way he couldn't function enough to do this one, tiny thing for her. He let that hate chew on him slowly, let it eat at him like an animal gnawing lazily on a bone for the last few morsels of meat.

He got back in his car and headed home to her.

*****

October sun crept over Nan's creased hand. Evan's chair creaked as he leaned into her bedside, pressing his nose into the blanket and breathing her in. His heart was ripping in half, he felt it so clearly. It was cruel that so much of Nan's remaining days were spent in slumber, her brilliant mind and warmth buried somewhere in a dreamscape he could not access.

The blanket stirred. Evan opened his eyes to see Nan watching him with a small smile.

"You have to stop watching me sleep, Evan. Don't be a creep." She started hacking but shooed him away when he straightened to try and help her.

"Stop fussing. Can you get me some tea?"

Evan scrambled. "Be right back."

He raced back to her bedroom with a mug of Earl Grey tea, spiked with honey and a bit of lemon. She always had it this way—the same mixture hot in the cooler months or iced in the summer. She took the mug from him with shaky hands.

"Have you heard from Dad at all?" Evan sank back into his seat. He regretted the question immediately as a twinge of tension moved across her face.

"It's not your responsibility to keep up with him, Evan. I'm just happy to have time with you."

Evan's eyes burned with his anger. His dad was such a piece of shit, out there skiing or something in Switzerland while his own mother was dying. He looked at her again. "I couldn't find the box you mentioned yesterday. Can you tell me why you need it?"

She glared at him. "You know damn well why I need it. Why *you* need it."

Not this again. Evan sighed. "You are not cursed, Nan. Curses aren't real."

She held up a hand, which used to be covered in jewels. "Don't patronize me. I'm doing this for you. You will not carry this after I'm gone."

Acid dumped in his stomach at that word. *Gone.* He tried again. "What do *I* need the box for?"

In between sips of tea, she said, "There are papers in there from my days on the city council and some other things from that period of time." She choked out another cough and gave him a knowing look. "Information you'll need to remove this curse from the family."

Family. Nan was his only real family. A family of two that would soon be a family of one. Evan had always considered Sawtooth Bay to be his real home, not boarding school, not at some up-state New York resort or bougie penthouse suite with his awful parents. He hated that Nan was spending her last days not at home in their Victorian house, but in a small cottage she purchased last year when her health deteriorated. It didn't matter that this cottage was easier to manage. The old Victorian house was only a seven-minute drive away but may as well have been across the planet. Or in another dimension, where he and Nan were outside in the sun, pottering around in her garden, his child fist full of lavender, the morning light warming his hair. Not here, crowded on top of each other in a two-bedroom cottage, the sounds of her hacking inescapable from anywhere inside.

Throughout his life, Nan was a force. Agatha Lawson, a force in business, in her private relationships, and in her role as his sole caretaker. Both mother and father. No one could have done the job better. Evan knew she loved him with a ferocity that no one could ever match again in his life. His childhood memories were filled with visions of Nan in a pantsuit, negotiating something on the phone in her office while he colored on the floor. Her voice was deep, husky. Her aura was regal and her attitude was take-no-shit.

She had built her fortune with her own hands and mind, no generational wealth to help her. Evan knew she was well-off, but they lived a simple, modest life. His father loved the money, not him. As long as he and Nan had their old house and time spent together, Evan didn't give a shit about whatever amount of funds were off in the ether somewhere.

Was it possible to mourn someone before they were gone? Or was that just stealing what time they did have away from them?

Nan had been watching him as his brain worked. She knew him too well, probably knew the exact words he had thought. She shook her head, grayish red waves swinging a bit. Brushing curtain bangs out of her eyes, she said, "I need you to run an errand." No, she knew he needed a distraction.

"Anything."

"There's a shop in town. A girl works there. She might be able to help us."

He typed out the few details Nan had about this shop on his phone and stood, glad for something to do. "Are you sure you want me to do this now?"

"Yes. I need a morning nap. Do this for me, please."

He nodded, gave her cheek a kiss, and headed out the door.

CHAPTER 3

October morning mist weaved through the square outside of Cool Beans, one of Sawtooth Bay's many cozy coffee shops. Punny name. Excellent coffee. Even better matcha lattes. And conveniently placed across the square from The Black Cat.

Frankie pushed up the lenses of her sunglasses to wiggle her fingers and make eye contact with Jack, who finally approached her café table. A classy thirty minutes late. Their blonde hair, buzzed on the sides and long up top, flickered like a candle in the morning breeze. Their face was encased by the high collar of a probably expensive, and definitely new, long, gray coat.

"Whaddup," Frankie said, looking them up and down. "And hello, new coat."

Jack cocked an eyebrow. "Two things: you don't need sunglasses when it's this overcast. And, you don't need to take them off to flag me down. There is zero mistaking this mane, bitch." They tugged on a lock of her black curls for emphasis.

Frankie frowned. "Third thing: you're late. My latte is gone already."

Jack rolled their eyes, scraping out a chair. "You are psychotically punctual."

Frankie settled back into her oversized cardigan as Jack ordered the usual with the table's QR Code—cappuccino. "And you're a wannabe European."

Jack flipped her off while they typed off a message with one hand, probably to this morning's client.

"Got a showing today?"

Jack's warm, light brown eyes flicked up to hers over their cat-eye glasses. "Yeah. That one-story mini-Tudor you cleansed like a month ago?"

"That was a cutie, it'll sell quick."

Jack and Frankie met in undergrad, back when Jack identified as female. The pair had ended up in each other's paranormal elective classes every single year and were fast best friends. Both studied spirits for different reasons—Frankie had talked to ghosts since she was an infant and planned to make a living with the skill. Somehow. And Jack had a clear vision of their future, to run a real estate business that could flip haunted properties. The business arrangement Jack and Frankie shared benefited them both, and they launched into work as soon as grad school wrapped up.

Jack bought houses for cheap.

Frankie slew 'em or sent 'em along.

Jack and their wife Bex hit it hard with high design and fast sales.

New England was haunted as fuck—Jack's brand-new, expensive coat was evidence of their successful business model. Now in their thirties, the pair was still inseparable. Frankie wouldn't have it any other way.

Jack's cappuccino arrived and they sank back in their seat with an airy sigh. "I love this time of year." They lifted their face up into some passing mist, the sound of dried leaves scratching along the cobblestones. "What do you have going on today?"

"No house calls in the inbox, thank the goddess. I can't handle too many people today."

Jack snorted and pointed to Frankie's storefront. "Except maybe you will."

Frankie spun around and scowled. "Mother fuck."

A gaggle of twenty-something year old ladies were waiting outside of The Black Cat. One of them was wearing a bright pink sash labeled "BRIDE."

She could already see herself giving love-themed tarot readings for the next two hours and cleaning up spilled spell ingredients from this group. Some influencer had listed Sawtooth Bay in a *Spooky Towns To Hang With The Girls*

11

post back in August, and the town could now rely on a very specific kind of tourist.

"They're getting an early start. What are the chances they've already had brunch and are hammered right now?" Frankie glared at the group.

One of the girls stumbled into "BRIDE" while laughing hysterically.

Jack choked on their drink. "Pretty good, my dude."

Frankie groaned and faced forward again. "I'm calling out sick. Hecate spare any poor soul who comes into the shop after they leave. I will not be my best self."

"If you end up not having any calls today, come over. Bex is making some kind of seafood risotto."

Frankie smiled. "Yes. I want that in my belly."

Jack glanced at their phone. "Shit, I gotta bounce. Good luck with *that.*" They nodded towards the gaggle waiting for Frankie.

"Please have whiskey on hand to go with my seafood risotto," Frankie whined after them, and Jack gave her a sarcastic salute. She stood and braced herself as she approached The Black Cat to get her very long morning started.

"Good morning, ladies—let me get the door for you. Oh! And it looks like we're *celebrating,* huh?"

*****

Frankie held an icy water bottle to her temple. Her oversized cardigan sagged off her shoulder, and she shed the layer to the ground for some relief, propping her boot up on a rail behind the counter. Sweat beaded on her neck as she let out an over-dramatic sigh. The broom was put away, and the spilled herbs were composted.

Her phone pinged, and she groaned, seeing that The Black Cat had been tagged on Instagram. "Please, no," she whispered.

She took a steadying breath and tapped on the notification. Up popped a post where "BRIDE" had shared a video. She clicked on it but knew what awaited her.

The start of the video was shaking and pointed at the ground—clearly, she was too drunk to edit but not too drunk to post. Frankie's mass of black hair whipped past the camera as a slew of profanity ripped from her throat in an embarrassing guttural tone. She roared as she shoved one of the ladies by the collar out of the shop and reached for another. The girls were all screaming at her, calling her everything from "witch bitch" to "crazy bitch" to "fascist bitch who doesn't support women and ruins bachelorette parties."

The video rolled on, and Frankie reached to grab the phone from "BRIDE," who then whipped the lens to her own face and screamed into it, *"Don't come here if you want a nice day to celebrate* you!*"*

She then pointed the lens back at Frankie, who stood with her teeth literally bared. Looking fully fucking feral.

Fantastic.

Aaaaaand swiping to the next slide in the post, "BRIDE" had taken a selfie with Frankie glaring up at her from the tarot table in the background. Frankie's tattooed grip on the tarot deck was white with fury.

Thanks, portrait mode. If there was any chance that someone wouldn't recognize her hair in the video, there was no hiding her identity now.

She could blame herself for this. True to form, the bachelorettes had wrecked the store. She had worked through back-to-back-to-back tarot readings, trying to deliver a nice message for their love lives (all falling on drunk ears) while trying to keep her eyes on the staggering girls crashing into her displays and digging into the cases of crystals.

At some point, lost in her rage and in the second hour of the girls emotionally dumping on her, Frankie had snapped.

So yeah, she could only blame herself for this. She knew she had gone too far and felt shame creep up her spine. Damn her temper. She was better than this.

Clementine finally came out from hiding in the office and wound around her ankles. She hushed her tears and picked him up, nuzzling into his shoulder. She set him on his counter bed with a heavy sigh, where he promptly went belly-up in a patch of sun.

*****

Evan paused in front of The Black Cat. He hated talking to new people. Especially about personal things. But he would do this for Nan. His palms went slick.

He ducked into the alley and pulled his phone out to check the shop's Instagram. Surely if he could get an idea of the employees or the shop layout, that might help calm his nerves. He clicked on tagged posts to see what was most recent.

It was a video. He jumped, startled by the volume once the video started playing. His mouth dropped open at what he saw.

"Bar fight" was the only way to describe the scene unfolding in this post. A woman with a lot of hair was violently throwing patrons out of the store. While... *snarling?* His eyes flicked down and saw that this was posted about an hour ago.

No, no, no. Was there seriously no other occult store in this creepy little town?

Evan checked the note in his phone's app again just in case there was any chance he didn't have to enter this building.

The Black Cat
Frankie
She knows about curses

Well, shit. He wasn't sure he wanted to meet someone who "knows about curses" and has violent tendencies. He slipped his phone back into his pocket and braced himself for an explosion. He gripped the door's handle and entered before he could rethink it.

Something shifted as Evan crossed the threshold into the shop. Something energetically. He was surprised by how well-lit the space was. He expected something dim, creepy, and reeking of patchouli. Instead, his blood pressure dropped as he smelled things that reminded him of his grandmother's garden: rosemary, florals, some kind of wood—cedar, maybe? Books lined two of the walls and a few free-standing shelves, and another wall offered containers and containers of herbs. Every item was meticulously placed, spaced out evenly, and labeled. The wood floor did not creak under his heavy footfall somehow, and he felt very big and loud in this calm, bright space.

He scanned to the counter where a woman was putting down an enormous tome of a book next to a dozing cat. The cat was not in fact a black cat.

It was definitely the woman from the video. He felt his jaw go slack. As she stood, Evan noted a pale face with cheeks covered in freckles, divided by a petite and almost delicate nose that softened her serious face into something youthful. But her eyes, a rich gray and heavily lined with black eyeliner, were hard and suspicious. She flipped long, curly black hair over her shoulder—a shoulder revealed as an oversized, chunky knit sweater slid down her arm and back with the movement. Her hair was like a vial of ink tipped into the ocean.

And, shit. Tattoos, lots of them. He suspected she had at least one full sleeve if the design snaking down her wrist was any indication. Both hands were covered in some kind of magic symbols, he assumed. The hands disappeared behind the counter under his gaze. Her expression was cold, and he couldn't imagine this woman smiling. Her skin had a luminous quality to it, set off by her pitch-black hair, and he noticed she had a very, very faded bruise on her cheekbone—yep, the bar fight type.

Her thick, dark brow arched in a question.

Fuck. He'd been staring.

Not bothering to hide her annoyance, she repeated, "Are you looking for something in particular?"

"Yeah. Yes. I'm looking to consult someone about a curse."

"A curse," she repeated, with zero interest.

Evan felt embarrassment crawling in and said, "Yeah, like a hex or something." Was she making this difficult already?

Frankie, he assumed, walked around the counter. Her build was *seriously* curvy, with a good amount of muscle tone. Thick, curly hair almost down to her butt. The tattoos continued up to almost her collarbones. Evan swallowed hard.

"Hexes and curses are not the same thing," she said with a hand on her hip, as if this was an obvious distinction. She was not helping this interaction and was not meeting him halfway—how the hell would he know any of this?

"Whatever you call it, you can get rid of it, right?" Evan gritted out, tone slipping into something sharp. Embarrassment turned into annoyance. Her lack of empathy was starting to grate.

She rubbed her eyelids. "Look man, my tank is empty and I'm actually trying to close early. I can't help you today."

Annoyance switched to anger. She was not grasping the lack of time he might have—*he* didn't even know how much time he had with Nan. Her doctor told them to expect to lose her before Christmas, perhaps in late November or early December. But who really knew? His hand fisted his hair. He tried not to yell, but it came out anyway. "I need a curse gone, and you have to help me."

He couldn't wait for this chick to be in a better mood. Evan was a task completer, and this was a task he could do while he waited uselessly for his grandmother to die.

A flash of anger struck her features. "Get out. You're not gonna come in here and act like a dick."

Huh? Okay, here she was, the crazy woman from the video. Unbelievable, this girl. Heartless. "Oh, *I'm* being a dick?"

"Yeah. Get the *fuck* out," she snapped. A slight rumble moved through the room—a teacup chattering against its saucer.

"Whatever," Evan growled. Not a good barb, not even a barb. *Fuck.* He stormed outside clenching his fists so hard that he felt tiny slices of pain up his finger bones.

He needed to be away from this situation. And he could regroup later with a plan. He stalked back to Nan's house, his head full of roaring.

CHAPTER 4

Frankie opened her inbox and groaned. Last night's seafood risotto and whiskey had run late into the night, as it usually did when Frankie ate with Jack and Bex: snorting with laughter and not enough hours for their conversations. And so much whiskey. She loved her friends, even if they sometimes led to mid-week hangovers.

The shades were drawn to block out the world while she planned how her day would unfold. And today held a fuckload of house calls. *Awesome.*

She read through an email message from one of her least favorite people in town—Margaret Oleander. Who was having an issue with the "faeries" in her kitchen again.

I need to have you come out for a THIRD *time it seems. They really are a pest, and my psychic told me they followed me from my previous residence—*

She may as well kick the day off with that mean old bat and then take a mid-morning break to recover before her other appointments.

A shadow from outside the shop's front door flickered over her laptop screen, and she turned around. Some dude was pressing his face to the crack between the blinds trying to see if anyone was there. No, not some dude. That guy from yesterday. The one she kind of yelled at.

She approached the door and opened it with a tiny crack. This guy wasn't a threat, but she had a feeling the gesture would irritate him. And it did, annoyance flashed over his features.

He cleared his throat. "Hi. Uh, me again. I know I kind of stormed out of here yesterday. I'm sorry about that." He scratched the back of his head sheepishly, seeming to be in a search for words.

Frankie opened the door all the way and snapped, "Get inside before someone sees you and thinks I'm open."

Right on cue, a group of young women came chattering down the block, and damn if they didn't have *rose quartz bath bombs* written all over them. "Like *now*," Frankie barked. She pulled him inside and shut the door.

She crouched, putting her ear to the door. And this guy, who could not read a situation to save his fucking life, started talking.

"Like I was saying yesterday, before you jumped down my throat, I need to consult you and see if your services would be a good fit for my family and—"

"Hecate spare me, *shut up!*" she whispered.

They both fell silent moments before the girlish laughter reached her shop door.

"No, you guys, I'm telling you, a friend of mine came here for her girls' night out a few weeks ago and it's the coolest. It's like, super witchy. Amazing crystal selection and I think she does readings and stuff."

A tug on the door, which Frankie had remembered to lock after pulling the guy inside, thank the gods.

"They're supposed to be open, I dunno, should we wait, or?" Frankie hung her head. *Please leave, please leave.* She glanced up at the guy who was watching her with an amused expression.

The girls finally mumbled something about their next destination, and she stayed silent until they wandered further down the block.

Frankie straightened and turned to her guest. He smiled. A really nice smile, actually. Obnoxiously so. His wavy hair was shorter on the sides with auburn curls spilling from the top of his head. The color of it shifted like a field of wheat in a controlled burn. Dark hazel eyes, perfectly confusing—she had a feeling they changed colors depending on his mood. His skin was on the paler side with faint freckles. Muscular build. Taller than her. Flannel shirt. He looked her up and down and she felt her cheeks heat.

"You're not meant for customer service. I have no idea why you have a shop. Did you know you're tagged in an Instagram post throwing people out of your store?"

She glared. "Did you need something or are you here to argue again?"

He paused, as if summoning some courage. "I need to consult you about breaking a family curse."

Frankie extended her hand. "Frankie Wolfe."

Evan gripped it with a respectable handshake. "Evan Lawson."

She steered toward the back room calling over her shoulder, "Well, Evan Lawson, I'm seriously hungover. Care to share your story over some tea?"

*****

After hauling out glass jars of various herbs, the girl started smashing some pinches of good-smelling things together with a mortar and pestle. Her gaze flicked up to him and back down at her hands.

"So, curse? Who's cursed? Are you cursed?"

"Not yet. Agatha—my grandmother—she's been battling some kind of illness over the last year. She's had a lot of bad luck too. Look, I don't know how best to explain this, I'm not knowledgeable on this kind of stuff and like I told Nan, I don't really believe in it." He was surprised she didn't glare at him. "Sorry, no offense," he added, lamely.

"None taken, Evan Lawson."

She poured the herbs into a metal infuser and stuck that in a teapot. Glancing at him over her shoulder as she threw on an electric kettle, she frowned, lost in thought.

She drummed her nails on the live edge of the wood countertop. "I'll need more details. Can you describe her illness?"

He swallowed. He could say these words out loud. He could do this. "She's dying." He barely got the sentence out without breaking.

Her face was warm with understanding, which was a relief. He still didn't quite know how to read her, but it seemed she wasn't cruel like he'd assumed.

19

"I'm sorry, Evan, you seem really close to her. I'm sorry this is happening to you both. What are her symptoms? Or did she get an official diagnosis?"

Evan braced with folded arms on the counter. "Mostly a respiratory thing. She's never been a smoker, but she suddenly developed a hacking cough. She started coughing up blood over the last few months, but her doctors couldn't figure out where in her system it was coming from. And more recently," he paused to steady himself, "she's gone downhill. The symptoms mimic COPD, but it's nothing her health team can nail down. All we know is that she's decided to not continue with any aggressive care.

"So, she's now in what are likely her final few months, at home in a little cottage, with round-the-clock nurses. I'm there a lot, but she's mostly sleeping these days, and she told me to get out of the house and stop being creepy, watching her sleep." He knew he was babbling but smiled to himself. Nan was still sassing him, even now.

"You said this came on suddenly?"

"Yeah, she was super healthy, and then things changed almost overnight, right around the time she was voted off the city council."

"And did you say she has bad luck?"

He straightened—this next part needed to not sound douchey or pathetic. "Nan is wealthy and has amazing instincts when it comes to money stuff, investments, that kind of thing. But when this all happened, a few of her deals fell through and she lost a huge amount of money."

Frankie's face was neutral, no sign of judgement, so he continued.

"When I was home this past winter break, after she developed a cough, she had a bad streak of investments, and several of the companies she owned went under. Any deal she made, anything she touched to try and right the ship just completely fell through."

The kettle popped, and Frankie poured the water into the teapot. "Where were your parents in all of this?"

"They've always been happy to leave me with Nan and fuck off to Spain, or Switzerland, or wherever they felt like. She gave my dad access to his trust when he turned eighteen, so he bailed Sawtooth and went to Boston, where he met my mother. After I came along, I was shipped off to boarding school most of the time, but when I wasn't at school, I spent every single break at her house in town. Nan raised me, she acted as both of my parents. I wanted to go into library science for my graduate degree, but my dad cut me off, so Nan paid for my education. And I came home to her about a week ago."

Frankie slipped a slight smile. "So, you're a librarian, huh? Interesting."

Evan shifted, feeling fully exposed with all of his childhood trauma spilled all over Frankie's counter. "Yeah, I don't know what's next for me, after she…" His sentence drifted off, but Frankie nodded in understanding.

He finished his story, adding, "She's asked me to break this curse before she passes. She thinks it will pass to me as being the next of kin that is closest to her, both physically and emotionally. I don't know about this stuff," he gestured around the shop, "But if this will give her any kind of peace, I'll do it."

Frankie nodded. "There could be several things causing this situation, and I'll need to dig more into details. Is your grandmother up for visitors at all?"

"Depends on the day, but yes, you could meet her. She said there might be some specific city council details from the lost election cycle in a box of files in her house. I still need to pick that up."

He didn't feel the need to add that he had a full-blown panic attack every time he tried to cross the threshold. Not relevant right now. Or hopefully ever.

*****

Frankie was too hungover for this today. This was not going to be a one-and-done kind of job. She might be dealing with Evan for weeks if she took this on.

He did apologize for the day before, and he wasn't hard on the eyes. So, fuck it.

Frankie poured them both a cup of tea in some very fancy thrift store-acquired porcelain teacups. "Unfortunately, I've got a full list of house calls today. So, I might not be able to chat curse details with you or go by her house until way later." Her eyes flicked up to him, expecting another argument.

A beat and then, "Um, can I come?"

She cocked her head at him. "You want to do a ride-along?"

His blush was pretty cute. "Caretaking is kind of my afternoon activity most of the time, and like I said, she's sleeping all the time right now and told me to get out of the house, so I don't have a ton going on…" He seemed to be babbling. Was he nervous?

"This might not be very fun for you." She leaned against the counter, palms pressing on the edge of it. "I thought you didn't really believe in this stuff?"

He gave an infuriatingly stunning smile, his blush remaining. "So, make me believe."

Uggh.

"Rules: don't complain about how long it takes—it's going to be a long day. Also, no commentary in front of my clients. It's a delicate balancing act, and I don't need anything fucking that up. And lastly, if you behave," she nodded at him, and could have sworn his blush deepened, "we can end the day at your grandma's house to pick up the files."

"Deal."

"Drink up." She pushed the saucer towards him.

"What is it?" He peered down at the herb blend suspiciously.

Calendula to brighten up her day, peppermint to soothe her whiskey stomach, orange peel to banish yesterday's shadows, and a strong scoop of Irish black tea for caffeine.

But Frankie said, "It helps me speak with the dead."

Evan stopped mid-gulp. "Am I gonna see some shit today?"

Frankie threw back her cup, much like a shot. "Hope blood doesn't make you squeamish."

CHAPTER 5

Evan watched as Frankie gathered her stuff. He realized in horror what he had just done—why had he asked to tag along? He blamed his subconscious. He must be bored. Or maybe this was a way to see how Frankie worked before agreeing to anything. Or, more likely, he was some kind of masochist, wanting someone to be mean to him. His brain was breaking from his grief. He snapped his eyes away when she turned to him.

"We'll need to get my truck, so I need to walk back to my house for a minute."

Evan nodded and watched her ancient cat stretch out its front feet on top of the counter, bony skeleton sticking out all over the place. It jumped down. He winced, hoping it hadn't hurt itself with the movement. "What's your cat's name?"

"Kevin."

"Seriously?" He laughed. "How old is Kevin?"

"He's got to be in his mid-thirties by now."

Evan was no expert on cats but was sure they couldn't live to be thirty-five. His brain emptied out for a moment. Wait, Kevin? In his mid-thirties? Surely this was not some kind of... man in cat form, right? Surely not. That's not possible.

Frankie strolled out of the front door, hips swinging. He followed her out, the cat also in tow. It seemed he was not a full-time shop cat.

"Kevin" leaped from the ground up to Frankie's shoulder and perched with no effort, like he wasn't a bag of dusty, fragile bones, and settled in for what must have been their routine walk home.

What the hell?

They headed north towards Frankie's house, walking in silence. Evan cautiously glanced at Frankie's profile and to his shock, she was watching him and holding in a laugh.

"Oh my god. You're messing with me."

She let out a surprisingly girlish laugh. A glorious, rich sound. So, she did know how to smile. He hoped it wasn't the only time he would see it. He examined how dimples appeared on her cheeks and how she hunched over a bit, gripping her leg. She laughed with her full body, fully giving over to the moment. The cat clung on to her, narrowing his amber eyes at Evan.

Once she regained composure, she noted, "His name is Clementine."

"And how old is Clementine?"

"Clemmie is thirty-five."

"Bullshit!"

Her expression flipped to something unreadable, like that cold mask she wore in the shop. "He is. I adopted him as an adult cat when I was in my twenties. There have been periods in my life when Clemmie kept me out of dark places. And when he turned twenty, I decided to keep him with me for a little longer."

Okaaay. "Can I ask what that means?"

She paused, deep in thought for a moment. "Everything has a cost, and I'll be called to pay it at some point. The price may be years of my own life. Or some part of myself."

She said it calmly like she hadn't just revealed that she'd traded possible years of her life to keep this ancient animal alive. Somehow, Evan knew Frankie wasn't messing with him about this. Even if he knew it was impossible, she believed it to be true. He sat with that horrible thought in silence.

They rounded a curve in the road and there, tucked away in the trees, was a spooky Victorian house, medium-sized. Evan guessed it was a four-bedroom. The entire thing was painted in a dark shade, the gingerbread elements in a slightly lighter color to highlight their shapes. Lots of turrets, a widow's watch at the top of the building, and a sprawling garden on all sides, framed in massive, ancient trees.

"Whoah." Evan's eyes trailed up the house's formidable face. "No offense, but how do you live here? Didn't this house cost a fortune?"

"Nope, it was dirt cheap. It was infested with a violent poltergeist and was on the market for a full year. My friend Jack couldn't sell it, so we worked out a deal. And now it's all mine." There was a devious glint in her eyes. She looked at him for a flash. "The ghost is gone now, obviously. Had to get a little nasty with it."

He had no idea what "get nasty with it" meant and didn't want to ask for more details.

She gave him a dismissive glance that made his temper flare. "Stay here, I'll let Clemmie in and grab my house call bag, then we can head out."

He crossed his arms and waited by the truck. It was an older model Ford, in vintage green. Shaking his head, he reminded himself that he signed up for this. Frankie came back out and tossed her bag in the backseat, and they took off, driving a little fast for in-town streets.

"So, where are we off to?"

"My least favorite person in town, living or dead." *Present company not included?* Evan guessed.

The truck pulled into position outside of a small house, painted a bright peach color. More garish than chipper. Frankie dropped the visor down for its mirror and pulled her bag into her lap. She slid some giant hoop earrings in and shrugged into a shawl-like floral duster. Stepping out of the vehicle, she pulled off her boots and pulled on some heeled booties from the backseat.

"Are you doing a wardrobe change right now?"

She rolled her eyes. "Trust me, this bitch wants Stevie Nicks." She strolled up to the entrance, and before her fist could tap the door, it yanked open.

Before them stood a short, squat, miserable-looking woman, dressed in pale pink everything. She glared at Frankie and gestured for her to come inside the also very pale pink interior.

"Ms. Oleander. I hope you're well?"

She narrowed her eyes at Frankie. "As well as I can be, given the circumstances. Did you read my email? The faeries are *back*. And my psychic told me I'm going to have to move *again*, but leave behind all my appliances so they can't follow me, which I shouldn't have to do because you've come out *five times* now."

This was a horrible woman. She was quickly becoming his least favorite person in town as well. Frankie smiled and in a breezy tone, replied, "Not to worry, this will all be taken care of in no time. I'll just get things set up, please feel free to wait in the other room."

The woman huffed and left the hall but seemed to linger nearby within earshot.

Evan leaned into Frankie and whispered, "Are faeries real? Is this a real thing?"

Frankie didn't smile as much as show him her teeth. "Not in the way she thinks," she whispered back. "But I'm going to have to put on a little show."

She floated into the kitchen, floral duster streaming behind her, and opened all of the cabinet and appliance doors. Dropping into a crouch before the cabinet of pots and pans, she retrieved a cast iron skillet and carried it with her. She smacked it with a wooden spoon from the counter over and over, a dull clang sounding like a drumbeat.

"I call now to the fae present—this is not your realm." She clanged the pan in time to her steps, pacing in a circle. This was a fully ridiculous scene, but her voice had taken on a strange, hollow, echoey quality. "Come out now, reveal yourselves to us."

Evan gripped his chin, fingers digging into his scruff, trying his absolute hardest not to laugh out loud.

Placing the cast iron on the stovetop, Frankie retreated to her bag and dug out a spray bottle. She sprayed all around the space, the scent of rose overwhelming the already cloying perfumery this lady bathed in every day. He felt light-headed and over-stimulated. He considered fleeing outside.

Ms. Oleander called from the other room, "Don't forget to cleanse the countertop toaster oven! My psychic said they live in there! I can't buy another one, that one is *perfect!*"

Evan snorted a laugh, then tried to turn it into a cough or a sneeze, which only made it worse. Frankie glared daggers at him, but there was a smirk forming on her face as well.

Her voice was cold, otherworldly, and a bit terrifying, but her words were absurd. "I call to the fae present in this toaster oven—*I cast you outside!*" She ripped open the back door in the kitchen with a flourish, sprayed herself in the face and chest with her bottled mixture, and tugged at her hair to mess it up. Just as he suspected, Ms. Oleander appeared in the kitchen doorway, just missing Frankie spraying herself.

Frankie braced against the counter, breathing heavily. "You were right, ma'am—they really didn't want to leave that toaster oven."

The woman sniffed, "I told you so."

Committing to the bit, Frankie held her massive hair away from her neck to "cool off" and rattled off some directions for her to keep the house guarded. Evan zoned out as she discussed how to hang some iron pots and pans around, or horseshoes. Then, she whipped out her phone for the transaction.

"Ms. Oleander, I think your persistence has done the trick this time. If they give you any more trouble, leave some honey out in your yard and they'll gravitate to that. And your total today will come to two hundred even."

Evan started. *Two hundred? For that?* He hated Ms. Oleander immediately after meeting her, but he had weird feelings about Frankie charging for this service. He tucked away those itching thoughts as they moved down the steps and out to the truck for the next stop.

CHAPTER 6

The librarian was okay. He'd held it together while she made a scene and lied to a woman's face. And then took her money. She got the feeling Evan didn't like the shadier aspects of her business. She also got the feeling that today was some sort of tryout for his curse job. Whatever. Better for him to know upfront what working with her would be like. This was *her* realm—he was just a guest in it.

She changed out of her Stevie Nicks costume and back into her soft-goth aesthetic. Onto the next: Old man Sherman and his arthritis.

Mr. Sherman lived down by the pier, and placing his stop at this point in the day was very intentional. Her stomach rumbled. Stepping out of the truck, she grabbed her go-bag. Evan fidgeted beside her, his shoes scraping across the rocks and sand. She could tell he was dying to say something.

"What?" she asked, watching his auburn hair float in the breeze like the leaves blowing by them.

"Can you give me a heads-up on the places we're going? Like, what we're going to do or see?" He avoided eye contact.

Wait... he was nervous? Oh. *Oh.* She had suspected, but this confirmed it. Evan had anxiety. He was an over-planner, an over-preparer, an over-thinker. Frankie understood this very well. She worked hard to let the world see a girl who thought on her feet and always had the right answer at the ready.

But the truth was, Frankie constantly ran through every possible outcome in her brain. If she planned enough, there would be no nasty surprises. The truth was, those right answers were dug out of her darkness with tremendous effort, like using a hand trowel to dig down to a coffin. It left her brain depleted at the end of every day.

Evan finally looked at her, his expression guarded. She nodded. "For sure. We're going to see Mr. Sherman now. It'll be a good stop, I promise."

They approached the front door to his cottage, but Frankie steered around back. Mr. Sherman was bent over a workbench, threading some kind of fuzzy bobber onto a fishing hook.

"Hey, Mr. Sherman, how've you been?"

He smiled up at her, one of his front teeth dipped in gold. His Massachusetts accent thick, he replied, "Frankie! You're a sight for sore hands."

Yeah, he could be a little corny. She smiled at him. "This is my friend Evan. And *this*—" she plopped onto his workbench a few vials of oil that she had mixed up several weeks ago. "This is your medicine. I made some modifications, more goldenrod, as requested. Smear it on your skin before you go to bed. It'll absorb better."

His gold tooth flashed as he beamed at her from his permanently hunched position. "Thanks, you're a doll. I'll let you know how it goes. What do I owe you?" His face was leathered and cracked like the pier itself, his white beard covered it like the season's first fluffy snow.

She shook her head. "No way—you're my test subject, you know that. If it works, I'll sell it in the shop. That's all the payment I need."

He shook his head right back at her. "Frankie, I'm at least going to feed you. *Don't* say no. You hungry?" He looked to Evan. "What about you? Hungry?"

Frankie feigned shock. "No, no, we couldn't. We won't take up your afternoon." She pretended to hug her bag and back away. They played this game every time she came by. She couldn't break the script now. But Evan didn't know that, and he looked disappointed. Mr. Sherman hobbled into the back of his house, calling for them to take a seat at the picnic table.

Fuck yes. She winked at Evan, who finally caught on. He settled in. "What was in those bottles you gave him?"

"It's oil for his arthritis. Some anti-inflammatory herbs, and then I blessed the oil under a dark moon." She dropped her voice to a whisper. "He does this every time. Brace yourself for the best lobster roll you've ever had." Evan's eyes widened.

*****

Mr. Sherman placed a plate in front of him, and Evan found himself voracious. He picked up the roll and took a huge bite. Frankie wasn't wrong— he was overwhelmed by the buttery, rich sandwich.

Frankie thanked Mr. Sherman and took a bite. Lost in her food, she let out an animalistic groan that brought heat to Evan's face. He choked down the oversized bite before his throat could close, and he drank deeply from the glass of water Mr. Sherman handed him with a gold-flecked grin.

Conversation came easily between the three of them. Frankie, it turned out, was very good with people. Mr. Sherman sat down at the table and continued to thread his bobber. "So, how'd you two meet?"

Evan jumped in before Frankie could say something to embarrass him. She had a devious look on her face. "Frankie is going to help my grandma out with a little problem."

Mr. Sherman squinted at him with one eye closed. "*That's* how I know you. You're Agatha's grandson, right? Wonderful lady. Damn shame what she's going through. You tell Agatha that Pierre will bring her fresh fish any time she wants it."

Evan's world started to narrow. He didn't want to have this conversation with a stranger and prayed for the moment to pass quickly.

Frankie snorted a laugh, and they both looked at her. "Sorry, it's just, I didn't know your first name is Pierre. So, you're Pierre, who lives by the *pier*?" She laughed and banged an open hand on the table.

The tension broke and the other two joined her in laughing. Did she do that on purpose? Mr. Sherman chortled, seeming to enjoy their company.

Evan's day grew a little brighter. He felt warm and watched Frankie as she chatted with client. Her hair was hypnotizing. It was pitch-black but with so many dimensions of other shades of black. It moved with so much life to it. Transfixed, he almost missed something slither between a few locks of hair. It disappeared around her skull.

What the hell? Did he hallucinate that? Could he casually ask Frankie if she had a snake in her hair? No, no. He imagined that.

He must've imagined that.

CHAPTER 7

It had indeed been a long day. After they left Pierre at the pier, they stopped to help a young boy with an upper respiratory infection. Frankie had prepared some herbs in a bowl with hot water and had the boy tent his face over it. "Vapors," she had called it. Then, they drove across town to collect a haunted doll from some guy who had purchased it at an antique store. Frankie had taken the doll from his shaking hands and placed it inside a black cloth bag to take with her. The man paid her one hundred dollars.

Evan wasn't sure how he felt about her business. But he kept his thoughts to himself, knowing the day would end with helping Nan. And get him away from Frankie and her creepy hair—he'd seen glimpses of something sliding through it all day and was seriously weirded out.

Frankie had promised this was the last stop before his grandma's house. For all her talk of ghosts and spirits, he hadn't seen much today that couldn't be explained by placebo effects or natural medicine. But he wasn't going to say that to Frankie. He knew all kinds of people practiced magic, whatever that looked like, but to make money off of people's troubles?

They now sat in a bright kitchen, in a cottage on the edge of town. Afternoon light flooded the space, but the house was eerie and made him uncomfortable. He kept finding himself looking over his shoulder, expecting to find something watching them from the shadows. The clients had requested some spiritual help, so he rallied his focus to get through this last appointment.

The clients were a mid-thirties couple, newly married Teresa and Allie. Allie leaned against a kitchen counter with her arms crossed, a black ponytail streaming down her chest and a furious expression on her face. Teresa tucked a short, strawberry blonde curl behind her ear and shifted uncomfortably in her seat while she chatted with Frankie. In short, over the last six months, her life had gone to shit, and due to her chronic pain, exacerbated by whatever this spiritual situation was, Teresa could barely leave the house these days. She sold pottery at the farmer's market each week, but with this new illness came back, hip, and joint pain, making it physically impossible to use her wheel.

Frankie dug out a penlight from her bag. "Okay, Teresa, follow the light for me." She moved the light back and forth staring deep into the woman's eyes. Evan leaned closer and stared over Frankie's shoulder, straining to see what she was looking for.

Teresa's blue eyes, which betrayed her fear and sadness, moved back and forth. A pitch-black shadow moved just half a second behind her irises—like each iris had its own little ghost.

He startled backward and nearly hissed in surprise. Frankie glared at him, but he didn't care—this should not be happening. The shadows moved like oil or slime. Evan's stomach turned over. It happened again and again as Frankie moved the light back and forth. Transfixed, it took Evan a second to notice a cool, greasy hand run up his spine and neck. He flinched and almost fell out of his chair, whipping around. But nothing was there.

He needed to get out of this house.

Frankie, the effortless image of cool when reality was breaking down, turned off the penlight and took Teresa's hands on the kitchen table.

"Alright, you've got a nasty hex attached to you. From what you've described, it sounds like it's a bit of an all-arounder, affecting everything from health to finances to your overall luck."

The woman teared up and stared down at the table. Frankie spoke in a soft voice, "Do you have anyone in your orbit that might have it out for you?"

Evan couldn't imagine how it would feel to know someone out there in your life wished you actual harm.

Teresa pinched her eyes shut to help the tears clear out of her vision. "I can think of someone. Someone chewed me out at my farmer's market booth about my prices, to an irrational point."

Evan could have sworn a flicker of something passed over Frankie. Like when the power in his house went out before coming back on. She smiled. "I don't need a name."

She let the woman's hands go with a gentle squeeze. "How do you want to proceed? We have a couple options. We can deal with your attacker or take the mildest option, which would be to treat your issues and give you materials to do a full house cleanse."

This timid woman seemed truly devastated by this diagnosis. She mumbled, "Yes, let's do that."

Frankie spent the next few minutes giving the couple a bundle of nails wrapped in red cord and a sheet of instructions on how to perform a house cleanse. Allie had moved over to hug Teresa from behind, her face filled with quiet fury at her wife's situation. Teresa leaned back into her, seeming to be more at peace already.

"If you can hold off for two days on the house cleanse, the new moon will kick this thing's ass." Frankie winked at them, and the women giggled, tired and giddy from having a solution in their hands. "In the meantime, I'd like to do a cleansing on you, Teresa. Allie, if you could stay nearby? This might get a little intense."

Frankie searched the floor for a minute and then positioned Teresa into a strong sunbeam. She retreated to her bag and drew out a bundle of herbs.

Evan stepped over to her. He had to ask a question or talk to her about anything at all. He was crawling out of his skin being this quiet. And he was seriously unnerved by whatever the hell touched him. Or was lurking in the hallway. Or was lurking in her hair.

"Burning sage? Is that a thing?"

Frankie frowned at him. "You *can* use sage, but I prefer rosemary and cedar for cleansings."

Sure, obviously.

Frankie snapped her fingers, and the ends of the herbs burst into flames. Evan felt the ground beneath him give way as his sanity cracked in half. *What?* His ears rang. A crazy, casual use of elemental magic. Frankie had just created fire from her bare. Fucking. Hands. Nan had a fascination with the occult and magic, but Evan had never believed in *anything* before. Certainly not this, not wielding the elements. Shaking, hot and cold, he mentally strapped in for whatever came next.

34

She blew it out like a candle, causing the herbs to release smooth streams of smoke that wound toward the ceiling. Then she stepped around Teresa in a counterclockwise direction. Evan could feel his heart batter against his ribs.

The herbs' smoke flickered blindingly white in the sunbeam, and the entire room seemed to warm. The smell was lovely. Calming. Evan's shoulders eased down. Frankie was saying some kind of spell, but she whispered it. He guessed she was trying to help keep Teresa calm by not coming at her with something like *"The power of Christ compels you!"* A shiver ran through him. He looked over his shoulder again, sure he heard something shuffle in the darkness.

As smoke surrounded her, Teresa began to cry and then sob, as if the entire weight of the situation was hitting her at once. Her breathing was frantic. Frankie kept moving slowly around her. When she reached her back again, Frankie paused and used the thumb of her free hand to rub on Teresa's shoulder, smoothing a knotted muscle. The tears softened and stopped as Teresa blew out a calming breath. Frankie raked her fingers through Teresa's short curls like a comb and the poor girl closed her eyes. Facing her again, Frankie came around to place a hand around Teresa's shoulder.

"Okay, that should do it. Cleanse the entire house on the new moon. In the meantime, mix up a solution with the herbs listed on that sheet, and use it to wipe down your front and back door sill plates."

Teresa stared at her with enormous eyes and lurched forward to grip Frankie in a death hug that made her look wildly uncomfortable. Evan stifled a snort. Customer service indeed. Allie joined in. That was his cue. Evan avoided the dark hall and made his way to the front of the house so Frankie could get paid and make her exit. He was relieved to see the sun again, even if it was fleeing over the hills.

Minutes later, they were outside heading to the truck. Evan had no idea what to think about the weirdness he'd just witnessed but suddenly felt tired and craved a few hours alone to process everything. He stole a glance and noted that Frankie looked exhausted. Dark shadows lined her face.

"Hey, we can deal with my grandma's thing later, if you're feeling tired," he offered.

Frankie was a million miles away. "Just one more thing left to do." Her voice was hoarse, her tone low.

Stomping to the truck, she yanked a little trowel out of the backseat, dropped down the tailgate to use as a table, and started stuffing herbs from her bag into some cheesecloth. She moved with a precise clip that unsettled him.

Gripping the cloth bag, now tied in red cord, Frankie stalked toward the edge of the yard, hair spilling behind her in a gust of October wind. Evan followed, a terrible feeling sinking into his guts. He didn't know what she was about to do, but Frankie vibrated with rage—he would stand far back from whatever was going on.

She stopped and counted steps until she was just outside the property line. She stabbed the trowel into the soil, digging a foot down. She plopped the bag into the hole and began chanting some kind of spell. Evan leaned in closer to hear what she was saying.

"Hex reversed and no longer needed, return to where you were freed. Release these victims from your grasp, find instead the one who cast."

What the—was she... sending a curse? His mouth fell open. He didn't want any part of this.

"Frankie, what are you doing?"

"What does it look like I'm doing, Evan? I'm sending it back to the original caster," she hissed at him, her professional mask falling off entirely to reveal the roaring demon beneath.

From the thick inky curls of her head, shapes began to expose themselves and morphed into shadows that writhed like smoke. He *knew* it—he had seen glimpses of them all day long. Only they were shadows, not snakes. And now they ripped out of her as if relieved to be free from containment.

Pulling a switchblade from her back pocket, Frankie sliced across her palm and squeezed hard, a stream of blood falling on top of the bag.

Panic rushed in his veins. "Oh my god, do *not* do this!" His voice was panicked, desperate for this to stop. He had come to her for help with a curse, something that plagued his family line and the only person he truly cared about, and she was shooting one off into the universe like it bore no consequences.

Frankie turned to him slowly, hair falling over her brow, her lips peeled back in that snarl he'd seen on Instagram. Here she was—Hurricane Frankie, raging in every direction in front of her. Shadows slithered up her legs, and Evan stepped back several paces. The thought of those shadows climbing onto him gave him the heebie-jeebies.

"Teresa might be too sweet of a person to not ask for a return-to-sender hex. But I'm not sweet. Know that right now, Evan, before you decide to work with me. I am not a golden girl or a shining light. I have no issue with the darkness—" she held up her bleeding hand, and shadows snaked around her wrist, leaked from her mouth, pooled at her feet. Her voice now a spooky, hollow tone as she continued— "and call to it if it suits me. I have done far worse than this casual hex and will do worse before I leave this world for the next."

Evan was shaking his head. "You know what? No. This is a bad idea. If you can curse someone so casually, I don't think this is going to be a good fit. I'll figure something else out."

Frankie stalked over to peer up into his face. His heart pounded as her shadows reached out for him, but he held his ground.

"Listen to me, you naïve little shit: to discount baneful spellwork is to condemn *hundreds* of years of magical practitioners' labor." She jammed a finger into his chest. "People have and always will seek out their community's magical person to heal an illness, get rid of a ghost, or poison an abusive husband. To heal and to harm—they grow on the same branch. And I will *not* be insulted by your Boy Scout beliefs."

He was incredulous, and yelling. "You are talking about harming people, Frankie! *Causing harm.* You are hurting people."

The Frankie storm slowed as if he had somehow slipped into the eye of the hurricane. He was afraid of what would come next. Was she going to shoot fireballs at him or something? How was he supposed to ride in a vehicle with her and escape this situation?

She spoke again, her voice an icy void that terrified him more than her screaming. "Get. In. The truck, Evan. I want this day to end, and I want to be done with *you.*"

He growled and walked back to the truck as quickly as possible. She could just drop him off at Nan's old house, and he would figure this out on his own. And then he'd never have to see her again.

CHAPTER 8

The vibe in the cab of the truck was really bad.

Evan seethed and gazed out the window at nothing. Frankie leaned an elbow against her open window, her temple resting on her fist. Cold wind wrapped around her pounding head and cooled her face down. She'd bandaged her hand and packed the wound with herbs, but it still throbbed a little. It would feel better tomorrow. And hopefully, so would everything else.

There was also the not-so-small problem of revealing to Evan her literal darkness. Her shadows had burst out earlier when they argued. She scolded herself for not being more in control. Something about him made her forget how to be cool-headed. Regardless, she was not a college girl picking fights at the local dive bar anymore. It didn't matter how tired or angry she was, this shouldn't have happened. She tried to hide her shadows from people outside of her inner circle, as well as the reason that she was never without them. Never truly alone. She didn't even know if they came from her own being or if they were a nasty reminder of the past. A physical manifestation of her trauma. No one needed to know any of that. But she'd gotten tired and then pissed, and, well, they would not be silenced any longer.

Fuck, she was so tired. How could today get any worse?

The sun was done with this day and sunk behind the trees with urgency. She checked out Evan from the corner of her eye as he continued to ignore her presence.

Fine. Fucking *fine*.

They pulled up the drive to a once-cute-but-now-overgrown little Victorian house. Her headlights lit murky beams into an old garden in the yard. Jack would love this place.

Frankie threw the truck into park with more force than necessary and took a breath before rounding on Evan with the least amount of venom she could manage. She needed him out of this truck and out of her life, and her ass on the couch, two glasses deep in whiskey with some bad TV. There was no way his family would want her services now anyway.

"Let's make this fast. What are we looking for?"

Evan finally turned to her. "You can just leave me here. I'll get what I need." His tone was cold and pissed. Frankie narrowed her eyes at him.

Evan got out, slamming the door hard enough to make Frankie clench her jaw. She let out a noise that was something between a growl and an exasperated sigh.

She wanted to throttle him. Asshole. Fucking asshole.

Evan approached his grandmother's porch and then slowed his movements. He curled and uncurled his fists a few times.

What the hell was he doing?

He stepped up a few steps and then froze, falling back on his back foot. Frankie saw his hand reach for the railing and miss, and he started to lean forward, his palms finding the step above him.

His back heaved huge breaths in and out as his shoulders shook. And Frankie knew what this was. She flung herself out of the truck and launched towards him.

*****

Evan's vision tunneled. His chest sawed through breaths and failed to find any relief.

Not again. Not again. Not again, *not again.*

He turned away from the porch as a sea of black curls and giant stormy eyes entered his vision. Two warm hands gripped the outside of his shoulders.

She was underwater asking, "Evan? Look at me. Look here—" She then lifted her pointer finger in front of him.

He focused on it.

Underwater, her voice came again. "Now look at that hydrangea over there," pointing to a bush in the side yard nearby. He did.

"Now look here again." Her finger reappeared.

"Now look there." She pointed at the hydrangea.

She did this a few more times. His back loosened up. Something shifted in his brain. Something about switching between those two tiny tasks unlocked his posture and his breathing came easier.

A warm hand found his forearm and steered him back toward the truck. His stomach lurched and he clenched his flannel shirt over his gut.

The hand guided him to the back tire well. "Lean here with your hands on your knees and look at the ground," she said. And disappeared.

Sounds came from the cab: objects moving, jars clinking, and then she was back. The tailgate of the truck fell, and he felt the breeze of a blanket getting spread out.

"Get in," she tried gently. He stared at her. "Now."

He heaved himself onto the blanket in the truck bed, not entirely sure what was happening or why he was following her orders.

"Lie on your right side."

He did as he was told. He started shaking, suddenly very cold. He pinched his eyes closed and tucked a sob down deep. He didn't want to let that out right now.

Something warm surrounded him. Rosemary overloaded his senses. He took a deep breath in and let it out slowly, his body loosening more. Another blanket drifted down on top of his frame. Her arm wrapped around his waist and pulled his back tight against her chest. She tucked her legs into the backs of his knees, tangling their legs together. A pair of boots knocked into his sneakers. His body began to warm from her heat—she was like a furnace.

Time slowed back down. His shakes faded into tremors and then into nothing. Her fingers—Frankie's fingers, he realized, stroked up and down the back of his head. Thinking of those lovely tattoos on her hands, he let out another deep breath.

"How are you?" Her voice was soft and careful, nothing like how they had argued earlier this afternoon.

"Warmer," was all he could manage, his voice hoarse.

The wind ripped through the trees, and leaves tore off to scrape over the pavement. Some hit the truck's windows. He listened to the sound with his eyes closed, tracking the paths of leaves by their music. A few floated down on top of them. He scooted back into Frankie more to keep the chill off. Some part of him knew this was a ridiculous situation. An hour ago, they were screaming at each other loud enough for the entire town to hear them. But he wasn't mad to be lying here like this with her.

He felt a flash of shame or embarrassment. He wasn't sure which. Why was this hateful woman taking care of him? She didn't know him, didn't owe him anything.

He could feel tears coming now. "Thank you," he said, barely audible, trying to disguise them.

She tugged her arm around his waist tighter in reply.

"What was that thing you did with your finger?"

She gave a low laugh that warmed along his bones. "It's called the Polyvagal Theory. It's a trick to override your nervous system using visual cues to help re-regulate things."

"That's crazy, I've never heard of that." He wondered why *she* knew about it.

Frankie was quiet for a minute, and he listened to the wind with his eyes closed. "Does that happen a lot to you?" she asked.

He opened his eyes as they started to sting again. "Yeah. Maybe a few times a week."

"I'm sorry, that must be exhausting."

He sniffed into the blanket. "Thanks. Uh, should we head back? You can drop me off at my grandma's house." He wondered if he should feel uncomfortable with her holding him. But he didn't. And he didn't want to move right now.

"In a few minutes. Let's let your system chill out a bit, then I'll take you home."

"Okay." The wind gusted again. "Do you always keep cozy blankets in your truck?"

She chuckled again. "You never know when you'll need to have an autumnal picnic in a graveyard."

He had no idea if she was serious, but mumbled, "Yeah, makes sense."

*****

Frankie slowed to a stop outside of Agatha's cottage. She had driven there slowly, keeping a steady eye on Evan. He looked exhausted. She started to tell him to give her a call tomorrow after he got some rest, and they could go back to the old house, but Evan wasn't listening.

He opened the door and stepped out, closing it gently. Without looking her way or saying another word, he meandered up the walk and into the house.

Damn. Poor guy. She sighed and sank back into her seat, a hand on the steering wheel and another running through her hair. Remembering how she slipped and let out her shadows in broad daylight. She felt relief now as she let some of that darkness release, seeping like a dark fog into the floor of her truck, cooling her aching feet.

She didn't think she'd be hearing from Evan again. At least she wouldn't have to explain the shadows.

Her truck drifted down the street, crawling its way home.

CHAPTER 9

Frankie stood at the kitchen stovetop, stirring ground turkey in a pan with something labeled as "stir fry sauce." The TV blared from the den over the kitchen island.

"Tonight, on Spirit Stalkers, *my crew of four fearless guys and I will lock ourselves into this abandoned, haunted lighthouse."*

Opening a jar of kimchi from the farmer's market over the sink, Frankie grabbed a fork and shoveled an obscene amount of the tangy, spicy cabbage into her mouth. It dripped down her chin. Very cute. Ah, the joys of living alone.

"Our tour guide tells us of a horrifying encounter just a few nights ago."

Chomping down on her bite, Frankie glared at the show's host. He was dressed in all black, wearing long sleeves and black fingerless gloves for some fucking reason. Even though they were filming somewhere in Florida. He stood with his arms crossed, stroking his goatee while interviewing a woman who was decidedly *not* camera-trained.

"Elain tells me how a dark force nearly knocked her off her feet one night when she was working here alone."

Now working through another bite from the jar, she rolled her eyes, first in annoyance, but it quickly faded into kimchi bliss. Through a full mouth, Frankie yelled, "Don't say it, I know you want to."

Brad's face shifted from color to black and white as his voiceover asked, *"Could this dark force be a demon? Could it be holding the other ghosts hostage in some kind of portal?"*

Frankie choked on her bite in laughter, the heat from the mixture making her nose sting. "Not everything is a demon and a portal, Brad." Such a tool.

She loved to hate-watch *Spirit Stalkers*. Her night was already improving. Rounding back to the stove as the show flipped to a commercial, she quickly stirred in some veggies and then dumped the mixture on top of some noodles. By the time the show had returned, Brad was creeping up the lighthouse stairs in night vision, whisper-yelling, *"What was that?"* And Frankie was plopping down on the couch next to a belly-up Clemmie to enjoy this... ground turkey, vaguely Korean-inspired dish.

Frankie's thoughts drifted again to Evan as she stroked Clemmie's tummy. He'd seemed thoroughly weirded out by her shadows earlier. And her entire life. Her job. Everything. Her eyes zoned out while Brad yelled into an empty hallway, shaking a digital recorder at the ghost.

"Here, I realize that the spirit wants to confront us. Alone. I quickly delegate to my team." Brad entered a screaming match with his castmate and camera guy, Taylor—also dressed in black—who always seemed to get sent to the scariest places solo.

She tucked her legs up beneath her, thinking of Evan's flaring, furious, hazel eyes and the way he clenched his jaw during their argument. She sighed. What a weird day. Had she overstepped when he had that panic attack? This was always Frankie's problem—she took charge in every single situation and never asked anyone else what they thought was needed. And he had been in no state to say what he needed. If Evan wasn't fully creeped out by shadows coming out of her fucking hair and body, he definitely must have been when she spooned him in her truck bed. What was she thinking?

She remembered her food and dug into it with urgency, working to clear her plate in record time. Was this meal a cultural abomination? Yes. Was it rich in garlic, ginger, and a sticky sweet sauce? Yes. Was this show a living nightmare that had somehow been running for over twenty seasons? Yes.

Was this moment on her couch almost a perfect night? Frankie propped her socked feet on the coffee table.

Also yes.

CHAPTER 10

The next few days passed in a busy blur. The Black Cat was hopping with tourists, and the more obvious items—candles, crystals, skincare products—sold out more than once. Frankie was glad for the distraction and the paycheck, but she had not had a day off in over two weeks and was desperate for a break.

Luckily, Jack and Bex had the same idea.

On a gray and foggy weekday morning, Frankie and Jack walked through muddy rows of squash. Bex moved ahead of them, pulling a wagon already loaded up with several pumpkins.

"Hey babe," Jack called up to her, "We're not even a third of the way through the patch. We might want to slow down on loading up so early?" They were right—hills and hills of orange speckled across the horizon. This place was huge. It would be a mistake to load up too early and miss the good stuff farther out.

Bex whipped her long braid behind her and turned to flash a giant grin. She wore shades of orange sherbet today, along with her wrecked Timberlyne boots. "We need like, a *shitload* of pumpkins. We're getting two houses' worth," she said, breathless from exertion. Bex was stunning in an almost goddess-like way. Tall and buff, her dark brown skin looked incredible in any color, and Frankie couldn't fathom how her hairstyles always looked pristine, even after a long week of contract work. Her personality was that of a breezy fairy. A fairy on a construction site. Bex was a bag of bizarre, and Frankie was so grateful that Jack had brought her into her life.

Frankie jabbed her hands in her pockets and glanced up at Jack, who ogled their wife's ass in those pale orange leggings. She jutted her hip against Jack to break the spell. Jack held their hands up in mock surrender. "You can't blame me, come on." A devious smile broke their face in half. Frankie scoffed.

Jack peered down at Frankie as they squished along another row of pumpkins. Frankie knew that Jack was dying to say something but wouldn't give them the chance. She didn't want to talk about her bad day with Evan. Jack and Bex knew that something had happened to rattle Frankie and that it was related to a client. They had given her space, and she was grateful, but she knew their family code demanded truth from each other. Frankie sighed, mood souring.

Bex then held up two, medium-sized pumpkins in front of her breasts, faced them, and made a honking sound while she flexed her hands on the gourds. Frankie and Jack collapsed in laughter. Jack dropped their coffee cup on the ground and clutched at their stomach. Bex was delighted with their reaction and danced back to the wagon with her boob pumpkins.

Frankie worked to regain composure and smiled at Bex. Bex gave her a knowing look back. They both faced Frankie, Bex blocking the wagon with her body so they couldn't proceed any further.

"All right," Bex began with her arms crossed. "Let's have it. What's going on with you? This is your favorite time of the year and you've been sullen all week."

Frankie glared at her. "Have not."

Jack snorted and perched on the edge of the wagon before tossing the empty cup into it and tucking their hands into their pockets. "We're in the middle of the patch, Frankie. No one's around. Just talk to us."

Frankie gripped her hands into fists a few times. Looked between the two of them. She sighed again, sinking back into her hip.

"I had a weird day with a client." She had said this sentence to them already, and the pair waited for her to go on. "It was just a weird day. He wanted me to help with a family curse and insisted on following me around during some house calls. He's a bit of a Boy Scout. Didn't like some of my methods. We got into it." She paused, clenching and unclenching her jaw. "And... and my shadows came out. And he fully freaked."

Jack's face fell into a sympathetic look and Bex's face twisted in concern. Frankie felt her eyes start to burn and hated the effect her loving friends had on her. To make her feel so safe that she could cry in a pumpkin patch, and they would still have her back. Always.

"How much did they come out?" Bex asked. "Like, Medusa?"

Frankie considered the best way to frame this. Nope, no good way to frame it.

"No… more like Hades."

"Damn," Jack said. "That hasn't happened in a while."

"Something about this guy got under my skin. He was so judgmental. And he's Agatha Lawson's grandson, by the way."

"Agatha's a good lady. Are you going to help them out?" Bex asked.

"I dunno. I haven't heard from him again, and I probably won't. Which means poor Agatha is stuck dealing with a family curse." That was the real reason she was upset. She was damning Agatha to carry this curse during the worst parts of her illness, all the way until her death, all because of Frankie's temper.

"Nuh-uh, stop it." Jack glared at her. "Stop doing that, I know what you're thinking, and you are *not* personally responsible for every person who lives in this town. You didn't curse this woman, so stop punishing yourself."

"Goddess, Jack," she smiled at them through watery eyes. "You're such a dick. Get out of my head."

Jack didn't smile in return but said, "You deserve to enjoy your October. And we want to enjoy it with you. Now come on." They stood, knees popping. "I'm sure Bex wants to try on more boobs."

She gave a soft laugh as the wagon started to move again.

Bex passed the wagon handle to Jack and fell back into stride with Frankie. "You know what we should do? Family dinner. Tonight. You've been hate-watching that stupid show every night this week, haven't you? No more." She looped an arm around Frankie's waist, pulling her into a side hug. "Tonight, we feast."

CHAPTER 11

Nan gasped at the obvious plot twist unfolding in the *Law & Order* episode they watched together. Evan smiled to himself. He knew she had long figured out the twist but feigned surprise, if only to trick herself into having more fun watching the show.

She muted the screen as the credits rolled. Evan waited. He knew what was coming.

"Evan. You're sulking. Did you go down to that shop and talk to that girl?"

"Yeah, I did. Have you met her? She's a loose cannon. Or a bomb. Or a... viper. She's got teeth."

Nan frowned, watching him with a disappointed expression. "Did something happen?"

"No." Yes. Yes, several things had happened.

Should he start with the fact that she herself cursed someone in his presence, not even at the urge of a client? Or that actual shadows poured out of her, her hair, her mouth, from her fingers, like some kind of demon? Or that he'd then had a crippling panic attack in front of his childhood home and ended up being spooned by that demon in the back of her truck?

The entire day had been disturbing, upsetting. Unmooring. He had not stopped thinking about it and had worked endlessly to drive it out of his mind.

Nan read all of this on his face. "Evan, there are lots of people in this world. Not everyone is going to share your exact values. It doesn't make them less

48

human or less of a person. Sometimes, you'll have to align yourself with someone you disagree with. Sometimes, it's the only way to get the job done."

He knew she was speaking from experience. Nan was a prism, every part of her a contrast: she was a shrewd negotiator in business, and soft as a marshmallow at home as the two of them dozed in the sunny grass. Her success in the business world had been built on diplomacy, not ego, even when having to partner with horrible men at work in the eighties and nineties. She believed someone had cursed her life, and she still told him to find the light in the people.

He felt his throat close. "I love you." It was the only thing he could find in his brain. The only true thing.

She laughed a hoarse laugh and coughed, patting her heart to say she felt the same. "Don't be stubborn about this, please. I need to know you're taking this seriously. She might be the only option we have." Hard-nosed until the end, this woman.

He leaned back in his chair. "I'll go talk to her."

*****

A hidden speaker blared Nine Inch Nails through the open windows of her house. Frankie balanced with one foot on a step ladder and one foot on the edge of the hall table, weaving a garland of bats around the chandelier to hang down in the most aesthetically pleasing way. This was not safe—she wore thick wool socks and could feel her foot's grip giving way, starting to slide. She tucked the garland into place right before she lost her balance and landed on her feet on the ground.

Nine Inch Nailed it, Frankie thought, making herself laugh at her own dumb joke.

She heard the creak of the front porch steps. Bex had offered to fix the creak, but there was no way in hell Frankie wanted to be surprised by unwanted visitors. Besides, her doorbell could be jarring, but she couldn't bear to part with it. Before it could sound, she slid on her socks over to the door and opened it.

Evan Lawson was on her porch, a fist raised to knock on the door. He looked as surprised as she felt. "Um, hey."

"Evan Lawson. Hi." She couldn't hide the surprise from her voice.

They stared at each other for a long moment before Evan's gaze found her hand gripping the front door. With no idea why, she pulled her large sweater's sleeve down over her hand, needing to feel less exposed.

"Come in?" she asked. He nodded and stepped through. She led him to the library where the decor storage boxes were all open, just off the hall. She was in the middle of decorating for Samhain and would not let this disruption stop her. She pulled her phone out and turned down the music.

"There's like twenty pumpkins on your por—" He stopped short as he rounded the doorway and beheld her library. "Whoah." His eyes widened. "Okay, I'm jealous."

This was the correct reaction. Her library was stunning, every wall lined floor-to-ceiling with books. Many of them were old occult texts or spell books, but she also had full shelves of classics and an entire wall of fantasy books. The floors were original and restored, and the room was stocked with a few vintage seating options as well as a huge, wood-burning fireplace along the far wall. The windows were tall and let in good light, one of them looking out onto the front porch.

Nonchalant, Frankie picked up another garland—this one made of cute, wooden ghosts with various spooky faces—and started to drape it over the mantle. Thank the goddess she had something to do with her hands. She looked over her shoulder at him.

"I'll be honest, I didn't expect to see you again."

He looked at the floor, a flush creeping up over his collar. "It was... an interesting day. It got a little weird at the end there." He dared to glance up at her. He had to be talking about her shadows. She schooled her face into neutrality, no idea if he was going to demand answers from her, act like it didn't happen, or be a dick.

To her shock, it was none of these. "I wanted to thank you. For taking care of me. You were kind to me. I was embarrassed and..." he trailed off, looking up at her again.

Frankie stopped her jaw from falling open. Well, this was unexpected. An awkward silence stretched a moment too long as he watched her. She cleared her throat. "That was a sympathy spoon, don't read anything into it."

He laughed, surprised. "A 'sympathy spoon?' Really? You guided me right into position. You sure you weren't trying to make a move on me?" His smile was infuriating. She wanted to hate him and was finding it difficult to do so.

She tapped her finger on a ghost's wooden face and decided it was worth it to get this out in the open. She said, "I know you don't agree with my methods. But it's how I work. And I'm not going to change." She put the end of the garland in place on the mantle—a period at the end of her sentence.

Evan nodded. "I know. I'm sorry for being a dick. We need your help, and it wasn't right for me to suggest you aren't capable of doing that."

Well, fuck her running. Even more unexpected. "Huh. You are not what I thought you were."

He pinned her down with an intense look. "Please tell me what happened during our argument. I can't stop thinking about it. I'm not judging you, I just want to understand."

She searched his face for panic or fear but found only curiosity. "Look, I don't know you well enough to share all of the things that have happened to me. I'll just say that you weren't in any danger. They come out of me sometimes if I'm angry or really tired. And it had been a long day."

"Do all witches do that?"

"No, I've never met anyone else who has them." She fussed with the garland.

"Are they always there?"

"They are. I'm sorry if they grossed you out, you weren't at risk or anything like that."

Alarm and guilt flashed across his face. "No, no, I was just startled. I had just seen actual magic happen for the first time in my life. I was not grossed out."

All of the apologies hung heavy in the space between them. Frankie couldn't stand the silence. "So, do you still want me to work on your grandma's case?"

"If you'll have me." Evan gave her a flirty smile. *Prick.*

"Alrighty then." Frankie knelt down to a box and dug for some skeleton plushies. Evan sat on the ground next to her. She stiffened. Did he have to smell so good?

"But I'm guessing right now you're busy?"

"I can multitask." She turned to find him sitting very close to her. He stared at her hair. "Looking for something?" she asked dryly.

Evan grinned. "Busted. Can I see them? Or is it not okay to ask that? Sorry."

She let two shadows pull free from her mass of curls and formed them into large horns that framed her head. Evan's face went slack. He unconsciously started to reach for one of them, then stopped himself.

"Shit, sorry."

"It's okay." She leaned the side of her head down so he could get a better look. "You can touch it."

Evan cautiously ran a finger along the side of the horn, and Frankie strangled the sound that tried to tear from her throat and swallowed it. This was an inappropriate time to be making *that* kind of noise. Her cheeks went pink, and she dug her nails into her palms. Her mind reeled. This had never happened. She realized in horror that no one had touched her shadows before, and the sensation was… unexpected. Oblivious, Evan kept stroking her horn.

"It feels solid! And tingly." He laughed to himself. "Huh, that's cool." He withdrew his hand and found her eyes again. His eyes were blueish green today, with a tinge of gold.

"I've got something going on tonight, but we can start to work on your case officially in the next few days," she said, her head lightly spinning.

"Deal."

CHAPTER 12

A doorbell sounded. No, someone had *rung* a doorbell, but the sound was not a *ding-dong*. It was the deep *dong* of a cathedral bell. Obviously custom, and obviously installed by Frankie. Evan laughed. "Wow, okay, Wednesday Adams."

She smirked at him and stood up from her seat on the library floor, her horns going away in a puff of shadow-smoke. "Want to meet the hands behind these built-in bookshelves?"

Standing on the porch with a cooler were two figures—a gorgeous woman and an androgynous person he knew from somewhere. Clemmie rocketed down from upstairs and wound in between their legs, the woman reaching down to scratch his ribs.

"Whaddup. So, we have an extra guest for dinner tonight." Frankie leaned into the open front door with a fist on her full hip. Her two guests gave him sinister smiles.

Evan raised his eyebrows. "You do?"

"Yes, dummy. Are you really going to pass up free dinner and drinks?" She gave him an incredulous glare.

"I guess not?"

The stunning Black woman stepped inside. "That's a good answer," she offered, her voice light and a bit musical. Long dark hair streamed in a braid down her back. She had a tall and muscular build and wore all pastel athleticwear with well-worn construction work boots. She pulled out of a baby blue puffer coat and hung it on a hall hook while looking him up and down.

"Evan, this is Bex, contractor extraordinaire. She built the bookcases and helped me renovate most of my house." The other person stepped over the threshold with the vibe of tall, steely cool in a long trench coat with a high collar. "And this is her spouse, Jack, my oldest friend from college. They contract me to help with haunted houses that won't sell."

That's where he had seen their face before—in ads all over town and his Instagram feed of the top-rated Sawtooth Bay realtor.

Jack peered at him through cat-eyed frames. "Frankie doesn't normally bring home strays."

"Well, I'm house-trained," Evan said, crossing his arms and nodding once as if he were proud of the fact. Jack chuckled and walked to the kitchen, Clemmie quick to follow.

They called over their shoulder, "Frankie, do you have any more of that migraine tea mix you made me? I had too much caffeine and I am *suffering*."

Frankie pushed her oversized sweater sleeves up to her elbows, tattooed skin sliding free. "Yeah, it's in the pantry, clearly labeled," she said, rolling her eyes.

"Bitchin'. I'm gonna make a hot toddy. Anybody else want one? Evan?" They stuck their head back into the hall from the kitchen.

"No thanks, I'm kind of a beer guy."

Frankie grabbed his bicep and pulled him out of the library, where he wanted to live for the rest of his life, and into the kitchen as if she were afraid he was going to run away. He didn't hate it. He caught himself grinning at this change in his evening plans, then quickly fixed his face when Frankie glanced at him.

"If you're staying, we're putting you to work. Do you cook?"

"I do."

She stared at him. "Interesting." She pivoted around. "Okay, fam, we have bison burger patties, we have corn, and you wonderful people have brought oysters."

Bex gripped a glass of whiskey and did a little squirmy dance, "Fuck yeah!

I'm starving." A little bit of whiskey sloshed over the rim of the glass and onto the hardwood. And control-freak Frankie didn't seem to mind.

Jack aimed straight for a drawer and grabbed a lighter stick, then headed outside towards the grill on the deck, leaving the doors wide open. Like they owned the place.

Evan dug through the fridge to find a beer. He spied Bex leaning over the patio table to talk to Frankie. He couldn't get over this little family she had. They were so comfortable with each other. His heart clanged a little with envy, a heavy anchor in his chest. He had friends in grad school. But that's the thing about grad school friends—it's an intense capsule in time, and then you mourn their loss.

Maybe he could rebuild in Sawtooth Bay after Nan passed. He sighed, mad at himself and full of guilt that he was even thinking about life after her. There would be so, so much life after her. He couldn't bear it.

He shook the thoughts free, determined to try and enjoy his evening. He could hear Bex and Frankie chatting and knew he shouldn't be eavesdropping. But how was he not going to eavesdrop?

Bex waggled her eyebrows at Frankie, who shucked oysters. "Soooo. Who's the sexy lumberjack? Is that the guy?"

Frankie smacked her arm. "Dude! Shut up! And he's not a lumberjack, he's a librarian."

She didn't say he *wasn't* sexy.

"Isn't he kind of cut for a librarian?"

Evan grinned into the fridge air. He'd never taken so long to get a beer in his life.

"Bex, for fuck's sake. He's a client."

"A little masculine socialization wouldn't kill you."

"Do you not see me holding this knife?" Frankie pointed her oyster-shucking knife at her.

Bex gave her a loud, smacking kiss on her cheek. "Yes, but you stab with love." Evan snorted, finally grabbed a can of lager, and headed out to the deck.

Bex gave him an innocent smile and then sauntered off to help Jack. Frankie glared after her.

"What can I help with?"

She pointed her knife at the stack of corn on the table. "You know what to do with that? It's going on the grill."

"I'm on it." He rolled his flannel sleeves up higher and settled onto the bench by the table. He looked around the backyard while he worked to clean the corn. The yard was spacious—a maple on fire in the waning sun, surrounded by a burning carpet of leaves, an oak tree stained in orange, a massive garden packed with end-of-season veggies and more herbs than he knew existed. A cool gust breathed through the trees, and they creaked and swayed in a gentle roar. Woods lined the back perimeter of the yard—woods so thick he couldn't see where they ended. Patchwork shadows painted the underbrush.

Evan glanced at Frankie as she worked with her knife, tattooed hands moving with alarming efficiency. Her sweater slipped off her right shoulder in a moment of concentration, and Evan was rewarded with a full view of a tentacle tattoo, reaching up like it was trying to climb out of her skin.

He wondered if it was an octopus or a squid.

He wondered how far down it went.

He cleared his throat, trying to focus. "We're keeping those raw, right?"

"Of course we are, we're heathens, not monsters."

After the food was prepped and grilled and devoured, they all chatted and drank and laughed into dusk and then into the evening, working through the pile of oysters. Fairy lights in the trees bloomed into life as the light faded. Frankie asked Evan about his library science program, and the group ranked their favorite classics. When their breath started to fog, they headed inside. Evan was delighted to see them head back into the library. Bex rubbed her arms and whined to Frankie, clinking around somewhere in the kitchen.

"*Frankieee.* It's too cold. Can you do the thing, please-please-please?"

After a dramatic, exasperated sigh, Evan heard Frankie snap her fingers, and the darkened hearth exploded into raging flames. Evan jumped back and Bex squealed.

She whispered in a conspiratorial tone, "I love making her do that." Evan heard a grumbled, grumpy complaining under her breath as Frankie joined them.

The meal and drink settled heavily into the group, and conversation quieted into comfortable silence, the fireplace crackling and snapping. Bex dozed against Jack's legs, who nestled back into the loveseat replying to emails. Workaholic. Clemmie passed out on a pillow throne in front of the hearth, belly up and feet twitching in a dream-heavy sleep. Evan could count his ribs in the dull light. Frankie lay on the rug, her back to the ground and legs up on the sofa next to Evan. Thick wool socks knocked together and wiggled, her eyes staring up at the ceiling, deep in thought.

He couldn't articulate it exactly, but this felt right, painfully so.

After the third time of nodding off, Evan excused himself for the walk back to Nan's. The temperature plummeted, but his head felt warm from conversation and his belly felt stuffed full of good food. Before he realized it, he'd made it back home and was falling into bed. He crashed hard into a deep sleep, not staring at the ceiling for hours or pacing the halls as he had for weeks. Just an immediate, blackout dreamless sleep.

CHAPTER 13

Saturdays at The Black Cat were long days filled with tarot readings, customers asking if she'd ever been to Salem and if it was worth the drive after they left Sawtooth, and wrapping up lots of spell candles at checkout.

Frankie felt profound relief when a young woman approached her counter with a list of herbs she needed. Finally, a fellow practitioner. She scanned down the page, fixing her face into a pleasant expression. Mostly generic stuff, lavender, rosemary, sage. Stuff she could buy at the grocery store. But further down in the list, things got interesting. This girl also needed calamus root, rue, and cayenne pepper.

Well, then. She glanced up at the girl, who shuffled her feet and avoided Frankie's gaze. Frankie raised her brows. She knew a baneful working when she saw one.

She hopped off her stool and gathered the herbs into brown paper bags, labeled them with approximate amounts for her customer, and rang her up. The girl's relief was palpable. She went to grab the bag from the counter and leave the store as quickly as possible, but Frankie held the bag firm. The girl finally met her eyes.

"Word of advice," Frankie said quietly, since there were still customers all around them. "Get some protective wards in place before you do any workings. Trust me." She gave her a wink.

The girl turned purple, yanked the bag from her grip, and ran out of the store. Frankie shook her head, laughing to herself. She'd been a teen witch. She understood how extra-charged everything was at that age and how desperate for personal power she had felt. She hoped whoever this customer was targeting deserved what they were getting—but that wasn't for her to decide. She just sold the wares. Regardless, the girl would learn the hard way if she didn't protect herself before doing any kind of hex.

Frankie's skin prickled. She glanced up to see Evan enter the store. Golden afternoon sun ringed his broad frame, cheeks pinked from the cold breeze.

"Hello again." She stood behind her counter.

"Hi." He stared her down for a long moment. Weird. He glanced around the store full of customers and asked, "Should I come back later?"

"No. Please save me from these tourists. I'm going to snap. And I left Clemmie at home today, so I have no one to complain to."

"Nan says she'd like to meet you, maybe tomorrow?" Evan moved out of the way so Frankie could check out someone purchasing a candle.

"Love to. Is tomorrow morning okay?"

Evan opened his mouth to answer, but a horrifying bellow burst through the shop door. Frankie craned her head to see over the pool of customers, now frozen in place by the scene unfolding.

Alexsy and Lena Kozlowski staggered into the space. Lena was holding Alexsy upright, which was difficult to do because the man was easily well over six feet tall. Lena was a short, plump woman with a normally sunny disposition. But now, her features were distraught. Black veins stretched up from Alexsy's shirt collar, and his lips were a dark indigo color. He tipped his head back to the star-painted ceiling and let out that horrible bellow again, a sound like someone having their legs crushed. A collective wave of tourist screams followed, and the tourist sea parted around the couple as it poured out into the square.

Frankie ran around the counter and tried to yell over the chaos. "Lena! What the hell happened?"

"He went down into that damned mine again! I told him not to go in there, but he stumbled home looking like this—"

On cue, Alexsy bent in half and vomited up a fountain of black bile onto Frankie's hardwood floor. "God*dammit*, Alexsy!" she swore at him, wanting to strangle him. Racing to the shop's door, she wedged a nearby broom through its handle to keep anyone from coming in.

Frankie's attention snapped to Evan. His face was pale and eyes wide, which was honestly a valid reaction. "Evan, get me the jar of black salt from the back office!" She had to yell over Alexsy's screams, sounding less and less human by the second.

Evan threw himself over the counter like it was a track hurdle and disappeared into the back. Frankie grabbed a large ceremonial knife encased in a glass display as Evan came back into view, holding the large jar. Frankie held her hand up, and Evan tossed her the salt over the counter.

"Now what?" he called to her. Frankie was impressed, he was handling this crisis well.

"Now you and Lena hold him down!"

The sunlight streaming into the shop darkened. Tourists pressed their faces against The Black Cat's glass windows, blocking out the light, and Frankie noted a few phones filming the scene. Nothing she could do about that now. She was not looking forward to getting tagged again on Instagram.

Evan came to Alexsy's side and eased him down to the ground while the man thrashed and tried to bite him. Lena sat on his other arm as Evan held a firm hand to his chest. Frankie quickly weighed her options. She didn't have any wishbones to snap. She didn't even have enough black salt to draw a proper circle to hold him in. But she did have something else she could use. She swore. This was going to be quick and dirty.

"I have to circle him in. When I get close to closing it, you two back out or you'll get trapped inside!" Frankie closed her eyes to center herself around the deafening sounds coming from the man and pictured her power like a vast lake before her. She saw herself place a palm to the water and let it flood into her.

Opening her eyes, she sliced her hand open with the knife. She slapped her hand down to the wood floor and ran clockwise around Alexsy's body. As her blood made its way around to close the circle, Lena and Evan scrambled. Encased by her power, Alexsy stopped screaming and moved into a crouch like an animal, a low rumble escaping his chest.

Lena quietly sobbed somewhere behind Frankie. Everyone panted for a few moments and watched Alexsy pace on all fours in the small circle. His eyes were fully white now, and Frankie knew a heavy fog would hold him under the possession until he was freed. White eyes usually meant an elemental spirit, and Frankie knew that mine spirits got bored and liked to hitchhike out of there.

This one might not respond to a simple handful of salt. But it was worth a try.

Frankie opened the jar of black salt and poured a handful into her non-injured hand. Her grip on the jar was slippery with blood, so she placed it down on the floor. She approached the circle and blew the salt in the spirit's face. The spirit hissed and spat black blood at her, which smeared and dripped down an invisible wall.

It didn't work. The spirit still glared out at her. Frankie sighed. Option two was going to suck. She retrieved the jar of salt again, steadied herself, and poured a large handful on top of her bleeding hand. She cried out a string of swear words so profane that even Evan looked shocked. Once the salt was truly soaked in her blood, she mounded it up into a snowball. Holding it to her mouth, she whispered in a banishment spell and poured in some shadows for extra oomph. She took another deep breath and threw it with all of her strength into Alexsy's face. It hit him square in the nose, and he flew backward, back cracking against the circle's invisible walls. Bloody salt exploded inside the circle. He slid down, head hanging onto his chest. His pale hair hung low on his brow, drenched in sweat.

They waited in silence. A white fog seeped out from his ears and nostrils, forming a thin river that flowed under the crack in the door. Frankie watched until it was fully gone. *Back to the mineshaft with you.*

Alexsky gasped and snapped his head up, white eyes gone. He found Lena's face and they both started to cry.

"I'm so sorry, Lena, I'm so so so, so sorry, sorry so—" he mumbled on and on.

Frankie leaned down and swiped her slightly cleaner hand through the blood circle, breaking it, and removed the broom door wedge. She then flipped the "Open" sign to "The witch is out." Any remaining onlookers seemed to have fled from the white smoke leaving the building, thank the gods. Lena pushed Evan out of the way and jumped on top of Alexsy. "You stupid, stupid man!" She gripped his face with her hands. "*Never* go down there again or I swear to god I'll leave you!"

Frankie walked behind the counter to wash her hands off in the back room. She returned to find Evan leaning against the counter, watching the couple hold each other on the floor. Frankie reached beneath the register and pulled out her emergency whiskey. She downed a few swallows and held her bleeding hand up above her heart.

"Evan, can you get me that jar on the top of the shelf there?" She pointed to a healing mix of herbs.

She picked the whiskey up again and braced herself. She moved to pour it over her hand but paused and called down to the couple. "I'm sending an invoice to your email in about ten minutes and it's not going to be cheap. Lena, get him on his feet and get out. Alexsy, if you go down into that mine again, I'll let the spirits have you and ban you from the store. That's a promise." She let some of her power seep out and rattle the objects in the room.

The two scrambled and stumbled out, yelling their thanks.

Frankie collapsed onto her stool. Thoroughly drained. Evan took the bottle from her. "Let me do this." He wasn't asking. "Ready?" He took her hand and poured the liquor over it. She hissed in a breath and stared at the wood grain on the floor. She looked up at Evan to find him watching her, an amused look on his face. "So why was he down in a mine?"

Frankie snorted. "I think he works for the city, but the dumbfuck has a YouTube channel where he goes to dangerous places and tries to contact ghosts. Both Lena and I have told him more than once not to go down there."

Evan reached for the healing herbs. "What do I do with this stuff?"

Frankie started to take the jar from him. "Oh, you have to chew it up and then press it in the wound. I can do it—" Evan pulled the jar from her.

"No. Just sit down." Remarkably, he poured out a healthy handful of the herbs, and without asking what they were, stuffed them in his mouth and started to chew. Once they were saturated, he pulled out the wad and spread it across the wound.

"*Mother fuck,*" Frankie groaned through clenched teeth. She breathed in through her nose and blew out the breaths slowly. "You know, you handled that like, really well."

Evan's hazel eyes flicked up to her and then back down at her hand. "I mean, I didn't have to cut my hand open, so I think you got a worse deal here." Frankie handed him a roll of gauze, and he wrapped it snug around her palm. She watched him stare at her palm, lined with long scars from slicing it open again and again, and forced herself not to squirm under his direct focus. He finally let go of her hand. "How long will it take for that to heal?"

"About a day and a half. I heal slightly faster than other people, and that's a pretty potent healing mix. Where were we? Agatha, sometime tomorrow?"

Evan made a surprised sound. "Sure, if you still want to. Come in the morning. She'll be less tired then."

The two spent the next hour cleaning up The Black Cat. Frankie tried to shoo Evan out more than once, but he refused to let her clean up alone. She finally relented, and they cleaned in comfortable silence.

CHAPTER 14

Cool, orange sunlight broke across Nan's backyard, where Evan sipped his coffee. He heard a truck door close out front. She was exactly on time. It only took a few of his long strides to get from the patio door to the front door. This house was so unbearably small.

He opened the front door just as Frankie was adjusting her bag on her shoulder. Her hair was pulled back. Enormous blackout sunglasses slid halfway down her delicate nose, and her eyes were lined with black eyeliner, which offset her porcelain skin to devastating effect. He took a sip of coffee to mask his stunned expression.

"Morning." He opened the door wider for her.

"Please tell me you have more of that."

"Obviously. How do you take it?"

Frankie thumped her bag to the ground inside the hall. "Today? Black." He could've guessed that. He handed her an oversized mug, and she gave him an honest-to-god smile that made him weak on his feet. She chugged down the boiling-hot drink for several seconds. This girl was insane.

"Right. Is she awake?"

Evan nodded. "Yeah, she's ready for visitors. Right through here." He led Frankie down the hall to the back room where Nan's bed had been set up in a chair position. She'd put in pearl earrings this morning when she woke up, and the extra effort filled him up like warm honey. "Nan, this is Frankie, the insane woman you sent me to go find."

Nan nodded. "Frankie Wolfe."

Frankie approached, took a seat to be on Nan's level, and leaned on the side rail a bit. "Agatha Lawson. I think we might know each other." She squinted her eyes a bit. "You've come to The Black Cat before, right?"

Nan hacked an awful, wet cough, but Frankie didn't flinch or pull away from her. His heart warmed. "Yes, a few times. You gave me a tarot reading last year."

Frankie's face fell. "Oh. Gods. I—" She was clearly trying to remember what she had foretold.

Nan spared her. "You predicted that my health was going to go downhill this year." Her laugh became another cough. "Well, it was money well spent." She eyed Frankie's forearms, now visible that she had pushed up her blood-red sweater's sleeves. "I like your tattoos. I'm thinking about getting one for my birthday next year."

There was a pause in the room.

Frankie burst out laughing and Nan joined her. "I like you," Frankie said as her laugh died down. Evan was not at all surprised that Frankie would appreciate Nan's gallows humor. He leaned against the wall and soaked in the sounds of their conversation.

The two chatted comfortably for a few minutes, both sipping their coffee. Finally, Nan put her mug down. "Alright you two, let's get to it. Evan tells me he's taking this all more seriously now. I hope that's true." She frowned at Frankie, who nodded to reassure her. "Good. As I've told him about seven times now, there's a box on the back sun porch. It has all of my city council things, including a log of initiatives I tried to pass. The ledger has a record of everyone who opposed my projects, voted no, that sort of thing." He loved Nan's voice—it was rough and deep. Leathery. Full of history and badassery.

"Do you have anything very personal to you during that time?" Frankie asked. "Maybe something like jewelry?"

She thought for a moment. "Yes, I always wore my grandmother's ring in those meetings. Do you remember it, Evan? It's a large ruby on a gold band?"

Evan knew immediately what ring she was talking about. He remembered sitting in her lap as a boy and spinning the ruby around and around her finger while she took calls in her home office. "I remember it. Do you know where in the house it is?"

She shook her head. "No idea. I stopped wearing rings last year when my joints started to hurt." Evan grimaced. Such a sudden illness. It was so clear now what had caused it.

"That would be perfect. If we can find it, I can use it in a few different ways to help undo the curse." Frankie tapped her knee in thought. "Agatha, I checked your yard earlier this morning for any kind of hexes placed or buried on the property, but I didn't find anything."

Evan suppressed his shock. Had he known Frankie was poking around in the bushes, he would not have made coffee in his underwear.

She continued. "I don't think this is a physical curse, like an object that I can destroy. It's going to be more complicated to unravel."

"I'm not surprised," Nan said, leaning back into her pillow. "The city council is full of vindictive assholes. I didn't get along with everyone at City Hall. But I did with the community. And after serving for years and years, I was suddenly voted out last November when my health nosedived. It's related, I'm sure of it."

Frankie nodded. "I believe you."

Nan straightened in her bed as much as possible—a C.E.O. in her element, ready to delegate. "You two need to retrieve that box of files. I don't know who did this, but I'm sure it's tied to my time on the council." She gave them a look that said they were dismissed.

Frankie stood with a warm smile for Nan. His insides liquified. "Great to see you again, Agatha. Your case has my full attention. I will find who did this." Her gray irises flashed silver, something dark lurking there.

Nan stared up into her eyes and was not alarmed by her resolve and intensity. "You do good work, Frankie Wolfe. Now, both of you leave. I need to make a call." She picked up her phone and waited for them to depart.

Evan kissed her on the cheek on his way out.

CHAPTER 15

Frankie liked Agatha.

She loved a woman who took no shit and bossed people around. What a badass. She could imagine Agatha in the nineties, decked out in a pantsuit and marching up the stairs of town hall for a council meeting.

Frankie and Evan stood outside of her truck before his childhood home. "Agatha is my new best friend."

Evan wore a sad smile. "She liked you, I can tell."

She watched him carefully. "Are you ready to do this? We can wait a bit if you need to."

Evan took a deep breath. "Can we just… go slowly?"

Anguish was written all over his face, bruising her heart as they approached the building. Frankie guessed this looming house had been his safe harbor in between months of getting dumped off at boarding school. She let fury spear through her at the thought of his parents. For casting off little, boy Evan to whichever boarding school was a million miles away from the person he loved most. Valuing high society institutions over kin. For thinking that money and a name counted as parenting. And now this safe harbor overwhelmed him with so much dread and awful feelings that he couldn't bear to be inside of it. All the memories he and Agatha shared in this house mocked him while she died slowly a few minutes away.

They should have had more time together. The injustice of it all felt like an abyss, something impossible to cross over. But she swore internally to his nervous profile that she would do everything she could to make this better. Somehow. She watched him look up at the house, his temple already a little beaded with sweat despite the chilly morning. She stepped closer to him. Leaves crunched under her boots, and he looked down as she slowly approached. She held his gaze and slid her hand into his.

"I got you," she said quietly. The intensity of her promise burned through layers of her being like a hot coal, and she worried she would frighten him.

He took a shaky breath. "Please don't let go," he whispered. She shook her head. She would not let go of him. She would not let go of this.

He took another breath and started up the porch stairs.

*****

Evan's heart threatened to give out as he gripped Frankie's hand. He made it up the steps. He made it up the porch. His free hand shook as he slid the key into the lock and opened the door. He paused just outside, letting Frankie's rosemary scent wrap around him as a gust of wind ripped by, her wild hair flying free.

Stepping into the hall, he muttered, "So far so good." Frankie was silent, but warmth radiated off of her and soaked into his arm. He was grateful for her quiet strength in this moment. She asked nothing of him, just offered to be there while he worked through it.

Evan closed his eyes and breathed in the smell of home. He was astonished to not feel panic's cold fingers wrapping around his lungs. His breathing came easy. And without the barrier of panic to buffer him, the emotions slammed into him at once. Everything he refused to feel from every time he tried to visit the house for this errand over recent months.

His breath flew out of him in a shudder, and he felt hot tears pour down his cheeks. Frankie stepped even closer, winding her arm around his waist, and placed her cheek on his chest. He pulled her into a hug without thinking because it felt right. She gripped him back just as hard and rubbed her hand on his back in soothing circles. He buried his nose in her hair to breathe deep, and they stayed like that for a while. The waves washed over him, and he let them— despair, anger, knee-wobbling nausea, dread. Frankie held him firm while the storm passed.

After some time, Evan released her. He hadn't realized that she'd been an inch or two off the ground as he held her. "God, sorry," he said, wiping his face with his sleeve.

She found his hand again. "Don't apologize. What can I do?"

"I'm okay right now, but can you stay nearby? I want to walk around by myself."

She pointed to the right wing of the house. "I'll be just over here." And then she left him alone with his memories.

*****

Frankie walked among Agatha's things and tried to not disturb anything, including the dust. Agatha had exquisite taste in everything from clothing to furniture. Her wing of the house was ornate but tasteful. She took care of her things. Frankie was dying to dig through her closet but kept herself in check.

This was a sacred space to Evan, and she would not jeopardize that. When the job was done, she wanted him to be able to focus on healing. She wondered if Agatha had arranged for her things to be taken care of after her death. Frankie suspected that Agatha was the type to think of everything, especially if it meant helping Evan.

Drifting through Agatha's home office, she found an enormous oak desk sleeping in the middle of the room, and a large window that overlooked the back garden. A deep, purple fainting couch lined one wall, and a bookshelf full of books and binders lined the opposite wall. She could feel the history inside these walls and listened to tiny footsteps thundering down the hall while Agatha held court over the phone. And heard through the windowpane the dull murmur of Agatha showing toddler Evan what each plant in the garden was. He must have felt so alone during school breaks with just Agatha for company. Evan needed community, she realized. He was back after years away from Sawtooth with no friends waiting for him and mourning the person he loved most in the world, thinking he had no one else to lean on. That burning coal of a promise she made climbed up her throat. She wouldn't allow that to happen to him.

Listening hard, Frankie turned to see if Evan was doing alright on his own. No sounds reached her, so she continued her search.

Finally, she made her way into Agatha's bedroom in the primary suite. A jewelry box seemed like the best place to start looking for the ring. Agatha's closet was just as she guessed: racks and racks of pantsuits, designer heels, and a large vanity against the back wall for dressing in her jewels. Frankie opened up the large cabinet as gently as possible and carefully sifted through the huge array of gemstones, gold, and silver.

Nope, no ruby ring.

*****

Evan found himself standing on the back sun porch. He found it strange that being in this peaceful place had caused him so much agony over the last few months. Nan took a lot of her Friday business calls out here when he was growing up, where she could keep an eye on him as he ran barefoot in the garden. Even now he could see her, standing in here with a hand on her hip in an emerald green pantsuit, watching him sprint through the herbs, chasing a bug.

He turned and spotted the box of files. *Finally.*

He made his way back to the foyer with the box under his arm. Frankie was nowhere to be found. He braced himself to enter Nan's half of the house. It smelled like her so intensely that he ached. He heard a light tinkling and followed the sound to find Frankie in the closet, looking through a string of necklaces with awe on her face.

"Agatha is a boss bitch," she said, giving him a little smirk. "Amazing taste."

"Didn't find the ring?"

Frankie straightened. "No. But I have an idea." She carefully extracted a gold necklace out of the cabinet and held it up for him to see. "Ruby pendant. I think there's a chance that the ring was part of a set. I'm going to try something."

She turned away from him and hunched over, whispering to the necklace. Evan loudly whispered to her back, "I don't think the necklace can talk to you, Frankie."

Frankie glared and flipped him off. "No, smartass. I'm going to use it as a pendulum." She held the ruby pendant and whispered to it, *"Help us find the ring, please."*

At first, nothing happened. Then the jewel began to rock back and forth on the chain. He raised his eyebrows. "You promise you're not making it do that?"

"Have some faith in the unknown, Evan." She strutted past him to follow whatever path the necklace was telling her to use. So weird. No way in hell this would work.

He followed in silence as they walked around almost the entire house. The path was scattered, and they walked through a few spaces more than once. The torrent of emotions he had worked through caught up to him, and exhaustion set in hard. After what felt like an eternity, Frankie came to a halt in front of a solid wall.

"Welp. No ring. Shall we?" He gestured to the front of the house.

"It's not a dead end." She ran her fingertips over the dark blue paint. "This house has an HVAC system, right?"

Oh. They grinned at each other. "The vent! Come on." Feeling truly energized for the first time in months, he ran upstairs with Frankie in tow. "Be right back." He trotted to his childhood bedroom and dug through his desk drawers until he found some duct tape and twine.

They stood over the floor's opening to the vent and peered into the darkness. Evan made a loop with the tape, sticky side out, and tied the twine to it. He handed Frankie the roll. "Can you back up and feed this to me?"

Heavy boots silent on the plush carpet, she walked backward to give him some slack. Evan lowered the string down, careful not to get the tape loop stuck on anything.

"Wait, wait!" Frankie called out and ran back to the vent. Holding her hair out her face, she leaned down and whispered into the darkness, *"Mother spider in the walls, return to us what was lost."* Evan raised a brow at her. "What? There could be a spider in there, you don't know."

Evan lowered the twine until it went slack and pulled it back up as slowly as he could manage. A gold flash shimmied in the darkness and came up into view, a large drop of a ruby like a ball of blood set in the band.

"Thanks, Ms. Spider!" Evan called into the vent.

CHAPTER 16

Sawtooth Bay had one and only one library. The selection was decent and contained a uniquely large number of texts on the paranormal and a backroom that held the really old, really special tomes. Tomes you had to read with white gloves and could not take with you. Frankie had long suspected that some witches of old in Massachusetts had fled their settlements and found themselves in Sawtooth with a bag of books. She'd spent endless hours in the backroom over the last few years. It was one of her happy places.

The outside of the building screamed *gothic* and *towering,* and *you better believe I'm covered in gargoyles.* High, arched windows, turrets, stone everything. It was gorgeous, and wouldn't look out of place on an old university's campus.

No surprise that Evan also knew this place. But she was shocked to learn he was friendly with Priscilla, an awful, forty-something woman who managed the front desk.

She greeted Evan as they approached. "Evan! So glad that you're home. Please give Agatha my love. Poor thing." Her smile was saccharine and fake. She glanced at Frankie, giving her outfit a dismissive glance, and turned back to Evan. Frankie stewed in silence. If Evan did the talking, they would have a better result. Priscilla never let Frankie stay long in the backroom, and they needed it today.

"Good to see you." He gave her a genuine smile. "I'm back for good, I think." Frankie blinked at him, stunned. She didn't know he was planning to stick around after everything that would unfold in the next few weeks.

Priscilla patted his arm in a patronizing way that made Frankie see red. "Please inquire if and when you're ready for work. There's a position here for you if you want it."

Evan looked surprised. "Oh! Uh, thanks." He shifted uncomfortably. "Can we rent the backroom for a few hours?"

Priscilla had yet to verbally acknowledge Frankie.

"Of course—please take your time."

*****

Evan walked with Frankie to the back of the library. She vibrated with anger, and it was hilarious. Waiting for her to explode, he said nothing, and closing the door to the backroom, he braced for it.

"Lovely lady."

"Oh for fuck's sake! I *hate* that woman. She never lets me come back here for longer than like half an hour."

"Lucky for you she likes me, then."

She grumbled and piled her hair on top of her head, securing a giant, wild bun with a hair tie. "Alright, you're on microfiche duty, I'm on ancient texts."

"We want city council news from that time period. Anything else?"

"I think that will be plenty."

"And what are you doing?"

Frankie slid on the required white gloves. "Looking up info on a Leshy."

"What the hell is a Leshy?"

She pointed at the microfiche machine. "News. Go."

Evan settled into place. The geek in him was elated to use this setup—the library had a microfiche machine as well as a scanner to import articles for digital storage. Although the library held *Sawtooth Bay Tribune* articles from its inception in the early fifties, he needed the nineties onward, and just city council-related news or legislation. And the only way to find it was to scrub through everything from that decade.

Something familiar worked its way into his bones as he started his work. Everything else up to this point—meeting Frankie, hanging out with her and her friends, the possessed guy in her shop—it had permanently altered his life. All of it revolved around the spiritual world. A world he had never had access to, understood, or even sought out. He wasn't sure he would ever actually come to invite strangeness and the unknown into his life. He was a planner. An organizer. This—research and data-organizing and report-building—this was his world. He didn't realize how much he had missed the familiar feeling until he fell into the groove of searching, uploading, categorizing, and storing.

The most effective use of time would be to transfer everything that looked related to the city council, then organize and study fine details later. A calmness always accompanied that flow state of work, and he sank into it like a hot bath.

*****

Three hours passed in swift silence. Frankie rubbed at a crick in her neck, cringing as the white gloves touched her skin. *Ick.*

After racking her brain during the slower hours at her shop, she could come up with only one conclusion: the curse had to have been purchased by someone who hated Agatha, and they paid a heavy price for it to be so destructive. A powerful spirit or entity out there had put it in place. And if that spirit contract could be bought, it could also be broken with a better deal.

Frankie had never spoken to or seen the Leshy that lived on the edge of town. She didn't know for sure if it existed at all, but she had noticed the wind patterns near that patch of forest made no sense, and those trees were impossibly quiet. It wasn't natural. After three hours of perusing Slavic texts and running phrases through an online translator, Frankie had an idea of how to access the Leshy and what to offer it. It was her best idea. If this didn't work, they'd be back to square one.

Evan stood and stretched, his spine cracking with the movement. "That might be all I can take today. Do you need to stay longer?"

"No. Do you have what you need?"

"I think so. I've scanned any articles mentioning the city council or laws passed during that period and set up a report to help me organize them from my laptop at home, along with Nan's files."

Frankie's stomach roared, audible to anyone within a fifty-foot radius. "Oof. I need to do something about this," she said, patting her belly. "How does a beer and bar food sound to you?"

CHAPTER 17

Soft, golden lights bounced in the evening breeze across the brewery's deck. Frankie closed her eyes and welcomed the salt spray to cleanse away the day's stress. She imagined the salt sinking into her skin to ease her headache.

"*Psst.*" Frankie opened an eye to see Jack trying to get her attention. "There she is. Worried you fell asleep over there. You feeling okay?"

Frankie drained the last of her beer, peeking briefly through the bottom of her glass like a telescope and hoping to project her dark fears out to the Bay. "Not really." It was an easier way to say, "*I'm nervous enough to shit my pants.*"

Bex leaned into the table with her forearms and squinted at her. Frankie reluctantly looked her way, receiving a frown in return. Evan finally returned to their table with a fresh round for himself and Frankie.

"*Finally.* Okay, gang's all here. What's going on? You two are acting weird." Bex crossed her legs and waited.

Frankie braced a boot on the rail of the table, chewing her lip. What was the best way to share this new development?

"I'm doing something a little dangerous tomorrow."

Evan nudged her arm, the brief contact surprising her. "Not by yourself, Ms. Martyr. Jesus."

Frankie rolled her eyes. "Yeah, he won't leave it alone. *We're* going into some deep woods tomorrow to look for an ancient forest spirit. A Leshy. I think there's one in Sawtooth out on the edge of town. I have a theory: whoever

76

cursed Agatha made a spirit contract with something really ancient. And a Leshy would be really ancient. I can't think of any other creature that's local with that kind of power. They'd have to be maintaining constant offerings to keep the harm active and ongoing, so it's probably local."

Bex took another sip of her drink. "What's a spirit contract?"

A bartender interrupted their chatter by approaching with another pint. He handed it to Frankie, who stared at it in confusion. "This is from the gentleman at the bar in a brown jacket."

Frankie leaned past him to see Alexsy Kozlowski give her a sheepish wave from his seat at the bar. She narrowed her eyes at him. He started to stand and come over. Frankie sprang to her feet and pointed a finger at him. "No. Do not." Alexsy cringed and sat back down in his seat, turning away from them.

Frankie accepted the pint with thanks and tried to remember where they were in the conversation. "Right. Spirit contracts. You know how you hear about people selling their souls in shows and movies? That would technically be a spirit contract."

Evan stopped mid-sip and asked, "Is selling your soul a real thing?"

"Not in the way that people think. A contract exchanges something from the practitioner for something given by the spirit, usually the spirit's assistance, knowledge, or power. In Agatha's case, I think someone on the city council wanted her out of her seat, so they made a deal to curse her life."

Jack was barely listening and tapped their empty glass on the table softly. "Leshy... they're fae, right?"

"Sort of. They're in that gray realm. Sort of an elemental being, *definitely* temperamental in mood. We'll need to be prepared. If the caster made a deal, we need to figure out what they offered, and maybe we can offer something better to break it."

Jack's gaze searched the table's wood grain, deep in thought. An idea formed there. "They're from the Slavic region." They put a hand on Bex's arm. "Babe, didn't you take Russian in college?"

"Da." Bex gave an obnoxious smile.

Frankie laughed. "Why is this relevant?"

"I'm just saying, if it's super old, maybe you'll get some brownie points by speaking its language." Jack looked at Frankie. "What? What is that face?"

"Bex, this is not a safe adventure—"

"Shut up. You can't stop me. You never let anyone come with you, so I'm coming." Bex drained her drink.

"Please don't?" Frankie tried half-heartedly. Bex shook her head. Frankie relented. "Fine. Come by mine in the morning tomorrow. I'm hoping if we approach it in the middle of the day, we'll have better odds."

*****

Frankie stood on her deck the next morning, wiping sleep from her eyes, and gazed out into the still woods behind her house. Clemmie trotted out of the kitchen and sat next to her bare feet, soaked in morning dew.

"It's a little cold and wet for you, my good man." She reached down and stroked a finger back and forth across his forehead, between his soft, silver ears.

Clemmie stretched and trotted down the steps. Frankie did not understand every facet of how their bond worked, only that her ancient cat showed up at her side when she did spell work, and sometimes he brought her what she needed for her working. She watched him slip into the edge of the woods and listened to him rustle around for a while as she sipped her black tea.

Spirit contracts. All those years ago, she had made a deal. No one in her life knew the details of it, not even Jack. Frankie's mind whirled, remembering that she made an open-ended promise with a spirit to keep Clemmie at her side for a while longer—the cost unknown, to be paid in the future. She didn't believe it was possible to sell her soul. But years of her life? Some pieces of her power? She knew those could be bargained. And they could be claimed.

Her therapist had told Frankie recently that she had a martyr complex and self-destructive tendencies. And today she would come face-to-face with a dangerous and ancient spirit without any certainty to her quest—just a theory. So, her therapist had a point.

Sleep had not come last night. She knew what awaited her in the deep woods and had stared up into her hand-painted star ceiling, waiting for dawn. She had tried to explain to her friends at the bar that she didn't want anyone to come with her, not Evan, and definitely not Bex. Frankie hoped the creature would be civil, but ancient spirits were nasty and unpredictable. Feral. A Leshy was a trickster, the kind that looked into your mind and played with your worst thoughts like shadow puppets.

Hours of research in those white gloves had led her to only one conclusion—today was going to be hard. She would remember and relive some of her worst moments inside those dark trees. Some of her past was locked firmly behind a vault door, and she knew that once it was opened, it would be very hard to close it again. She hoped she would return from those woods with her sanity intact.

Her creepy doorbell sounded, and she checked her phone. Evan was early.

Tugging her sleeves down over her hands, she trotted inside to let him in. The morning mist spun around him, casting an illusion that his amber curls were swirling too. He studied her face with a warm expression. In recent days, Frankie had begun to realize with a swell of blushing aggravation that she was thinking of Evan a lot. With a frequency that did not match her other client relationships.

And fine, yes, Evan was hot. Frankie had noticed it ages ago when he came crashing into her life, and the thought nagged at her constantly over the last week and a half, ever since he showed up that afternoon on her porch—just like this—to apologize. She had a burning urge to strangle him half of the time but also wanted to straddle him and lick up his throat. It was mortifying. A slow afternoon at The Black Cat this week had left her daydreaming, wondering what he looked like with his shirt off. She could tell his arms and shoulders were *huge*, based on how his shirts fit, and wanted to prove that theory with her hands and mouth. She had thought about running her fingers through his hair. Evan had endless, deep eyes and a stare that made her feel fully exposed. She hated herself for how much she craved it.

"Morning," he said, stepping inside and wiping off his boots.

"Another day, another flannel?" she asked, eyeing him up and down.

He returned the gesture. "Another day, another sweater? Keeping up with my outfit choices, are you Frank?" His eyes glittered down at her, burning a hole.

Frank? Was that supposed to be some kind of nickname? Frankie already was a nickname, for Francis. She glared at him and retreated to the deck, leaving Evan to decide if he would follow her out or not. He did.

"There he is," Frankie muttered as Clemmie came trotting back into view.

The gray tabby's mouth was full of a mass of red feathers. "Oh gods, Clemmie. Please tell me you didn't hunt this poor thing down."

He dropped it at her feet and yowled, his fuzzy face lit up with pride. She leaned down to inspect the dead cardinal.

"Dude, birds have diseases. I am *not* touching that." The cat yowled a long, sustained note, sounding despondent. "Hecate spare me. Yes, okay, thank you. I'll take it with us."

Great. She made an addition to her mental checklist of things to bring: dead bird. In a plastic bag.

Her phone buzzed with incoming texts from Bex.

> Bex:
> *I'm coming I'm coming*
>
> *Am I supposed to bring anything*
>
> *Nvm I'm already driving*
>
> *Texting at a stoplight I promise*

Frankie tucked the phone back into her black jeans. "We should pack up."

Into her go-bag, Frankie packed a large ceremonial knife, a suet cake, and three protective charms. She tucked a small notebook and pen inside next to Clemmie's dead bird. She didn't want to have to make a spirit contract with this thing, but she wanted to be prepared, just in case. Evan moved around in the kitchen, fixing himself something caffeinated in a thermos for the drive. She watched him and tucked a switchblade into her boot.

Bex let herself in the front door without knocking, which made Frankie smile. She loved her family.

"We ready to roll?" She was dressed in a baby blue athletic set, her work boots, and huge, white-framed sunglasses perched on her head.

"You're a vision of subtlety, as usual."

Bex grinned. "Let's go talk to a tree!"

CHAPTER 18

Evan watched from the backseat as shadows coiled around the back of Frankie's head. She drummed a nervous thumb on the steering wheel, sighing every few minutes. Bex chattered in the passenger seat, mostly to an audience of herself. He glanced back to find Frankie watching him in the rearview mirror. She looked away. She was on edge this morning. Weird.

Before he knew it, they had arrived on a service road outside of town. Frankie dropped down the tailgate to double-check her bag.

"Alright, crew. Tie this to your wrist." She handed them both what looked like a bird's foot wrapped in red cord.

Evan wrinkled his nose. "Eww, seriously? What is this from?"

She breathed out slowly as if barely containing a fountain of rage. "It's a crow's foot, blessed by the goddess. *Put it on,* Evan." His cock twitched at her sharp tone. Evan had a vague idea that Frankie was barely holding herself together. He held his wrist out for her to secure the *dead crow appendage* to his skin and suppressed a shudder.

Strapping her charm to her wrist, she asked them, "Do you two know how to do grounding?"

Bex stretched an arm over her chest and twisted at the waist. "Duh, I do yoga twice a week."

Evan had no idea what they were talking about. Frankie sighed, and said to him, "It's a way to keep connected and shield yourself, mentally. If you can try to put a mental shield in place, that will help as we approach him. He'll try to mess with your head."

That did not explain anything. His confusion was apparent, and Frankie stepped closer to him. "Okay, if you had to think of one place on earth that feels warm, feels like home, what would that be?"

"Nan's garden at the old house. In the morning."

"Perfect. Picture that and think in terms of sensations. What it smells like, the way your skin feels, the garden's sounds. Stuff like that. Hold onto those sensory things and focus on them as much as possible. It'll create a barrier that will be more difficult for him to break through."

With that, they paused just at the edge of the tree line. Evan heard Frankie whisper some kind of spell under her breath, her fingers moving in a creepy, unnatural formation. Finally, she stepped through.

Evan focused on "grounding" before entering the forest. *Lavender, coffee, the sun in my hair. Nan's hands harvesting herbs, her rings glittering in the sun.*

As Evan stepped through the trees, he felt the temperature drop several degrees. The world inside was painted in deep blues and blacks. Damp forest air breached his clothing, and he grew fully chilled to the bone. The light dimmed to a murky dusk despite the time of day. Unnerved, he turned to get a last glimpse of the bright, autumn morning light behind him, as if he could catch it and carry it with him. But he found nothing but dark, dense forest for miles all around. His head spun. *What the fuck?*

Frankie trudged ahead as if she knew where she was going. He caught up to her. "How do we know where to go?"

Her shoulders shifted, tight with tension. "The wind will point us to him." And as if she had spoken it into existence, a brisk gust ripped past the trio, pointing a straight shot deep into the trees.

Bex looked around nervously. "There's no bird song."

Frankie paused. "Guys, it's going to get worse from here. Mental shields up. You won't be able to keep him completely out, but it will help."

"Help with what exactly?" Evan asked.

She trudged forward again. "Right now, he's trying to work his way through your mental barriers so he can pick up each of your memories and fears, and use them against you. He'll conjure voices and images. Don't trust anything you see or hear that isn't one of us wearing one of these." She held up the bird's foot tied to her wrist.

Evan began moving again and felt a sensation like long, cold fingers brushing the inside of his skull. He hated this place. He fingered the dead bird's foot, seeking comfort in its ridges and edges.

His thoughts drifted to Nan earlier that morning. Guilt panged through him. He shouldn't be tromping around in the woods. He should be at her bedside, not spending a moment away from her until she passed. Hadn't she said something along those lines this morning?

He could now hear her voice so clearly, like she was walking beside him. *"Evan, don't leave me. I need you—please just stay home. I've only ever wanted you at home with me. What if I die while you're gone?"* His throat burned. They had so little time left together. He shouldn't be out here. He should turn around and leave and go back home like Nan wanted. Nan wanted him with her, right?

He slowed his walk and swam through his thick thoughts. No, wait, that wasn't right. Since he'd returned to Sawtooth, she had shooed him away from her bedside every single day, told him to go out and enjoy the adventure of curing this curse. Make some friends. She didn't want him wallowing beside her. Or to be alone when she was gone. She'd never said those words exactly, but her motivation to push him toward this new group of friends was obvious.

He could smell her—coffee and cashmere. Evan stopped walking and ran his hands through his hair. *It's not real. It's not real. It's not real. Nan is still alive, and I am doing the right thing.*

"Don't be an ungrateful shit, Evan. I've given you everything in this life. And in my hour of need you abandon me?" Her leathered, rasping voice was right behind him, practically on his shoulder, her hand cold, firm, and bruising as it gripped his arm, but he didn't turn around. Even if he was desperate to do so. Desperate to fall on his knees and apologize. He clapped his hands over his ears and ran towards Bex and Frankie.

As he caught up to Frankie's stride, he lowered his hands and found them shaking. He stuffed them in his pockets and glanced at her. Her eyes were locked on something in front of them that he couldn't see. She gnawed on her bottom lip. Her eyes were haunted and gave her face a youthful appearance that hurt his heart. He wondered what the Leshy was doing to her to send her so far back into her past. And what horrors she found there. She wrung her fingers and cracked her knuckles over and over. He reached out a hand to her arm and she jumped, letting out a shuddered breath.

"Sorry," she said, keeping her voice low. "You okay?"

"Better when this is over." He looked behind him and saw Bex furiously wipe tears from her cheeks, tears that would not stop.

She shook her head at him. "Keep moving, I... I need this to end."

Frankie looked between them. "Fuck this. Let's make a run for it—*now*."

The trio bolted on pounding feet in the direction of the wind. Or maybe those were voices, and not wind? A thousand chattering whispers ricocheted in Evan's mind, shredding his focus, dizzying his vision, threatening to bring him to his knees. *Just keep going,* he thought, *just keep going.*

Frankie, running ahead, suddenly threw up a hand to stop them in their tracks. Campfire smoke curled through the tree canopy before them. A tall, dark shadow drifted around the clearing. The air felt thick like a storm approaching.

Evan swallowed hard. They were there.

*****

Frankie wiped her wet, nervous palms on her jeans and opened her bag. "Bex, I'm going to approach him with the offerings. Walk up behind me and translate, okay? Evan, keep an eye on the surrounding trees for any extra movement. I read they sometimes keep wolves as pets."

"*What?*" Evan whispered to her. "You're just telling me *now* that there might be a fucking wolf?"

Ignoring him, she pulled out the suet cake and the bag with Clemmie's dead cardinal. She stepped slowly and deliberately, watching the giant form bent over its fire. Taking a deep breath, she spoke in a soft, confident voice that was at complete odds with her warring insides.

"Good morning, Grandfather. We come as guests to your camp. We mean you no harm. I have gifts." She tried to keep the language simple. Bex would never admit it, but her use of the Russian language was not stellar.

Bex rattled through the Russian translation, and they waited, barely breathing. Frankie became aware of the smell of rot and death streaming towards them.

With its back turned to them, the Leshy straightened, cracking its pointed spine joints to their full height—easily over thirty feet tall. Frankie felt nausea boil through her gut, hot and acidic, as the stench of carrion flooded her senses. The Leshy turned to face their group, a dark cloak fluttering in the movement, revealing a lanky, gnarled body that was somewhere between a skeleton and a tree. She fixed a neutral expression on her face. Showing visible repulsion at this moment would be catastrophic. She prayed to Hecate that she didn't lose her breakfast at this thing's feet. The smell was overwhelming, and her vision swam. She realized in horror why the stink was growing. The Leshy's campsite was full of animal carcasses—some of them hung from tree limbs, others were splayed open, roasting over various fires. Others littered the forest floor.

Her vision traveled up and up to find its face near the canopy, and she beheld a massive head like the skull of a deer, and antlers (or were those branches?) covered in ripped, fuzzy skin that dangled and swayed in the breeze. Its eyes were not eyes but icy blue flames stuffed inside of the skull's eye sockets. Two skeleton hands and hoofs for its feet.

Holy. Fucking. Balls.

Fighting against every instinct to flee for their lives, Frankie forced her gaze down and bowed, removing the bird from its plastic bag and placing it with the suet cake at the Leshy's enormous, hoofed feet. She cautiously stepped back and said, "I bring you breakfast to purchase a question."

Bex stumbled through the translation and Frankie winced. She hated not having the outcome of this interaction within her control. Bex gave her an apologetic shrug, worry lining her face.

The Leshy's bones creaked and snapped like trees in a storm as it leaned down and ignored the bird breakfast to smell the side of Frankie's head. The strong inhale pulled some of her hair into the skull's nostril holes, pinching the hair slightly at her scalp. Her shadows writhed in protest at the invasion. It snuffed out her locks of hair, and she started a mental countdown to when she could shower for several straight hours. She clenched her jaw and dug her nails into her palms. Her breathing was fast and shallow, and she knew she must reek of fear. Bex whimpered behind her.

But Frankie rooted herself to the spot and waited for it to speak. She'd read that they could indeed speak. Instead, it nuzzled the bird and took it into its mouth, swallowing it whole without chewing, completely ignoring the suet cake. *Clemmie, you are getting an entire can of tuna for dinner*, she thought, breathing slightly easier.

Finally, the Leshy stood once more. Its mouth opened and hung down at an angle like the jawbone was disconnected. A few rows of fanged teeth jabbed upward as the maw swung wildly to form words. A voice like gravel falling down a mountainside rumbled through a phrase she couldn't understand. She looked at Bex, who stared up at the creature dumbfounded.

"Well?" she whispered, glaring at Bex.

"Shit," Bex whispered back. "I have *no idea* what he just said. I think that's ancient Old Church Slavic?"

Shit, shit, shit, shit. Before the scene could unravel, Frankie spoke again. "Please, Grandfather, I have only one question."

Bex translated, and the Leshy's body groaned in a strong breeze. It nodded down at them.

Fucking thank the goddess, holy hells. She clasped her hands together to keep them from shaking. "Our friend here—" she looked over at Evan who stood behind them, completely white in the face, "—his grandmother is cursed." She paused for Bex to translate. "We ask if you have a spirit contract with a human in town?"

The Leshy rumbled as if in thought. It spoke again, and Bex shook her head at Frankie, panic setting in. "I have no idea, dude, I'm so sorry!" Tears formed in Bex's eyes.

We are not going to die today, Frankie told herself. "Grandfather, can you nod for yes, please?"

Bex began to translate but stopped when a stuttering gale wind ripped from the skull—the Leshy was *laughing.* Dread curdled low in Frankie's stomach. *We are not going to die today*, she thought again.

The Leshy dropped—joints snapping like a body falling through the trees— onto its hands and hind legs, looking now like a giant, demonic deer made of human bones. It placed its skull face so that it filled Frankie's vision. Blue flames clawed into her, freezing her in place. The voice came again, but this time, they could all understand it.

"I keep no deals with fragile mortals, witch. Any who seek such an agreement do not leave this clearing with their lives."

"Understood," Frankie said, swallowing her bile. "Thank you, Grandfather, we will leave you now." She took a step back, her boot squelching in something wet and bloody.

The creature purred. "*But you said you brought me breakfast, mortal. I need more than a bird to warm my belly.*"

"Wait, what—"

The Leshy's skeletal hand flung out from its side, gripping Bex with enormous bone fingers, and pulled her into the air.

CHAPTER 19

"BEX!" Frankie yanked the ceremonial knife from her bag and ran at the creature. "Drop her *now!"*

"I am not obligated to you, mortal." The Leshy kicked with its hind leg, colliding with Frankie's torso. Evan watched in horror as Frankie went airborne before her back cracked into a large pine.

"Frankie!" Evan sprinted across the camp. She dry-heaved, her lungs fighting to pull in the air that was taken from them. "Can you stand?" Blood ran from her temple as she nodded, and he hauled her to her feet.

Evan searched the ground wildly for the large knife and spotted it on the other side of the clearing. He communicated this to Frankie with a look, and she gave him a devilish grin.

"Let's do this."

He broke into another sprint as Frankie screamed up into the creature's face to distract it. Bex shrieked and punched her fists into the Leshy's fingers, desperate to be released. The creature seemed amused by their pathetic attempts to save themselves and laughed, the wind stuttering around them with its exhale.

Evan tore across the ground. *Five feet, three feet, now*—he wrapped his fingers around the blade's hilt and used his velocity to launch toward Frankie with their only weapon. Before he could reach her, shadows exploded out of her hair, bursting from her fingers and legs, and wrapped around the creature's feet.

Her voice was hollow and terrifying as it echoed through the clearing. *"I said to release her, beast. I will not ask again."*

Evan thought back to Hurricane Frankie, squeezing her blood into a hole in the ground, sending a curse out into the world. A force of pure destruction. He felt very glad indeed to be working on the same side as her.

The Leshy paused and leaned down to get a better look. "*Well, aren't you unexpected. I knew I smelled something on you.*" It tossed Bex like a ragdoll, and she fell hard into the earth. Something wet and blue leaked down her shoulder. She didn't move again.

Scared shitless, Evan approached Frankie carefully. He had not seen her this intensely buried in her power and didn't know how far gone she might be. "Frank, here it is, I'm putting it in your hand." He pushed the hilt into her palm, and she gripped it without turning.

Staring up into the creature's face, Evan was reminded of the Goya painting, "Saturn Devouring His Son." He ran for Bex as Frankie raised her empty fist, shadows winding from the Leshy's feet to her grasp, and then pulled down. The creature fell with a deafening crack, shaking the ground, and Evan was sent flying into Bex's side.

"Ow, *fuck*, Evan!" She cried out, pushing him off her. He nearly wept with relief as they scrambled to their feet.

Frankie approached the Leshy with her blade as it thrashed on the ground, ready to slice. A blur of red movement caught Evan's attention at the edge of the camp.

A howl rang through the trees.

"*WOLF!*" he screamed as a bloody, half-rotted wolf the size of a meaty horse prowled toward them. Bloodied saliva ran from its mouth onto the brown leaves, the rumble of a wild growl unfolding like rolling thunder. It wore its ribs on the outside of its body. This was a monster made entirely of carnage. It was official—when they crossed into the treeline this morning, they had slipped directly into hell.

And it hit him suddenly—white-hot, burning fear, realizing that this could be it, and Nan would never know where he went or that he died brutally in this violent hellscape. Even if it seeded agony in his heart, he was supposed to outlive Nan and live the rest of his long life without her.

Frankie's form, completely draped in shadows, materialized at their side— the Leshy restrained on the ground for the moment with shadow chains. But that wasn't going to last. The creature wailed with the sounds of a monstrous elk as it worked the chains off its body.

The wolf lunged at them, and they broke apart in all directions. Frankie swung the blade and embedded it into the beast's neck with a grunt. The wolf yelped but did not fall.

"*Goddammit,* die already!" She screamed and swung again, but a skeletal hand gripped her waist, and she lifted from the ground. The knife slipped from her grasp.

Bex scrambled to the other side of the camp. Was she running away? Evan's confusion cleared as he watched her grab the wet fur of something dead from a low-hanging limb. Demented glee glimmered in her features with this new challenge.

"Evan! I'll distract, you stab, okay?"

The wolf looked between the two of them, deciding who to eat first. It charged for Bex.

*****

This ancient forest deity would die at her hands today. And the gods would just have to forgive her.

Hot rage sluiced through her veins as she let the darkness pour out of her spirit and wrap around the creature's giant form. She gave herself over to it, letting go of that last shred of control and diving down into that internal lake of power. She was so far gone, her voice was that of something as ancient and terrifying as the monster that held her firm. "*You have lived for ages, Grandfather, but you will find no mercy here.*"

The Leshy's body groaned as it straightened to its full height. "*What spirit speaks through you, child? Whose shadows do you wield?*"

She snarled, vaguely aware of Bex and Evan screaming so far down below them. "*This darkness is mine, beast. I command the shadows, and they answer to me.*" She wrapped a dark tentacle around its throat and wrung a tight knot—but the Leshy didn't breathe and was not deterred.

In the intoxicating haze of her unleashed power, she struggled to focus but glanced down to see Bex distract the wolf with a dripping animal skin like a matador waving a flag. As it charged, Evan sprinted and leaped onto the wolf's back with the knife, bellowing with the effort to grip its matted fur and stay on. A glorious, animalistic sound came from his throat that made her blood run hot. She watched as he stabbed and stabbed until the wolf collapsed in a bleeding heap. Evan was thrown onto his side with the beast's death.

She glared back up at the giant. The Leshy opened its mouth and ran a rotted tongue up her face. It shuddered. *"You taste like ancient power, mortal. I will enjoy you in my belly."*

Frankie raised both of her hands as if she bore claws and roared up at the Leshy. Flames burst into life from her fingernails, and she sank them deep into the Leshy's skeletal grip. Fire raced up its arm. It shrieked and smashed her form into a large tree trunk twice, pinning her there, squishing her guts. She waited for her ribs to crack and puncture her lungs.

But she had one more trick up her sleeve. Or rather, her boot. A small shadow tentacle reached into her boot to retrieve her switchblade. She palmed it as discreetly as possible, her vision blinded by pain. Blood in her mouth. The Leshy opened its fanged jaws and leaned in to bite her in half.

Frankie drove her switchblade into the blue-flamed eye socket before her. Her hearing left her as a deafening screech shook the earth. Icy flames burned her hand with a brutal frost, but her blade found the other eye socket and burrowed deep. Her hand went completely numb from the pain, her vision dimming by the second. A feral scream torched out of her throat as the ground came up to meet her.

And then, the dark pulled her completely under.

CHAPTER 20

Evan was sure his soul left his body as he watched Frankie stab the Leshy in both eyes with a small knife. The monster's form collapsed with a prehistoric roar that rattled his bones, still gripping Frankie around the waist.

Her eyes were closed, and blood ran down her chin.

"No no no no no—" Evan was there in an instant. The Leshy appeared to be dead and was smoking but still gripped her in a grasp he couldn't pry open. Evan swallowed hard and brought the knife to its skeleton fingers. "God help me."

He began to saw through the joints, one by one. Hot and cold raced up and down his spine. He sent himself to a warmer, happier place. A place that wasn't soaked in blood and bodies. And hellhounds and bones. He thought of Nan's garden. Of the sun on his skin. The smell of rosemary.

Frankie's form fell completely into the dirt. Her right hand was burned and blistered to hell. He propped her up, gently cradling her head and neck, and checked her pulse.

Thank fuck, she was alive.

Shadows swirled around her body, and he felt a strange current move through them both with the motion.

"Frankie? Can you hear me? Come back to us, please come back." His throat tightened. He held her blistered right arm outward so it wouldn't touch anything and cause more pain. He looked back to her filthy, bloodied face and found her eyes open and fixed on him.

They were black. Fully and completely black. No pupil, no iris, no whites. Black.

"Frankie, it's dead. You killed it." He cupped her cheek. "Please come back to me. We're okay, but we need you to come back."

She looked confused. She shoved him off her and stood slowly. Grabbed his knife. She cocked her head at the dead creature.

"I want its heart."

He surely heard her wrong. "What? Why? Let's go, it's dead. We can just go home." He was pleading now.

She ignored him and climbed on top of the corpse, her blistered knuckles white on the hilt of the knife. She sank to her knees on its chest, raised the knife over her head, and brought it down with a sickening squelch. Her face was blank, dark, and horrifying as she carved and carved. Evan felt his stomach threaten to empty.

In no time at all, Frankie stood with a bloody mass of an organ in her hands, the size of a watermelon. The thing's blood was blue, staining her hands and burns.

Bex approached the scene, gripping her wounded shoulder. "Okay, Frankie. You've got your heart. Let's go home now."

Frankie slipped unconscious and slid down the Leshy's body to the ground, the massive heart at her feet. Bex sighed heavily and picked up the disgusting form with her good arm, cradling it to her hip. "Can you carry the Princess of Darkness? And I'll carry this repulsive souvenir?"

*****

Her throat was bruised, both outside and internally. Bruised from being squeezed until she lost consciousness, bruised from her screams as she pleaded for it to stop.

She found herself in a filthy bathroom she didn't recognize, staring at her face in the mirror. She felt her cheeks split into a grin so wide it hurt. The smile so completely wrong on such a young, battered face. Her dead eyes. She realized she was wearing pajama shorts and a tank top, despite it being winter.

Cuts lined her arms. Fingers were filthy, gripping the disgusting sink. Her stomach cramped in hunger, caving in on itself. She felt her head tilt down to get a better view of her legs, also peppered with cuts, some fully scabbed, some fresh, and worse yet, some that had fully scarred over, betraying the amount of time she had lost already. And a view of what was to come. A promise.

She didn't know how much more her body could withstand before it gave out.

And she just wanted everything to stop.

*****

The world came back to Frankie in blurry slits of light. Her eyelids ached, and she pinched them closed again. She was being rocked a bit, the sound of birdsong drifting down to her. No, she wasn't being rocked—she was being carried. She recognized Evan's masculine scent and the feel of his flannel on her cheek. Her thoughts were heavy and murky, and she tried to be patient with herself as things came back to her.

Her torso throbbed—it was definitely bruised. Nothing seemed to be broken. Everything felt stiff and sticky. Bex walked with a gingerly gait ahead of them, clutching a massive bleeding object to her hip. Her left shoulder was soaked in dark blue.

Frankie focused on her own black jeans and realized some of her shadows were circling her legs as well as Evan's arms.

She tried speech. "E-Evan?" It was a croaky, awful whisper. Barely audible.

She heard and felt him take a sharp inhale. He kept his voice low. "Hey, you're awake. Try not to move, we're almost at the truck."

She looked ahead and saw the edge of the woods, the bright autumn sunlight welcoming them back to the land of the living. Without the Leshy's grip on these woods, life poured back to the area. Animals moved in the underbrush, and she could hear birds up above in the busy canopy.

The Leshy. That's right, she had led her friends straight into a hellscape deathtrap that they barely survived, and they had no new information to help their case. Her insides turned to acid as she chewed on her guilt and self-loathing. Evan and Bex should have just left her on the forest floor with the Leshy's smoldering corpse.

As Evan reached the edge of the trees, she pinched her eyes closed again. She heard Bex give a long exhale of relief.

"Frankie, I'm driving us back to your house. Do not fight me on this, I am bloody and exhausted, and I will get *mean*."

"Whatever you want." The words came out as a hoarse whisper.

Bex stared at her. "Okay, well, now I'm worried. Evan, get in the backseat with her and keep her from falling off."

Evan hoisted Frankie into the backseat to cradle her in his lap. A drunken, slurry thought crossed her mind: this was not how she would have preferred to visit the back seat for the first time with Evan. Or his lap. A laugh bubbled out of her, causing her ribs to scream in pain.

"Jesus, I think she has a concussion. Should we take her to the hospital?" She could hear Evan's voice muffled through her ear as she buried her face in his shirt.

"You smell nice," she mumbled. Evan gave a long-suffering sigh.

"No," Bex's voice came from the front seat. "She'll heal up in the next few hours, but she needs to get home. The fewer questions we have to answer about what happened, the better." She felt the truck lurch into reverse and then fly down the gravel road back towards town.

CHAPTER 21

Finally back at home, Evan carried Frankie inside and started to set her down on the loveseat in her library.

"No!" she cried out. "This is vintage and I'm covered in gore!"

"For fuck's sake, Frankie, you need to sit still somewhere."

"No."

"You know what? *Fine.*" Evan yanked her back to his chest and started up the hall stairs. Bex grinned up at Frankie, waggling her eyebrows. Frankie flipped her a middle finger as they went around the corner and out of sight.

Evan seemed to instinctively know where her bedroom was. She flushed. *Also not how I was expecting him to be in my bedroom for the first time.* He carried her into the bathroom and sat her on the edge of the soaking tub.

"Um, I'll go get Bex to help you." A blush touched the tops of his cheeks.

"No, I'll be fine," she slurred. Dizzy and swaying, she started to stand and pull off her sweater.

Evan steadied her by lightly touching her hips. Shocked still by his hands, Frankie's matted curls tangled in her bloody sweater, and she found herself trapped with her arms over her head.

"Oh my *god.* Just hold still and let me help you." Evan's tone was sharp. Past annoyed. She couldn't help but smirk a bit. He carefully lifted the sweater from her head, pausing to untangle her bloody locks of hair. When she was freed, she looked up at his face and found him blushing. "I'll just get your boots and then I'll go." He kneeled at her feet and started to undo the laces.

She stared at the top of his head while he worked through mud and blood and bits of bone. His hair was such a nice shade of auburn. His curls had a bit of gold to them when the light shone a certain way. Gilded. She reached out a disgusting, tattooed hand and ran it through the curls. *Soft. Really soft.*

Evan froze at her feet. She heard him swallow. She looked at her fingers and found them gripping his hair a little too firmly. "Oh, my hands are gross. Sorry," she added, breezily, with a look up to the ceiling. A shower. She was ready for a shower. And pizza. Evan yanked off her boots and fled the room as quickly as a walk could take him. He then stomped back in and pointed at her, red in the face.

"I'm going to get Bex. Do *not* move until she comes up here."

"Bossy boots," she mumbled and leaned back onto the edge of the tub. Then he was gone.

She loved this bathroom. Dark, emerald green tiles and muted gold fixtures. Moody, soothing walls. She'd picked out a gorgeous starburst tile pattern with Bex to match the celestial aesthetic in her bedroom. Both ceilings were hand-painted with stars and whorls, and every time she either lay in bed or took a bath, she felt like she was floating at the edge of a galaxy. This was her safe place. She was safe. *Wait, where did he go?*

Bex sauntered into the bathroom with a knowing smile on her lips. She edged the door closed and listened for Evan. When she was sure he was gone, she nearly jumped on top of Frankie.

"You need to let that happen."

"Fuck off," Frankie's speech was slurring again. "I'm gross."

Bex snorted. "You just need a shower, you concussed bitch."

Bex ran a piping hot shower for her and sat on the edge of the tub while Frankie bathed to make sure she wouldn't pass out again. Bex picked at her clothes. "Uggh. You owe me a new matching set. This was one of my favorites."

The water's scalding heat and her healing rosemary soap started to clear her fogged mind. Her witch blood was healing her body already. She winced as she poked at the giant, handprint bruise across her ribs and belly. "I do. I'm so sorry, Bex. Today was a shit show. Are you okay?" Her nose stung from shame. And her burned hand stung from the water pressure.

"When we're sure you aren't going to drop unconscious, I'll have you look at my shoulder. It's… bleeding blue." She made a disgusted noise.

That can't be good. "Hey, just toss those clothes on the floor and grab my robe from the closet. You're getting a shower next." She heard Bex moving around while she wrung the blood from her hair.

After scrubbing her skin raw, especially her open cuts and slices, Frankie stepped out of the steaming shower to towel off. Bex sat in her robe on the edge of the tub, inspecting her bare shoulder, which was indeed bleeding blue.

"Oh, gods. That looks bad." Frankie gently prodded the area, and Bex hissed a little at the contact. "Sorry. Get a shower, get that wound nice and clean, and come down to the kitchen."

*****

Evan pounded his fifth glass of water in the kitchen, heart pounding in his ears. Clemmie sat on the counter, watching him with narrowed eyes. He sighed at the cat. "Don't look at me like that."

He was sure he would feel the ghost of Frankie's hand gripping his hair for the rest of his fucking life. And he was also sure he would be half hard every single time that happened. He shook his head, trying to clear the fog.

"Soft," she had mumbled to herself. *"Really soft."* Nope. She was just concussed. Nothing to read into there.

He was still covered in the mess of their morning and was desperate to feel clean again—inside and out. He padded out to the deck and found Frankie's garden hose on the side of the house.

She had a nice grip. He liked it. A lot. He frequently found himself staring at her hands, her fingers. Trying and failing to push those kinds of thoughts from his mind, he picked up the garden hose and cranked it full blast. He turned the nozzle on himself from up above, letting the cold water soak him through.

He gasped and felt a small relief from the shock of cold. This would have to hold him over until he could get back to Nan's for a proper clean.

Evan felt like he was being watched and turned off the nozzle, shivering a little bit in the afternoon wind. Frankie stood on the deck leaning onto the railing with folded arms, watching him with a huge smile on her face. Her right hand was wrapped in a bandage. Dressed in a black tank top and short gray gym shorts, she looked alert and coherent again. He could see new tattoos that had been hidden by her sweaters. Under the tentacles on her right upper arm was what looked like a pirate ship.

Damn. He hoped it wasn't obvious what he was doing right now. "Is your hand okay?"

"It'll heal."

"What about your tattoos?" He stood with his hands on his hips, trying to redirect her attention from his current actions.

"Supernatural injuries don't usually affect them. You don't need to bathe outside, Evan. Bex is almost done, then you can shower."

Evan scoffed. "I'm not putting these clothes back on. I will be burning them, thank you."

"No, dummy. I've got some clothes out for you in the bathroom."

"I seriously doubt you have anything that would fit me." The thought of her having an old boyfriend's things still in her dresser made him feel itchy inside. *Nope.* He shut that thought right down. None of his business.

She gave him a feline smile. "Oh, it'll fit you." Bex called to her from the kitchen and Frankie turned, the creamy, porcelain column of her throat exposed in the movement. Her hair was wet. "I'm coming, bitch."

Jesus Christ. Evan needed a drink. A strong one. He rolled up his pants legs so they wouldn't drip too badly and reluctantly headed inside.

Bex stood in the kitchen in a fluffy, eggplant-colored robe. She handed him a glass with a shot of what smelled like whiskey. "Down the hatch, doctor's orders." He threw it back without question.

As he headed toward the stairs, he heard Frankie call out, "So it's the Juicy velour tracksuit on the counter. Have a nice shower!"

Bex cackled and slapped her hand on the quartzite countertop. *Just another day with her friends.* Evan shook his head as he climbed.

He had been too distracted earlier to actually take in the design details of her primary suite. The bedroom, all deep blues and purples, had a dreamy, starry quality to it. She had a king-sized bed, immaculate, tucked, neat—no surprise there—and the dark bedding looked like it was a soft cotton. Exhaustion hit him hard. He wanted to dive into those glorious sheets, but he forced himself into the bathroom.

Thank god, Frankie had been fucking with him about the velour tracksuit. Folded neatly on the counter were a pair of black basketball shorts and a huge shirt with a skull on it. He snickered. And next to that was an enormous, black hoodie. Evan stripped off his shirt and pants, dried blue and red blood cracking off in pieces from the cloth and denim. He checked his chest and back in the mirror, noticing a few bruises and small cuts. But otherwise, not too bad.

Lucky. They had been very, very lucky today.

He leaned against the counter and checked his phone. A text from Nan had come through over the last few minutes.

Nan:
Going to bed early. DO NOT come home
early tonight and wake me up.

I mean it.

Guess he had the night off, then. Another notification let him know he'd been added to a group text with Frankie, Bex, and Jack, called "Sawtooth Baddies." Evan felt a warm chord move through him. Without knowing why or how, he'd fallen into a very tight group of friends. The fact that they made room for him made him want to weep. Or maybe that was just the trauma and exhaustion talking.

He instead gazed around the large bathroom, which had the same aesthetic as the bedroom, but in dark greens. There was a large soaking tub, separate from the shower. Evan was not surprised that there weren't tiny bottles of products littering every surface—Frankie was a neat freak and a minimalist. Only one big, glass container of bath salts sat near the tub. He felt his blood pressure drop the longer he was in this room. He looked over to the enormous shower with its rainfall shower head and felt a ravenous desire for boiling hot water on his skin. He nearly ran to it.

CHAPTER 22

"So. He's up there right now. In your shower. *Using your soap.*"

Despite her worrisome injury, Bex was in rare form tonight. They had video-called Jack to catch them up on the day's events. After Jack chewed Frankie out for a few minutes for putting their wife in danger (deserved), Jack agreed to pick Bex up in a bit after the day's closing wrapped up.

She now sat on the counter while Frankie worked on her shoulder. And it seemed she would be teasing Frankie relentlessly about Evan until she left.

"*Shut. Up.*"

Frankie had spent the last twenty minutes digging the blue substance out of her wound. Bex hadn't so much as flinched. Quite the opposite, she had not stopped wiggling as Frankie tried to remove the blue poison with surgical precision.

Bex's braid hung down her chest, across Frankie's plush robe. Bloody, crusty, and ruined. "Oh, gods. Your hair!" Bex plucked the braid up and tossed it over her shoulder, trying to wave her off. "No, it's so bad, Bex!"

"Forget it. I booked an appointment tomorrow morning with my hairdresser while you were in the shower." Bex avoided eye contact, making Frankie feel worse.

"Send me the bill. I'm not asking." Frankie gave her an uncompromising look. As she switched her grip on the knife to get at a different angle, Frankie looked past Bex and spotted the Leshy's heart dumped unceremoniously on the patio table on the deck. "So, I didn't hallucinate that."

101

Bex giggled. "No, and I carried it for over a mile for you. *You're welcome*. Why did you even want it?"

Frankie's mind felt like a swamp. Hot, buggy, and full of sludge. She reached into the murk to try and remember what happened before she collapsed. She cringed, remembering that she shoved Evan off of her before yanking the knife from him. She owed him an apology.

She pressed a cold compact to the inflamed skin on Bex's shoulder as flashes came back to her.

Oh. Gods. She had carved out its heart. Frankie stifled her unease. At the time, her instincts had told her she couldn't leave those woods without it. Nothing would have stopped her. "I wanted a trophy."

Bex shook her head. "You're a psychopath." She took the ice pack from Frankie. "I can do that."

Frankie took the opportunity to inspect the heart. The organ's overall appearance had begun to shift from more meat-like to more plant-like. The blood still ran blue, but the heart's surface now resembled a wet mass of leaves. Frankie approached with her blade and pried open a section slowly, unsure of what to expect. The autumnal smell of wet, rotting leaves hit her hard in the face. Within, a slurry of dirt and oak leaves ran like streams past her blade and onto the patio table. The mass twitched and pulsed, like a large, mossy human heart. Figuring out what to do with this seemed like a problem for another day.

Jack's voice floated out to the deck from inside, followed by Bex's flirty giggle. As Frankie returned to the kitchen island, she found Jack in between Bex's knees, giving her a sweet kiss. They frowned at Frankie. "Bex says you had a concussion. You shouldn't be alone for the next few hours. Want us to stay?"

Frankie desperately wanted some alone time. "No, leave. Please," she added, but knew her tone was biting.

Jack's eyes lit up at the sound of Evan coming down the stairs. They gave Bex an evil look and grinned at Frankie. "Well, we can't stay, but someone should be here for a few hours." The words timed perfectly to match up with Evan entering the kitchen.

Frankie glared bullets at the two traitors.

"I mean, I can hang out for a bit," Evan said.

Of course he fucking can.

*****

Evan texted Nan's nurse to make sure she was in fact asleep and found himself relieved to have an excuse to stay. He watched Frankie dive onto the large sectional with a cream-colored knit blanket to wait for their frozen pizzas to cook. She clicked buttons on the remote with purpose, queuing up something.

The clothes did fit, and Evan wanted to know why she had them. But how was he supposed to bring that up in a natural, I'm-not-trying-to-hit-on-you-right-now-well-not-that-much way? He grabbed a beer from the fridge and joined Frankie on the couch.

Panning through her DVR menu, she paused to look at him. "I shoved you earlier today. In the woods. I shouldn't have. I'm sorry." She held his gaze, waiting for him to say something.

"I was honestly just glad that you were alive. And feeling feisty enough to push me off of you." He couldn't keep the flirt out of his voice. It felt too easy with her.

She rolled her eyes, then looked down at the hoodie he wore. "Told you they'd fit."

Now, now is the perfect time to ask.

"And who do these belong to?" He plucked at the hoodie. "They're huge."

"In case you haven't noticed, I'm not a small girl." She gestured to her gorgeous, thick thighs. Oh, he'd noticed. Constantly.

She continued, "They're mine, I wear the shirt or hoodie like a short dress with sneakers. It's cute. Wait, wait!" She stopped and pointed at him with her bandaged hand. "You thought they belonged to a guy, didn't you?"

He felt himself go red. *Damn her teasing.* She was always catching him off guard. "I was just asking, that's all."

"Mmmhmm," she noted dryly. She started up an episode of *Spirit Stalkers.*

"What?" Evan exclaimed. "You watch *Spirit Stalkers*? Are you serious?"

She glared at him. "I don't *watch* it, I *hate-watch* it. There's a difference. Look at this douchebag and tell me you don't want to yell at him."

He couldn't disagree. "He has… an unlikeable face." Was it the goatee or the sunglasses after sundown that bothered him more? No, it was the fingerless gloves. Because it looked like they were filming in summer. "But you actually *do* ghost stuff, right? How can you stand this?"

"It's weirdly cathartic."

He propped his feet on the coffee table and tried to get comfortable, but his legs were bare aside from the basketball shorts. Goosebumps broke out all over them before Frankie's cream-colored blanket flared out in the air to cover them. He looked at her in surprise. "Are you sharing your blanket with me?"

"I can't hear the show over your chattering teeth," she replied, eyes still on the television.

Evan became immediately aware of how close their legs were. Anything could have been happening on the screen—a murder could have happened live, and he wouldn't have noticed. The next few hours passed in a cozy blur— Frankie yelling or laughing at the douchebag as he screamed and ran down hallways in night-vision, frozen pizzas, another beer. She was sitting closer to him now, and he was certain he would split in half from being so tightly wound.

The deck and yard beyond the windows had long since grown dark, aside from the fairy lights in the trees. Clemmie dozed on the floor under the coffee table. That cat had saved their asses and bought precious time today with his dead bird offering. Without it, the Leshy might have eaten the three of them whole and not tried to play with its food. Evan shook his head in wonder. The day had been bizarre and traumatic. Bloody. The memory and feel of sawing through the Leshy's hand to free Frankie's body hung heavy in his ribs. But even worse would have been not having her here, on the couch, eating frozen pizza and sharing a blanket.

He felt her shift closer to him, their shoulders brushing, the back of her head hitting the cushion. He debated if it would be weird for him to put his arm around her. Then scolded himself for turning into a teenage boy. Sure, he was an adult man in his thirties, but Frankie was intimidating and very intense, and he always worried he might scare her off or cause her to shut down. Then again, she had to like him *somewhat* to risk her life defending him in the woods, right?

Fuck it.

He moved slowly to stretch his arm across the back of the sofa, and Frankie slipped to lean against the left side of his chest. He prayed his pounding heart wasn't as loud as it felt like it was. Her wild hair was strong with her scent, making his head spin. She leaned back into him, so Evan brought his hand down to test out brushing his fingers on her arm. She didn't balk, didn't squirm away.

He couldn't believe this might happen. But he wanted to be sure. "Hey, Frankie?" he asked quietly, not wanting to break the spell of the moment.

He waited.

And then a light snore sent a javelin through his pounding heart.

Shit. The shadows in her hair seeped out a bit when she slept, he realized, watching them trail down to the floor and wrap around Clemmie. He also realized with some discomfort that she was in a deep sleep and if he moved, he would wake her. So, Evan watched two more episodes of *Spirit Stalkers* in the quiet den, which confirmed that the show was unbearable without her roasting it, and waited for her to shift on her own.

Finally, as his phone neared midnight, Frankie shifted in her sleep to lie flat on the cushions and tugged the blanket down with her. Evan's legs chilled over again without the blanket or her body heat, and he took it as his cue to leave. He quietly stuffed his bare feet into his boots and slipped out the front door, flipping the little switch on the handle to lock it behind him.

CHAPTER 23

Frankie woke from a blissful, dreamless sleep to the smell of Evan. Her eyes snapped open, a cool morning sun rising over her backyard. Looking around the den, she found Clemmie snoozing by her feet where Evan had sat. He was gone, but the blanket still smelled like him.

She remembered falling asleep watching her show and nothing after that. A burst of urgent fear slipped through her. She had a precise routine every night to lock the house up and check every room but did not do it last night. Wrapping the blanket around herself, she jogged to the front door and found it locked.

He locked it.

Every door was locked.

Every door was locked.

The chant repeated in her mind until she believed it. She sank down the door to the floor and mounded the blanket around herself. *I am safe. He locked up. No one got in. I am safe.*

She waited patiently for her breathing to even out. Cold, orange light streamed through the hall. She watched it grow for a few minutes, and when her joints started to ache, she reluctantly retreated back to the den. Backyard grass glinted in the breeze, dusted in a wet, fall frost. On her patio table, sat a soaking, disgusting mess. Its energy called out to her like someone had grabbed her arm and was dragging her outside. Cautiously, she stepped out into the morning mist and approached the table.

106

Last night, it had been more plant-like. This morning, the Leshy trophy was once again more meat-like, the shape and size of the giant's heart.

Huh? That can't be good. She sniffed the mass, lip curling in repulsion. But there was no smell. Blue blood had drenched the table and was now tacky to the touch. Had the heart healed itself? She didn't know what to do with that information. The plan had been to throw it onto the grass and set it aflame, but this development gave her pause. Would this organ have healing properties? Or something else she might utilize in the future?

This thing should have smelled to hell but did not. It looked fresh. An insane idea seeded in her mind.

I should keep it.

But she'd need to be careful with how she stored it. Her house was a frequent stop for the Sawtooth Baddies, and with a stab of guilt, she remembered Bex being thrown across the clearing and Evan having to carry out her unconscious body after killing an undead wolf. No one could know about this. Turning back to the door in thought, she watched Clemmie trot out to her feet.

"What do you think?" She gestured to the heart with her thumb.

Clemmie gave her a slow blink and meowed around a yawn.

"Hmm, good point." No, Clemmie wasn't using words, but she understood his vibe. "Basement?"

He stretched his front paws out and headed back inside to the kitchen.

"Basement it is."

Unlike the rest of her house, she had left the basement untouched during the renovations. It was unfinished and had a few sectioned-off areas in its layout. She stuffed the Leshy's heart into a garbage bag and threw it over her shoulder like a sack. Stepping down into the darkness, she said a mental *hello* to the shadows present, and they led her to a large, empty crate in one of the back rooms.

It seemed that fate wanted her to keep this. Perhaps it wasn't *that* grandiose of a situation, but Frankie trusted her instincts above all else. And they screamed at her to hide the heart down here in her basement.

She slid the lid closed, giving the monster's heart one last glance.

CHAPTER 24

Nan reclined in a patio chair in her backyard, wrapped in a large, plaid blanket with sunglasses covering the top half of her face, her bare hands holding a steaming coffee. The image of cozy. Evan warmed next to her in the autumn sunlight, doing everything he could to drive the other day out of his mind.

It seemed the Gang, as he'd taken to calling them, had also needed a break for a few days. He hadn't heard from Frankie directly about the next steps but had heard from all of them in the group chat. He'd assumed they made a new chat to include him, but no, it appeared they had dropped him right into the middle of their own group chat.

His phone buzzed again.

Jack:
Frankie, wtf

Frankie:
*… Yeah I'm gonna need more info
than that?? What are you on about*

Bex:
Popcorn emoji

Frankie:
*Did you just write out
the words popcorn emoji?!?!?*

Evan laughed, aware that Nan was watching him stare at his phone.

Jack:
You know what I'm mad about
Are you seriously going to act
like you don't know anything about this??

Jack attached a photo of them glaring up into a selfie in front of a house, wearing bright blue latex gloves and holding up a large jar with a bunch of gross stuff in it. Evan zoomed in to try and see the details but could only make out bones, crow's feet, and some kind of herbs.

Jack:
It smells fucking terrible
WHY WAS THIS INSIDE THE
FLANNIGAN HOUSE FRANKIE

Frankie:
… Please tell me you didn't
move that from where it was

Jack:
Please tell me why there are
fucking TEETH IN IT?!?!?
The buyers ran for the hills
OBVIOUSLY

Evan laughed harder with no idea what was unfolding, but absolutely wishing he had popcorn for this exchange.

Frankie:
This is an all-caps situation.

THE FLANNIGAN HOUSE HAD
A FUCKING MONGOLIAN WORM
IN THE BASEMENT

YOU ASS.

Jack:
Wait wut

Frankie:
PUT IT BACK OR
THE WORM WILL COME BACK

Evan wiped the laugh from his eyes and swiped to do a quick internet search for "Mongolian worm." He grimaced. Phrases popped up like, "between three and five feet long," "long-distance killing," and "spray its victims with venom." Evan looked up to see Nan reading the entire exchange over his shoulder. He held the phone so they could both read.

Jack:
What would you say if I told you that the jar was no more?

Frankie:
Jack, I swear to the goddess if you destroyed that jar

You and I are officially in a fight

Bex:
Jack has exited the chat.

Jack:
Oh fuck off both of you

Nan and Evan burst out laughing. The worm argument continued, but Evan hadn't heard Nan laugh that hard in a while. He soaked up the sound, wishing he could record it and listen to it over and over again. Instead, he waded into the moment, letting it surround him.

She settled back into her patio chair, laughter becoming a warm chuckle. "Evan, I like them. Do you like them?"

He considered the last few weeks. "I have no idea why they've made me part of their group. They don't know me beyond this month, they don't owe me anything."

Nan snatched off her sunglasses and glared at him. "You sound just like your father right now. Companionship isn't a transaction." She shook her head. "Your father did a number on your head as a boy, but I've worked too hard to drive out that *nonsense* for you to be talking like that."

He dropped his eyes in shame. Because she was right. His father had given him the gift of expecting the worst. From people, from situations. Taught him to never have any needs, so he would never owe anyone, and they could never come to collect. It had been a lonely existence trying to make friends through that lens.

These last few weeks had been terrifying—because of blood-soaked horrors, obviously, but also because he was relying on these people in the heaviest way he could imagine: to save his family. The feeling was brand new, the pathways in his brain for trust and hope still being built. Those pathways felt very fragile, liable to collapse in the slightest breeze.

Nan was the missing voice in his head that kept him human and allowed him to be vulnerable. When she was gone, who would remind him that he was not his father?

"I'm sorry." He reached over and took her hand, still warm from her coffee mug.

"I want you to spend more time with these people in the next few weeks. Promise me." Her eyes were closed, warming in the sun again.

"I will spend more time with these lunatics, I promise."

CHAPTER 25

Frankie swiped a cloth over a glass case inside The Black Cat. A few days had passed since they escaped hell out in the woods, and although her ribs were feeling better and the giant skeleton handprint had faded, her guilt had only grown. Cleaning took her mind off things. She had begun by dusting every book and straightening them on the shelves, then moved on to arranging her ceremonial knives by size, then decided it was a good time to refill the herb bins. She'd stopped herself when she began to neatly stack leaves inside of the herb bins, which was next-level absurd. She instead tried stacking her display pumpkins from the pumpkin patch in different variations. There was nothing left to fiddle with, so she'd spent the last few hours wiping off the glass cases.

So today, the shop was very, very, clean.

Everyone was due to come over in a few minutes and plan out what to do next on Agatha's case. Frankie's heart wouldn't stop galloping in her chest. Anxiety coursed through her, and she took some steadying breaths.

She could still vaguely smell him on that blanket. It was impossible to describe with any accuracy. He smelled masculine and woodsy, but not anything she could easily name. The door tinkled, and she knew he was there without turning around. She flexed her hands in the rag and faced Evan.

"Hey, how have you been? How's Agatha?"

"Good. Yeah, she's doing fine. She's been up and moving around over the last few days." His eyes betrayed something she struggled to place. Frankie never lied when doing tarot readings, would never let a cold read of a client direct her tarot spread. She would never be *that* kind of practitioner, even if she could size up a customer at a glance, know their motivations, their stresses, their desires. And yet, sizing up Evan was like trying to look inside of an obsidian wall. Impossible. Only her own frustrations mirrored back to her. It made her want to throttle his skull.

And then pin him up against a wall and find out what his neck tastes like.

She banished the thought before a blush crept up her face. Thankfully, she was saved by Jack and Bex strolling into the space while holding hands. Jack was impeccably dressed in a bold blazer and slacks without a wrinkle in sight. Frankie gave a dramatic gasp as Bex came into view.

"Dude!"

"I know, they're so good, right?" Bex turned in a circle, showing off her new Bantu knots. The back of her head revealed a starburst design made with the parts of her hair.

"They look so good. I love the back!"

Bex beamed as everyone settled in different places and chairs. Frankie perched on the counter with the register.

"Okay, I'd first like to address the Leshy in the room and once again apologize for us almost getting killed over a possible lead."

Jack rolled their eyes. "That's old news. What's next?"

Frankie shrugged. "Okay. Well, I have no idea what kind of spirit Agatha's attacker contracted with. I know it has to be very old, but that's it. I've got Agatha's ring, so I can use that to do some channeling and see if someone on the other side can give us some direction."

Bex leaned back in her chair. "Who are you trying to reach?"

Frankie shook her head. "A spirit guide? Ancestor? Mine or Agatha's. Someone who can see behind the veil. I haven't done it very much, I honestly don't like to."

"Why not?" Evan asked.

"There are too many assholes in my family line. I don't want them following me around. If I reach out, they might try and drop by more often." It was a good reminder to refresh her door wards before beginning any kind of séance.

Jack snorted. "Antisocial even with spirits." Frankie glared at them.

"I'll need to pull some things together before I can attempt this, so it might take a few days. Evan, what's going on with the research?"

Evan straightened. "I've just about sorted everything I scanned from the microfiche into the report I made. It's taken longer than I thought. There were hundreds of individual articles to pan through. Once I've got everything in the report, I can sort and filter to see who Nan butted heads with the most often. Should also only take a few more days."

Frankie's mood brightened. "Killer. Finally feels like some progress."

Jack raised their hand like they were in class. "And what can Bex and I do?"

"Nothing right now, but I'm sure I'll need someone to keep watch while I break a few laws at some point."

"I'd be great at that," Bex noted. Her shoulder was healing well, only a few blue streaks still present under her skin, peeking out of her mint green zip-up.

"I was mostly joking. The other thing you two can do is accompany me over to the Flannigan house. Need I say more?"

"No," Jack mumbled, sheepish.

"What do we need to bring?" Bex looked around the shop eagerly, her gaze falling on the case of ceremonial knives.

"Yeah, we'll need some of those," Frankie said. "This will be a physical extermination."

Evan stood up. "I'm coming too. I call dibs on a sword."

*****

Evan carried the bag for the Gang that held several knives (Frankie, he was disappointed to learn, didn't have any swords for him to wield), some small pieces of wood, and a baseball bat shoved halfway inside. His curiosity over this so-called deathworm destroyed any lingering trauma from a few days ago. He'd seen more crazy shit in the last few weeks than he could have imagined he'd see in a lifetime. Now, the thought of a ceiling keeping him closed off from the rest of the unknown universe made him panic—he needed to know it all.

He felt a bounce in his step as they approached the house he recognized from Jack's pissed selfie. "What's the plan?" He was full to the brim with crackling energy after a few days stuck indoors on nursing duty. Astonished, Evan realized that in just a few days, he had rewired his brain regarding the unexpected. How violent could he expect this adventure to be? Didn't matter. He needed to feel something. Anything. Anything other than the grief that was barreling towards him, that would be shackled to him for the rest of his life.

Frankie jerked her head toward the house. "The floor of the basement looks like a huge sand pit. I think the worm has been there for a few years loosening the ground up. We're going to have to wade through it, unfortunately. We need to kill it by slicing the head off."

"Cool," he said, not believing that this was his life.

Frankie turned around and ran a pointed finger across them all. "Do not lose sight of it. If you see it opening its mouth, it's either trying to shoot you with its venom or lunge and latch onto you."

Jack wrinkled their nose. "Eww, like a leech?"

Frankie nodded. "If it latches, do *not* cut its head off. You need to bash it with the bat first so it unlatches."

Inside, Evan was amazed to find a sandpit in the basement of this normal, suburban house. It would come up almost to their waists, and they would have to move slowly. Nerves tingled in his body. Everything appeared to be still, but he heard a strange, low hiss that set him on edge. Frankie stopped on the stairs, the sole lightbulb swinging on its chord. "Bex, stay up top and keep it from leaving the basement. Evan, you're with me in the sand. Jack, take the baseball bat and intervene if it latches on anyone."

Jack, still dressed in their slick trousers and blazer, perched a few stairs up, the bat across their knees. Assuming position, Evan waded slowly through the sand, praying he didn't step on the damn thing. Frankie gestured for him to circle the opposite way from where she was moving.

"*Ready?*" she mouthed to him. He nodded, raising the longest knife available to him from Frankie's case. She held up a knife with a curved blade, like a scythe, and scraped hard against the wall with the blade. In an instant, a tubular shape rose from a far corner and started to circle in the sand. Acid filled Evan's stomach. *Here we go.*

Frankie stilled as the worm slid towards where her knife scraped the wall.

She waited until the last moment before slicing straight down at the shape. A shriek rang through the room, but the worm kept circling. Frankie held up her blade to see a bit of brown substance staining the tip.

"I think I nicked it, it's gonna be pissed now."

Evan watched the form retreat to the corner of the room and go still. The hissing grew louder before a head emerged from the sand. It was way worse than the photos on the internet. Rows and rows of needle-like teeth, a gaping hole that undulated into blackness. He backed as quietly as possible in another direction. The worm appeared to be blind and relying on sounds. It shot a brown-colored stream toward where he stood moments before, the drywall hissing and collapsing under the goo.

Evan waved his hand at Jack to get their attention. He gestured to the bat and mimed hitting the wall near the base of the stairs. They nodded and smacked with the bat several times. The worm dove down, then rose again from the middle of the sandpit and was airborne.

Time slowed. The worm's body speared through the air, revealing foot after foot of the hideous, writhing shape. Evan slowed his breathing and swiped down with an exhale as it crossed in front of him, chopping the worm in half with his blade. The shriek it let out pierced the basement, and brown blood sprayed across his front. But the worm kept its path forward and lodged teeth into the wall next to Jack.

"Evan!" They held out their hand. He pulled another sheathed knife from his back pocket and tossed it to them. Jack ripped the knife from the sheath and plunged it down into the worm's hissing skull until the creature fell silent.

Frankie stood with her hands on her hips. "Damn, I should bring you guys with me more often. I would have been here all night."

*****

The Gang stood out on the driveway, where Frankie stacked the small pieces of wood they brought with them and laid the two pieces of worm corpse on top. She had to wrap the snake-like body into a few coils for it to fit. She snapped with fingers on both hands, and the mass burst into flames.

She looked at Jack. "I hope for your sake it's a male." She narrowed her eyes. "I'm not digging through that basement all night for eggs."

Jack looked legitimately worried. Not sure what they were waiting for, Evan

117

crossed his arms over his brown-stained shirt and stood patiently. A neighbor from across the cul-de-sac had come out to "walk the dog" near a smiling, ornamental scarecrow and observe what was going on. Evan looked back to the fire to see skin melting off of the giant deathworm that they were burning on a driveway. He laughed to himself.

"Ha! PENIS BONE! That's a penis bone! YES!" Frankie cried, loud enough for the entire neighborhood to hear. Jack and Frankie high-fived.

Evan glanced back to the neighbor, who had suddenly dragged his dog back inside. Frankie did a little victory dance and Jack sighed. "Yeah, okay. You won. I'll clean it up."

CHAPTER 26

Stirring her medium-sized spelling pot, Frankie sighed at the mid-October breeze floating through the open window. Leaves scraped in a musical current along the deck below. Clemmie perched in the window, the breeze ruffling his whiskers. He sat there with his eyes closed, even if it was far too chilly for him to nap. Gorgeous. Autumn in Sawtooth Bay was gorgeous.

From her heaping pile of herbs, she snatched mugwort and dried yarrow and sprinkled it into the simmering water.

"Where did I put the bee balm..." She mumbled, glancing around the counter space.

Her phone buzzed.

She leaned over, seeing Evan's name on the notification, and felt her insides jump a bit.

Evan:
Wyd

She smiled to herself and typed back.

Frankie:
What the fuck is wyd

Evan:
What are you, 100?

Frankie:

Over 400 years old, actually. My ageless
beauty spells are unmatched

Was she flirting?

Evan:
It means "what are you doing," grandma

She paused, tapping the back of her phone in thought. Cute witchy selfie? Too much?

She tugged her ponytail down and fluffed her hair. Before she could overthink it, Frankie scrolled to the camera and lined up the phone from above at a flattering angle.

Then adjusted her ingredients to be more aesthetic.

Then paused again and gave a little tug on her tank and bra to prop up the girls.

That looked natural, right? Not trying too hard? She snapped a few photos, then picked the one that made her feel the least panicked about this decision. Just the right amount of cleavage, her tattooed arms looking muscular, her face fixed in a you're-annoying-me-but-I-might-think-you're-cute smirk.

And, send.

Frankie put the phone back down and stirred her pot, pretending that she wasn't completely on edge waiting for his reply. Several minutes went by before anything came through, and just as panic was settling in, she started to tip a jar of angelica into the pot. Her phone buzzed again. Half of the contents of the jar dumped in, and swearing, she dropped her spatula with an unnecessary amount of force to grab the phone. She winced—this mixture might be a little potent tonight.

Evan had "loved" the photo and was now typing.

Gods, this is ridiculous, she scolded herself. She never got hung up on people like this.

Evan:
Gotta say, you make being a
400 year old witch look pretty hot

Her face burned. Full blush. She typed back, biting her lip.

Frankie:
Naturally. And "wyd?"

Again, a long pause. Frankie left the phone unlocked this time while she stirred, watching the screen.

Finally. Oh, he sent a photo.

She enlarged it. Evan was lounging on what must be Agatha's couch, the late afternoon sun lighting up his hazel eyes a bit. His flannel shirt sleeves were rolled up, revealing very muscular and delicious forearms. And his shirt was riding up slightly. And she did not miss the sliver of his hip.

Fuuuuuuuuck. She swallowed hard. Fuck, fuck, fuck.

*****

Evan had no idea what had come over him when he stopped mindlessly scrolling on his phone and sent Frankie a text. Didn't know what sass he thought he'd receive from her. Or teasing. When instead Frankie had sent that selfie, he stared at the screen stunned. His tongue felt thick in his mouth.

Fuck's sake. Smirking up at him, a bit of cleavage on display, perfectly framed—maybe she didn't realize she'd done that. Or maybe she did? *Shit*.

His brain emptied out at the thought. Evan then realized he'd been staring at the photo for several minutes wondering what it would feel like to lick up that strip of cleavage. And hadn't texted back yet.

Fuck, fuck—

Evan:
Gotta say, you make being a
400 year old witch look pretty hot

What the hell kind of lame flirt was that? Thankfully, she got back to him quickly with a snarky,

Frankie:
Naturally. And "wyd?"

He needed to reciprocate, right? Pulling up his camera, Evan adjusted himself so he wasn't visibly hard on the screen, then snapped the photo. He realized after the photo clicked that his shirt was riding up…

Fuck it. He sent the photo anyway.

He knew most of the time they had spent together was based on trying to undo Nan's curse, but there had been social time too, and he felt like he and Frankie could be something else. Friends. Maybe something other than friends if Frankie would unscrew some of her titanium walls. But if he was honest with himself, after the terror-soaked day in the Leshy's woods, after watching her drive a tiny knife into a giant's burning eye sockets, he knew he wouldn't be able to be just friends with her. And then be near her without imagining grabbing her hips and hauling her toward him. Plunging his hands in her hair and kissing her. His face burned at the thought. His phone buzzed.

Frankie:
I see your research is going well

She included an eye-roll emoji. He grinned, happy his photo hadn't shut the conversation down. He propped his feet on the coffee table and tapped them together while he thought of what else to say.

Evan:
What can I say, I'm a devoted student

Frankie:
Hmm. I was doing it wrong all those years
I spent in the library learning about
poltergeists and different kinds of summoning salts

The last few weeks had been the closest to death as he'd ever been—keeping himself and his new friends alive, working to help Nan before she died. Being so intimate with death was exhausting. It blew his mind that this insane woman spent so much of her mental capacity surrounded by the dead and spirits. The damage and healing cycles Frankie put herself through every day. And in that time, with her endless crankiness, Evan had learned Frankie's dirty secret: despite all her spikes and her fangs, she really, truly, actually cared about people. And wanted to improve their lives.

But *fuck*, her fangs. He wanted that vicious, fanged mouth on him. Anywhere. Everywhere. As quickly as possible.

Evan:
So you're doing the witchcraft

this evening?

Frankie:
"Doing the witchcraft"???
Now who's a grandma

I'm making a mixture to take with
me to a graveyard later

It's for your case

He shut down visuals from his brain of doing things with her. In her truck. Parked at the edge of said graveyard. He cleared his throat.

Evan:
Do you need backup for this venture?
It sounds like a potentially dangerous
situation

All those weirdos out in the graveyard

Frankie:
"We are the weirdos, mister."

Okay, he'd walked right into that *The Craft* reference. But she still hadn't answered his question. He waited, forcing himself to let her take the lead on this possible extra hangout.

*****

What was the worst that could happen? She needed to talk to a ghost or two and negotiate some grave soil, and that *would* be impressive for Evan to witness. Might make her look cool. He did seem eager to hang out—not that she was thinking about him being eager.

Or hooking up with him in her truck.

Straddling him in the passenger seat.

Their hands down each other's pants.

Frankie:
Have you nothing better to do
with your evening then hang

around with me doing creepy shit??

Evan:
Frankie please don't make me beg

Frankie:
I might very much like seeing you beg

Whoops. That had slipped out of her fingers too quickly to stop it. Was it possible to have a Freudian slip over text?

Evan:
Duly noted

He sent a smiling devil emoji.

Fuck. He was better at this than she was.

She padded over to the fridge, fixed herself some iced water, and started to chug it, staring at the open window between gulps like it was the most interesting thing in the world while her brain imploded into filthy stardust.

She tried typing a "sure, let's hang out" text over and over, but it kept coming out like, "If you promise to behave you can come," and then her face started burning all over again.

Time to pour some iced water on this.

For now.

So she wouldn't die.

Frankie:
I'll pick you up at 9. Dress discreetly.

CHAPTER 27

Evan stood in front of Nan's house. Nan had finally taken her meds and gone to sleep and would be fine for the rest of the night. He wasn't counting on staying out all night with Frankie anyway.

Not *that* much.

Frankie's truck rolled up with the headlights off. He approached, heart racing.

"You don't have to arrive in stealth, Frankie. We're adults and no one knows where we're going."

She leaned toward the open passenger window. "Hmm. Sounds a little dangerous for you, then." She frowned. "Why aren't you wearing black?" She eyed his clothing: the sleeveless hoodie and joggers, sneakers. None of it black.

"I just left my gym clothes on when I got back. Figured we'd be moving around."

Actually, he'd gone to the gym for a few hours to take his mind off things, and to give his hands something productive to do. He'd fallen so hard down the workout rabbit hole trying to distract himself that he ran late and barely made it home, got Nan settled, and raced out front before she pulled up. He hoped he didn't smell.

She scowled. "I can't believe you double-booked doing crimes with me and going to the gym. You're going to embarrass me in front of the ghosts dressed like that."

"Wait, doing crimes? Are we seeing ghosts tonight?"

She gave him an unsettling smile. "Hop in, we got crimes to do."

*****

They parked along a back alley a few blocks from the cemetery. Frankie grabbed her bag out of the backseat and motioned for Evan to follow silently. When they reached the bars of the side fence, she peered around the area and then chucked her bag over the fence.

Ah. They were breaking in. So, "crimes" then.

He watched Frankie back up, then take a running start and launch herself at the fence before scaling it with cat-like grace. He was not looking at her butt. Evan climbed over and landed with a loud thud on some crunching leaves. She glared at him as they started walking.

Taking the lead as usual, Frankie gripped her flashlight, eyes scanning in all directions, but didn't turn it on. Out here in the gloom, the rattle of leaves blowing across the grass sounded too much like Leshy bones to him. Evan breathed in the night fog and cold wind behind her as they walked. In the front of the graveyard, the most ancient graves were scattered all over plots with no coherent lines of gravestones. Bodies had to be everywhere under their feet. A light whispering skittered across the back of his head, playing with strands of his hair. Startled, he whipped around to find only more swirling fog. He turned back around and jumped, a sea of black hair and intense eyes now in his personal space.

"Stay close to me, the veil is thin," Frankie said in a low tone. Whatever that meant.

Her eyes gleamed, two glowing moons in the cemetery darkness. Evan did stay close. He found himself wanting to follow this woman anywhere—into battle for his family's salvation, into a basement infested with a deathworm, into hell itself. Into a graveyard on a weeknight to convince a dead lawyer to let them take some grave soil. She'd mentioned this was a necessary ingredient in finding the identity of Nan's attacker. She said she'd be "harnessing the power of justice" in her ritual. And this apparently had to be done at night when it was illegal to be here.

After wandering for a few minutes towards newer graves, Frankie dropped her bag to the ground and dug out a bouquet of marigolds. Her eyes flicked up to him. "Never come without an offering, and never take more than you give."

Flashlight on and placing marigold blooms on several graves, Frankie located the person she sought.

She dug into her bag again, removing a jar of liquid and mixed herbs. She poured the mixture directly in front of the tombstone and knocked on it like a door. Bizarre. Frankie arranged herself cross-legged on the ground, so Evan copied her. He scanned around for anything moving in the mist, swearing he could still hear faint whispering. He shivered.

A rumble. Then, green light cracked through the stone like streaks of lightning. Sound disappeared into a mute roaring—the pressure in his ears was painful. His pulse pounded in his neck, his wrists. He felt a sense of growing dread, like something was galloping towards him and he needed to move out of the way. But Frankie remained still, so Evan fought to not squirm.

With a pop, an actual fucking ghost came up out of the grass and sat against its headstone, displacing earth all over. Casual. Illuminated in green light, his quaffed blonde hair floated on a phantom breeze. Evan worked to fix his face. Per usual, none of this was normal.

"Eugene, been too long," Frankie crooned, with far more charm than Evan had seen her use before with anyone living.

The ghost crossed his arms. Evan realized that Eugene was wearing a suit with shoulder pads from the eighties. A high-powered attorney?

The ghost glared at Frankie. "No. Whatever it is, the answer is no."

"Aww, come on, man, you haven't even seen what I've brought you." She pulled out a bottle of Lagavulin. What the flaming hell was going on? Ghosts couldn't drink things, right? Eugene straightened a little, feigning disinterest.

"No. Whatever bullshit you're up to Frankie, I don't want my soil to be part of it."

"Who else in this cemetery had the amount of power you had in life?" She was switching to flattery now.

"I don't want my grave soil mixed into your black arts, *witch*. Oh, and cute, you brought backup." The ghost sneered down at Evan.

Evan shifted, uncomfortable. He didn't like this ghost's tone, the disrespect towards her, and he moved closer to Frankie on instinct. Frankie, unfazed, removed the topper of the bottle and threw back a generous pour. Eugene's throat bobbed. Ah. He must have liked to drink in his life. Evan was starting to get the game.

She glanced at Evan and wordlessly handed him the bottle. Evan smiled, making eye contact with Eugene and throwing back a shot. His nose burned and his eyes watered. He hated scotch. But he kept a straight face, playing it cool.

He was not thinking about Frankie's lips on the bottle as he handed it back to her.

Eugene was breaking. His knee bounced, tongue poking out of his mouth. He looked ridiculous.

Turning away from Eugene, Frankie took another swig, ignoring the ghost. "I bet I could drink you under the table, Evan. Wanna find out?" She gave him a wicked smile that turned the scotch in his belly over like a barrel wave.

He scoffed. "Not a chance. I've been partying in grad school for the last few years while you were manhandling bachelorettes in your shop." He was trying to get a rise out of her. He took another swig and handed the bottle back.

Frankie's eyes flashed and bounced down to his mouth. Nope. He imagined that. Surely.

Her gaze slowly dragged away from him and back to Eugene. Evan missed those silver eyes already. Christ, the liquor was hitting him fast. He should've eaten something before he left the house.

Eugene jiggled the balls of his feet, his leg bounces becoming more frequent. Frankie took another swig and dangled the bottle in front of Eugene. "Damn you," he rumbled, his tone turning nasty. An unpleasant thought struck Evan. Was this ghost able to hurt them?

"Hear me out. It's a simple trade. I just need a vial of your soil, and you get this whole entire bottle to yourself. Well, if we don't finish it first." She downed another shot before Evan grabbed it and took another swig. He was going to be hammered very, very soon.

"Ok, *fine, fine*! Take it. Take it!" Eugene held out an expectant palm. Frankie, a queen triumphant, handed the ghost the bottle, its edges turning green as it passed into whatever plane Eugene existed on. He was gone in a green flash.

"And not even a goodbye, the jerk," Frankie grumbled, getting to her feet.

She held a hand out to Evan who gripped it and stood, not needing the help but wanting to hold it anyway. His feet landed very close to hers, their faces almost touching. *Damn*, she smelled good. His mouth watered.

She blinked up at him before leaning down with a vial, scraping up some of the loose topsoil Eugene disturbed on his way up to the land of the living.

"Now what?" Evan felt himself sway on his feet.

"Now we can take an illegal stroll through this gorgeous graveyard unless you're too drunk to walk?"

"Yes." His voice husky, he stepped into pace with her.

They twined through the stones and gnarled trees for a while, moonbeams reaching down for them. He again heard whispering and felt phantom fingers trailing on his exposed arms. He should have worn a full hoodie, not a sleeveless one. He shivered again. "Do you hear that?"

She smiled, teeth showing. "As I said, the veil is thin. Stay close." There was a note of something in her voice. Was she flirting? He'd been playing their text exchange on repeat in his head for hours and was not equipped to handle this situation wisely, especially several shots deep in scotch.

While staring deeply into his eyes, Frankie gave him another wicked smile, the shadows in her hair creeping around her face. Suddenly, the dark swallowed her whole and a giggle sounded too far away.

Fear and aggravation licked through him. *Where did she go?* Evan called out to her but got no reply. He stomped towards the giggle off in the mist somewhere, praying to whichever gods were listening that he wouldn't stumble upon a Hound of Baskerville. *"Frankie?"* He stopped to listen again.

"Here." A whisper directly in his right ear. A brush of her lips against the lobe.

"Shit!" He jumped away, but she was already gone.

Okay, so *that's* how it was gonna be. He crouched down into the fog bank and scurried along, hiding behind a disturbing statue of an angel weeping. He waited for a few minutes, still as he could be while swaying, holding his breath when possible. In the gloom, a darker shadow crept slowly, silently toward his hiding place.

He grinned, getting into position as the shadow wrapped around the other side of the statue.

Evan leaped out, growling, and grabbed it around the middle as Frankie's astonished face fell out of her shadows. She squealed and ran away, cloaking in darkness once more.

Evan liked this game. A lot. He hunted her form, and now that he could see it, had no idea how he couldn't find her before. Her shape was ingrained in his brain, stained there. He drunk-stumble-sprinted toward the darkness, rounding on a small mausoleum, and crashed into her, pinning her to a large, gnarled oak. The shadows fell off of her body like smoke evaporating.

He snarled into her ear with his arms wrapped around her. "Got you."

She giggled, a little breathless from the chase. He pulled back, boxing her in, his nose brushing hers. Her breaths were fast and foggy, her stormy eyes searching his face over and over. He moved a hand from the tree trunk to her hip and touched it lightly, giving her plenty of opportunity to stop him. He gave her a questioning look. Her posture softened as she leaned back into the tree, pushing her chest out toward him. Holding him in place with her stare. His hand gripped her hip with more pressure, her bottom lip tucked up into her teeth. She stared now at his mouth. He let out a strangled groan involuntarily. His other hand rose to her face, thumb brushing over her cheekbone. Her breathing hitched. He leaned into her and she leaned into him. Holy shit, finally, finally, finally, *finally*—

Beams of flashlights lit them up, shattering the perfect dark. They both swore, whirling around to see a large group of tourists on the other side of the fence, a ghost tour guide droning on and not yet aware of them. But that was about to change, as some people in the group laughed at the sight of them. The guide started to turn around as Frankie tore away into the dark, ripped her bag from the ground, and retreated further into the night, Evan racing after her.

They giggled and sprinted, giddy children racing through the graves, life pumping through them, drunk-stumbling and snorting with laughter. They slowed to a halt near a larger mausoleum wall. Her bag thumped to the ground. Breaths heaving. He looked at Frankie's grinning face again—her inked fingers swiping away tears from laughing too hard. Evan's bare arms weren't cold anymore. He was burning up. He was going to burst into flames.

Frankie caught him staring at her and her smile morphed into something anticipatory, pupils flaring. Her brow raised. A dare. He stalked toward her, her grin growing as he backed her up against the mausoleum wall. Caging her in again, he ran his nose up her neck, smelling her deeply. Frankie shuddered and arched into him, a small sound leaving her. *Fuck*, he wanted to hear that sound again, more sounds. All of her sounds. He nuzzled his way up her neck and gripped both of her hips. Her beautiful, tattooed hands trailed up his bare, burning arms, one coming to rest behind his neck, the other falling to hook a finger in his waistband, pulling him closer, pulling him flush with her.

He was going to combust, and he hadn't even kissed her yet. Still feeling like an animal from their game, he growled into her neck, picked her up by gripping the back of her thighs, and pushed her into the wall. She wrapped black-legginged legs around his waist, gasping when ground himself against her core. Her fingers knotted into his hair and tugged hard. He remembered another tug in his hair when he was kneeling at her feet. The memory sent another jolt of need straight to his cock.

His hands shifted to grip her butt as he ground his hips in pulses against hers—she needed to feel exactly how badly he wanted her. She rolled her hips against his and moaned out a sound through a clenched jaw, hunger etched all over her features at what she felt pressed against her. He was going to eat her alive.

Another goddamn flashlight beam ran over their tangled bodies, her eyes going wide as footsteps thudded toward them. He placed her down on the ground, ready to rip the head clean off the body of whoever was disturbing them. His eyes focused through the fog on a cop racing in their direction.

"*Run!*" Frankie's amused voice rang out, and they were off again.

"I see you, Frankie!" A man's voice echoed through the cemetery, bobbling, huffing and puffing, clearly having trouble keeping up. "And this time… you're really… going… to… get a citation… for trespassing!"

She ran backwards calling back to him. "Sorry, officer, there's nobody here by that name!" She cackled, sprinting toward the fence, her bag smashing into her side.

They made it to the fence where they entered, the cop's flashlight just starting to crest into view. She flung her bag over the fence and looked at Evan. "Come on, come on!" They scrambled over the bars, Frankie laughing in near hysterics over her "crimes." Evan hard to the point of pain in his gym pants.

"Shit, we should split up and get away from here, or he'll see my truck in the alley. Can you make it home from here?"

Evan swallowed a lump of disappointment, nodding. "Yeah, it's not far."

"Okay, I'll see you soon." She grinned and took off, wrapping herself in shadows.

Evan jogged down the alley and out of sight of the cemetery. Once he was certain he was alone, he placed his hands on his hips, catching his breath.

Fuck.

He folded his hands on top of his head to expand his lungs and walked toward Nan's. He had a very, very cold shower in his future.

CHAPTER 28

Frankie dragged a needle-sharp line of black eyeliner across her lid with surgical precision, the warm light from her vanity chasing off the previous night's scotch-fueled confusion. The movement could be done in her sleep from a lifetime of practice.

"Then what?!" Bex's voice was shrill in her earbuds, grating against her lack of caffeine on this too-bright morning.

"Do you have me on speaker? Because I am *not* repeating this again to Jack. Or possibly ever in my life."

Jack's low, smug laugh flitted in the background.

Frankie scoffed. "I'll take that as a yes." She paused, eye pencil balanced in between her fingers, and took a large gulp of coffee.

"We're waiting," Jack drawled.

Frankie groaned and gripped her face with both hands. The rest fell out of her mouth in a rush. "And-then-I-wrapped-my-legs-around-him-and-we-basically-dry-humped-against-the-mausoleum." Her face was burning.

Bex shrieked in delight, banging her hands on what sounded like their kitchen table, and Jack laughed until they choked on their morning cappuccino.

"Thanks." Frankie deadpanned, turning back to the mirror. She sighed. "And then we got interrupted by that cop, Dave? I think? He doesn't like me. So, we ran for our lives and split up."

"Wait-wait-wait," Jack was walking toward the phone. "You split up and went home alone?"

"Yes?"

"Frankie. Are you serious?"

"What was I supposed to do? None of this makes any sense to me!" She glared at her phone.

Bex cackled and Frankie heard a light thump, like Jack had whacked her arm playfully.

Frankie went back to drawing black around her eyes. "Guys. I don't know what to do. He's a client, his grandmother is going to die soon, he's relying on me to get this job done—"

"I'll bet he is." Bex said suggestively through a laugh. Jack let out a snort.

"Frankie." Jack's voice, close to the speaker, was the calm steadiness she needed this morning and had relied on for almost two decades. "This seems complicated. But it doesn't have to be. You have amazing instincts, always have. It's how you survive facing literal demons on a weekly basis, throwing salt in their dumb faces or some shit. I don't know what you do, you know I always wait outside. You can face a monster from the depths of hell? I think you can handle this."

Frankie's eyes watered. She was glad she opted for waterproof today.

"If things between you two are meant to happen, it's gonna happen. Stop fretting." Jack sensed her snivel.

"What if it's awkward when I see him next?"

"Yeah, I don't think that's going to be a problem." Their tone was dismissive and casual.

"What do you mean?" Frankie switched to mascara.

"My dude. He is so hung up on you. Do you not know this?"

Frankie froze. She honestly hadn't let herself consider it, didn't want to get it wrong and break her own heart. She had been telling herself he was just a shameless flirt. That it was just the number of life-threatening situations they had shared over the last few weeks. That it was just the scotch making them grind on each other in a fucking cemetery.

Bex called from across the room, "The next time you see him, try pinning him up against a wall. And then please report back in detail."

"*Goddess*, Bex!" Frankie choked on her coffee, but now she was laughing.

The sound of Bex trotting to the phone came through her earbuds. "Frankie, when we had family dinner at your place, he did not stop staring at you. At all. Once."

Frankie was not able to cope with this. "Fuuuuuck," she groaned into her coffee.

"When do you see him next?"

She blew out a puff of breath. "A few days, I think? We might meet up at the library to look at his research, but I don't know."

"Oh! Perfect!" Bex leaned into the phone, and said with dead-seriousness, "Wear a short skirt with high socks."

Frankie laughed, "What? Why?"

"Trust me," her voice was sage, like she was bestowing ancient wisdom on her. "You are going to be channeling dark academia, you'll be in a library—his element—and he's recently out of school. He might drop dead at the sight of you."

She sipped her coffee. "How high of socks are we talking?"

"How high do you have?"

"Mmm, I think I've got an over-the-knee pair."

Bex and Jack spoke as one.

"Do it!"

CHAPTER 29

As October eased over the halfway point, Sawtooth Bay erupted into a riot of fiery color. The streets were packed with tourists, and any shops that had dragged their feet decorating the storefront upped their game to keep up with their neighbors in the square.

Naturally, Frankie took this holiday very seriously. The Black Cat's front window displayed a trio of skeletons: one was dressed as a stage magician sawing a second, screaming skeleton in half for a magic act while the third was dressed as an assistant in a glittered leotard, arms wide in a grand gesture, trying to steal the scene. Obnoxious and suggestive, but not so overly gory that it scared the kids. Perfect.

Shop traffic over the last few days had been constant and unending. More than once during a tarot reading on some poor soul from out of state, Frankie had zoned out, remembering the feeling of being pinned against a mausoleum wall, then quickly crossed her legs and barreled through the reading, fully distracted.

Evan hadn't texted her directly but had finally started chiming in on the group thread.

She wondered what he was doing right now. If he was thinking about her at all.

After another long shift, Frankie decided to close up early as soon as the last cluster of customers dripped out of the shop. Jack and Bex had both stopped by at different times of the day to make sure she was still coming with them to the orchard. Apple magic was one of her favorite fall-time activities. And the fresher the product, the closer to its place of creation, the more powerful the working would be. She planned to load up on enough apples to bake an apple cobbler, stew some stovetop applesauce, make some protective apple charms, do some fortune telling for the season ahead, give thanks to the goddess for her bountiful harvest this summer, the list was endless.

And she needed an assload of apples to make it happen.

Ready for some drama-free, stress-free, boy-free, goof-off time with her friends, Frankie's truck creaked into park at the orchard. She spotted Bex and Jack being silly, having already purchased some apple slices and trying to toss them into each other's mouths. And missing every single time.

"You two are absurd."

Bex lit up. "Hi! Are you ready to do this?"

Frankie stretched her neck, bones popping. "Gods, yes. I need this."

Jack handed her an apple slice. As she popped it into her mouth, her phone buzzed in her back pocket. Fishing it out, Frankie froze with the fruit hanging halfway out. It was the Sawtooth Baddies thread.

> Bex:
> *We're parked over on the right*

Frankie bit down on the apple slice, sending half of it tumbling into the dirt. She whipped around to Bex, who gave her a shit-eating grin. "Dude? What the hell?"

"Don't worry your scary little head about it—hi, Evan!" She beamed and waved beyond Frankie's stiff form.

"*Traitor!*" Frankie hissed at her.

She turned to watch Evan stroll up to meet them. His eyes immediately found hers, and she felt the noise of the parking lot fall away. Had it only been a few days since they saw each other? She was sucked back to a foggy night earlier in the week, drowning in the smell of him, chasing each other through gravestones. So close to kissing.

She watched emotions move through his features and wished she could pry his head open and see all of his secrets. Vaguely aware of Bex and Jack making themselves scarce, Frankie tugged her sleeves down over her hands as he approached.

*****

Evan found himself swallowed by her gravitational pull, and before he'd realized he'd parked, opened the door, and gotten out of his car, there she was. Heart-rendingly beautiful, all-consuming.

In truth, he worried nonstop for days that things had gone too far in the cemetery. Blamed it on the Lagavulin. He lay awake every night, staring at the ceiling, re-reading their text thread, thinking of the pressure of his hips against hers and how he didn't even get to kiss her. Running his fingers through his hair and gripping hard, trying to make sense of it all. But now in front of her, his brain emptied, useless emotions flicking through him like projector slides. Fully beyond words. So he said the first thing that popped into his head.

"Do you know how absolutely terrifying you are?"

Wait, what? He'd intended to compliment her and *that's* what came out his mouth? He prepared himself for the parking lot to swallow him whole and end his misery. Or for an apple tree to fall on top of him and splatter him across the pavement. Death might not be so bad, comparatively.

Her stunned face broke into a bewildered full smile, and she cackled, bending a bit to grab her knee.

"Why, Evan Lawson, that's the sweetest thing anyone's ever said to me." He loved her laugh— it was so at odds with her tough exterior.

He couldn't stop the laugh that came out of him, meeting hers. He looked down and saw she had hidden her hands in her sleeves again.

Be brave.

He reached for her hand and gently slid the sleeve back to her wrist. He wove his fingers into hers, glancing at her face at last. She watched him, riveted, unreadable, aggravating. He summoned courage that he did not at all possess and ran his free fingers across the back of her hand, trailing over her sigils.

He stepped closer. "I really like your hands, Frankie."

A blush splashed across her cheeks. She stuttered. "I—Oh."

It was all she said. Evan realized with a jolt that she was nervous. This gorgeous maniac was nervous around *him*? Frankie disarmed was just as scary as Frankie with her claws out, but he went in for the kill while he still could.

"That was the most fun I've ever had in a graveyard." He searched her face. "But how are you feeling?"

It was strange seeing so much pink on Frankie's pale face. "Y-yes. It was almost a perfect night."

"Almost?" After everything she had put him through, he enjoyed seeing her squirm like this. Fighting a smile, he brought her hand to his mouth and placed a few small kisses on her palm. Her eyes were wide and her breath hitched. "Frankie, am I making you nervous?"

That snapped her out of her spell. She narrowed her eyes at him in a challenge.

*****

How dare he? Two could play at this game.

Frankie removed the space between them and stood flush with him. She grabbed his chin and tilted his face up a bit to expose his neck at a good angle. Holding his face firm with one hand, she trailed a fingernail down his throat. Her mouth watered. What the fuck was wrong with her?

Evan swallowed hard and she giggled, watching his throat bob. He clenched his fists at his side. Gods, this was satisfying. She was delighted to know she had a similar effect on him as he had on her. She leaned up and whispered in his ear.

"And do I make *you* nervous, Evan?"

He couldn't look her in the eye from this angle, but he didn't pull away and just let her control him. "Obviously. You scare the hell out of me."

She pressed a finger to the pulse in his neck and felt it pounding up to her fingertip. Evan letting her position him wherever she wanted was extremely hot. If she wasn't careful, she was going to climb him like a tree in this parking lot, surrounded by screaming children. But she wasn't ready to pull away just yet.

Not caring how many tiny eyes or their parents were around them, she dipped a fingertip in his waistband and turned his face to look at her. He was fully flushed, shaking with restraint.

She looked him dead in the eye. "It's too bad we got interrupted that night." Then she gave his cheek a featherlight slap and turned around to go find their friends, leaving him gobsmacked. She didn't have to glance behind her to know he was following.

*****

Evan was fucked. No, he was a goner. A dead man.

He stayed right on Frankie's heels for the next hour, aware that they were not alone, but physically unable to keep his eyes off of the sway of her hips, the way the shadows in her hair glittered in the sun. He ached to throw her over his shoulder and go find a secluded spot off in the trees somewhere to break some of this tension.

Instead, the Sawtooth Baddies sat around a picnic table with their apple hauls and goodies. Frankie dipped an apple slice into some apple butter, then topped that with a piece of white cheddar cheese before scarfing it down. Jack returned with a bucket of drinks—three canned whiskey cocktails and a can of IPA for him.

Children shrieked and crashed into their table before sprinting away to their parents. Jack frowned at them through their sunglasses. "How does anyone go to places packed with kids and *not* drink?" Frankie snorted in agreement.

"I don't want to know. Hit me with that." Bex yanked the can from Jack's grip and took a huge gulp. "Oh, it's good."

Frankie took a huge sip and hummed in agreement. "Who's free tomorrow night to help me with the séance?"

"I'll be there," Evan heard himself say. She gave him a little smile. He couldn't wait for whatever weird, creepy shit that would entail.

"Not us!" Bex said. "We have a date night tomorrow. Sorry." She batted her eyelashes.

"Uh-huh. And it's not because of my… what did you call them? 'Creepy dead eyes?'"

"No, I said 'possessed doll eyes.' I hate watching you do that. I don't sleep for weeks."

"Fine," Frankie said, exasperated.

Jack spoke around a bite of apple pastry. "But send us a text when it's all done so we know everything went okay. Promise me."

"Promise."

CHAPTER 30

The next day was Sunday, and Frankie spent the morning and most of the afternoon pottering around her house, procrastinating any sort of planning or prepping needed for the séance. She refreshed the protective wards on every door. Mopped the kitchen floor. Carved two pumpkins, even though she knew they would rot within a few days and she'd have to bring more home. Made elaborately decorated Halloween cookies with Clemmie's supervision—orange blossom round cookies with intricate spider web designs, pumpkin-flavored cookies shaped like jack-o'-lanterns with different faces, and chocolate-and-coffee-flavored cookies shaped like coffins.

But dusk fell, and she knew it was almost time. She fought through her nausea and ate a few cookies, trying to settle her stomach. It had been ages since she attempted to channel the spirits. Some of her ancestors were abusive assholes, and they were not welcome in her home. A séance was like calling a phone in the middle of a public space—anyone could answer it. She just hoped she would get lucky.

More importantly, channeling was dangerous, and she knew by doing this working, she would be a beacon of bright light for any and all surrounding spirits. A lighthouse calling them to the shore. She didn't like visitors of any kind, and definitely not of the spirit variety.

Her doorbell sounded, and Frankie swore, checking the time. *Why is he always early?* Entering the hall, she watched Evan's shadow move across the porch. Part of her was glad that Jack and Bex had a "date night" planned and were finding pathetic excuses to push her and Evan together.

As she opened the door, her anxiety over the next few hours momentarily swayed. Amber porch light illuminated Evan's wavy hair and eyes, and she was dumbstruck for a long moment. *Gods, he's really beautiful.*

"Hey, Frank." She wouldn't admit it under threat of torture and death, but the nickname was growing on her.

A little bit.

She opened the door for him to come inside and started to pull her sleeves down over her hands but stopped herself.

"I really like your hands, Frankie."

The sentence looped in her brain on repeat. It kept her up at night.

"Thanks for coming," she mumbled.

Evan took off his coat and frowned at her as he hung it up. "What's wrong? You look stressed." Without saying anything else, he pulled her into a hug.

Shock and aggravation moved through her in waves and then the floodgates opened, her eyes threatening to ruin her makeup. She sniffed a bit, and he tightened his hold. After a few moments, he released her. "Are you nervous?"

She stared at her feet. "I am. Things might get a little weird tonight." She chanced a look up at him and found him holding in a laugh.

"As opposed to barbequing a deathworm on some rando's driveway?"

She couldn't stop the giggle that came out of her. She hated her laugh—it was so girlish. But Evan beamed at her, at the sound. Which made her itchy and confused.

He took her chin in his hand. "I got you," he said, his tone tender. Her eyes swam, remembering when she said that to him outside of Agatha's house and her silent, burning promise to take care of him, to help him through whatever came next. "What can I do? How does this work?"

Frankie aimed for the kitchen. "I just need to paint my face a bit and then we can get started." She sat on a stool at the kitchen island and resumed the work she had begun before Evan arrived. With a liquid eyeliner pen tip, she began to draw on her cheeks and forehead.

Evan grabbed a coffin cookie and watched. "What's that for?"

"I'm painting on some protective runes. Trying to stack the deck in my favor, you know?"

"Do you wear those at any other time?"

She thought for a moment. "Sort of. If I'm doing any kind of summoning or big working, I'll paint my entire face up to honor the spirits. I call it my Spirit Face. Not needed for tonight, but I'll take any extra protection I can get."

When she was satisfied that the lines were sharp enough to hold through any sweating or moving around during the séance, she led Evan into the library.

"Help me move this," she said, pointing to the coffee table. After shifting some furniture around, she rolled back the area rug to reveal an encircled pentagram of red and black tiles built into the floor. It was a particular sticking point when renovating the library. She had demanded that this pentagram be placed into these gorgeous, original floorboards. Bex had been hysterical, but Frankie expected to live in this house until she croaked, so fuck it.

"This was under our feet the whole time that we hung out in here?" Evan asked.

"When it's permanent, the circle can't be broken as easily."

"Do I get in there with you?"

"No!" she snapped, then cringed and said, "It's not safe for you to be in there. I need someone on the outside in case I need to be pulled out."

"Pulled out of the circle? Meaning you couldn't do it yourself?"

Frankie nodded. "You can get in, but I won't be able to get out unless I dissolve the circle, or you drag me out." She pointed to a bright orange bucket from the hardware store next to the fireplace. "If things go tits up, use that bucket of salt water. Just throw in on the whole scene."

"Seriously?"

"Promise me." She knew her tone was too sharp.

"I will. I promise."

*****

Frankie and Evan spent the next few minutes aligning all of the pieces for her séance, which included a small FM radio, Nan's jewelry, the vial of graveyard dirt, and lots of lit candles. Evan noticed that her hands shook. He burned to grab and hold them until they stilled, but with Frankie in this kind of agitated state, he would only do exactly what she needed for as long as she needed it.

"Okay, guess I can't put this off any longer." She sat down in the center of the pentagram and pulled out Nan's ruby ring, which she had threaded onto a chain. She handed it to Evan, and he began to swing the ring like a pendulum in front of her face, her eyes glazing over. Shadows poured down from her hair and up from the floor to fill the space of the circle, giving her the illusion of sitting on a dark cloud. Clemmie appeared from nowhere and watched her intently, his tail wrapped around his feet and furry toebeans pressed to the very edge of the circle.

Evan immediately understood the phrase "possessed doll eyes" as Frankie's eyes darkened to two glossy, black mirrors reflecting the room back to him.

He turned on the radio to a low static, hit "scan," and set it just outside of the circle. He felt crackling energy everywhere in the room, down to his bones. He started to pace so he wouldn't crawl out of his skin. Her voice sunk into the dark quality he had only heard when she was accessing a huge amount of power.

"I call now to the spirits that know me. Come forth and speak, either through me or through the radio."

Nothing but raw radio static and silence greeted them. *Speak through Frankie?* Evan resumed his pacing. This suddenly felt like a terrible idea.

"Are any ancestors present? Any spirit guides? You have permission to speak."

Again, they were met with silence and static.

*****

Frankie saw herself standing inside of a dark fog bank, looking all around for any sign of life, of movement, of anything familiar. She found nothing but the void.

She tried again. *"I offer this grave soil to you, Spirits, as I seek justice for a crime committed. Will someone please answer me?"* she asked, fumbling for the vial and pouring it in a line in front of her.

Several minutes passed, and just when things seemed pointless—and a bit of relief worked its way under her skin—she heard a low creak off in the fog. Her head snapped in that direction.

*****

Evan jumped as a genderless voice scratched through the static of the radio. *"I will answer you. What do you seek?"*

Frankie snapped her head toward the radio. *"Thank you, spirit. Who has cursed Agatha Lawson? Can you see what arrangement was made?"*

A long pause of static.

"I see not blood promised but life itself—in exchange for life."

Frankie's face twisted in frustration. *"What does that mean, spirit? Can you see who made the bargain?"*

The voice came warbled through the radio speaker. *"Something old... Something... Wait. Child, who is with you?"* The spirit's voice sounded panicked. Evan felt his skin prickle. Clemmie stood and backed away from the circle, his ears falling flat against his ancient head.

"He is a friend, he's no threat to you. We come in respect and mean no harm."

The radio began to pop as a buzzing white noise interrupted the spirit's speech. *"Not—man in the room w—you, child, what is it that follows you?"*

What do they mean "what"? Clemmie let out a low growl while staring at Frankie. Evan's bad feeling began to flood his entire system. Events were unfolding on the other side of the veil, and he could do nothing except watch Frankie, one foot in both worlds as she held onto a metaphysical lightning rod.

Frankie's brow pinched in confusion, and she opened her mouth to ask another question. The radio crackled in a deeper tone and fell silent. No more static. Frankie's face fell into flat shock at some realization. "No, no," she muttered to herself. "Oh, shit."

*****

Though she never questioned the "how" of it, it was strange how Frankie could read people so quickly. She could read spirits, too. And though the first spirit's energy felt old and familiar, something very wrong had slipped in behind them into the fog bank. She strained to peer through the fog, electricity building around her as if she now stood in a thundercloud. A rumble shook her body like a great beast moving beyond her field of vision. The stink of a sewer seeped through the atmosphere to her mixed with something floral—freesia? The awful combination stroked down her memory with cold fingers, and something dislodged from the past.

Then, familiar feelings. Repulsion. Terror. Loathing. Confusion. A tummy ache. A loss of time. A head and body that moved without her consent. A physical reaction that she had buried so deep behind a vault door that she had forgotten its markers, the all-consuming quality that it carried.

Suddenly, she was dumped back in time, her tiny body crashing through the surface of the water, her child legs swimming to right herself again.

She knew where she was. And that no one was coming to save her.

*****

Evan toed as close to the circle as he dared, not sure if he needed to interrupt. If he needed to pull her out now. Or wait? Clemmie stood in front of Evan, back arched, hissing and yowling.

Evan paced around the circle, frantic for any sign of what he should do. His instincts told him that something had shifted, something was very, very wrong.

He crouched in front of her, her face still frozen in shock. "Frankie? Can you hear me?"

"Evan?" Her voice was so small.

"I'm right here."

Tears streamed down her cheeks, runes smearing a little bit.

"Evan. Run."

CHAPTER 31

In the same moment, Frankie's eyes went from glossy to a matte black—a void. Black veins streaked down from her eye sockets into her cheeks.

Frankie's face pulled wide into an awful, ear-to-ear, feline smile. Unnatural, the skin not meant to stretch that way. She cracked her neck and stood from the floor, shadows scattering into the corners of the room.

"Frankie? Can you hear me?" Evan's voice shook. He hated how much it shook.

She looked at him, slowly, unblinking, still showing her teeth.

She spoke.

"*Oh, what a lovely little life this one has built.*" The voice was a hiss, a harsh whisper. This was not the scary, ancient voice of Frankie wielding her shadows. Clemmie sprinted into the kitchen to hide.

"Frankie? Please, can you hear me?"

The spirit laughed, the sound more like a snake's rattle than anything else. "*Not Frankie, boy.*"

His head spun before remembering the salt water—he had no idea if the spirit was trapped in the circle, but the salt water was his one and only defense against whatever the fuck was happening. He charged at the bucket and snatched it from the floor.

"Sorry for this!" he called out, hoping that somewhere in there she could hear him. He swung the bucket towards the circle, watching the water arc out and fly towards the creature in the center. Not-Frankie raised her hand, and the water froze in place, then crashed to the ground in a thousand ice shards.

Shit.

Not at all bothered, the spirit reached out one of Frankie's lovely, tattooed fingers—the fingers that had shaken in fear not long ago—and tested the barrier of the circle. Watching the spirit inside Frankie's body made him nauseous. She didn't stand right, her shoulders sagged down to one side, head cocked, as if not knowing how to move in a physical form. He'd never seen her smile this constantly, this horribly. The spirit wore her body like a skin suit not fully inflated.

He whipped his phone out and texted the Sawtooth Baddies thread.

> Evan:
> *SOS SOS 911, whatever the fuck*
> *Séance didn't go well*
> *I think I need help*

He held his phone to his chest and considered taking a photo to explain what was going on, but he thought of Frankie in the future, learning that evidence of this violation existed. He couldn't do that to her.

> Evan:
> *FUCKING SOMEONE*
> *OH MY GOD*
> *WHAT DO I DO*
> *I THINK SHE'S POSSESSED*

Fucking finally, a message popped up.

> Jack:
> *WTF EVAN*
> *Are you serious??*
> *We're not even in town right now!!!*

Evan felt his guts melt. No, no, no, no, no.

> Bex:
> *WHAT WHAT WHAT WHAT*
> *WHAT IS HAPPENING*
> *We're in fucking Bar Harbor*

He realized with complete certainty that he was alone. Alone out here in this creepy old house, with the creepy girl who was very important to him held hostage inside of her own body. Not-Frankie trailed a finger along the circle's circumference, a spark following its path like it was welding an exit.

Evan didn't have hours. He had seconds.

He thought of Frankie standing in front of Nan's house with him on that afternoon taking his hand, her gray eyes set in resolution, some kind of unspoken promise sparking there while he was drowning. Drowning in the fear, the panic, the grief. She told him in that moment that death wouldn't come for him all alone. She would block its path.

He would not let this dark force take her. It couldn't have her.

He welcomed the rage that surged through him now, and as if coming from outside of his body, he heard his voice speak, strong and unwavering.

"You can't have her, spirit. Leave now."

The spirit looked delighted by this declaration and flicked a pointer finger into the side of the circle. A loud crash signaled the fall of the circle's walls. *"Silly boy. She said we could speak through her. We were invited."*

Oh, no. The spirit was right—her language in the séance had allowed for that to happen. He sorted through his thoughts, seeking an answer, summoning calm and reason and logic.

"You know damn well that's not what she meant."

"Doesn't matter now. Here we are." Not-Frankie held her arms wide and stepped out of the pentagram. As if remembering she had arms, it pulled up her sleeve and ran a fingernail down her inner forearm. It chuckled. *"She covered them up."* The nail scraped over tattooed skin. *"Let's make a new one."*

The fingernail pierced her wrist and sliced straight down towards her elbow.

"NO!" Evan launched towards Frankie's body and pinned her arms to her sides. Already, he could feel the blood pouring into his slippery grip, making it hard to hold her tight. The spirit jerked its shoulders and sent Evan flying into the loveseat. It flew on top of him, slicing into his arms with Frankie's fingernails and dragging him to the floor.

*****

Frankie waded in the neighborhood pool, sinking down into the depths. She loved how cool it was down here. She liked the feeling of sinking, like she was being safely held by something. Something that calmed and soothed her.

Sound faded away and she surfaced in a burst of bubbles, finding herself all alone. Had there been other kids around?

After a hum of thunder, the oncoming afternoon storm unleashed, sending droplets striking up to her face and goggles.

But something was wrong. She couldn't place it. There was no one around, but she wasn't alone.

Swimming over to the edge of the pool, she heaved herself out and stood. Peeling her goggles up on top of her mass of curls, she looked around. Afraid.

She pretended she was holding hands with a bolt of lightning and stepped around towards the gate. If she hurried outside, she might be able to figure out where everyone went.

Who did she come here with?

Then, she felt an invisible lasso loop around her middle and tug.

She turned, eyes wide, the band of her goggles digging into her scalp. Her body dripped onto the pavement. Her bathing suit had pineapples on it. She hoped she would still love this bathing suit tomorrow.

Something waded in the center of the pool. Dread filled her and she was overwhelmed by an intense floral and sewage stink. Fighting through the sensation, she tried to make out its form through the rain. It was sort of the size and shape of a thin man but made up entirely of a void, a pitch-black nothingness. Not a color, but more of an absence of light. Except for its teeth and the whites of its eyes, which were white as snow. It was smiling wide, which made no sense. It lifted its long, clawed hand out of the water, a gold chord wrapped around its wrist. The same chord, she realized, that held her waist.

"Knock, knock," it said. And yanked.

*****

Frankie's hands gripped Evan's throat, squeezing him out of consciousness, the grin on her face now dripping with spit. Her tongue hung limp from the side of her mouth.

"This one was fun as a small thing. Imagine what we can do now. And with these?" It raised up a hand. Shadows pulled out from her fingers as if being dragged by force. They quickly shrank back under her skin. *"They will kneel for us soon enough."* Evan felt his head rise up several inches before it was slammed back into the floorboards. Ringing pain erupted between his ears, and his vision spotted and went white.

The world tilted diagonally, and he felt the spirit climb off of him, walking disjointed on all fours like a spider before remembering to walk like a person. Feeling returned to his limbs, and he rolled to his side, coughing and sputtering.

Frankie's body angled towards the front door, and before Evan knew it, he had tackled her to the floor.

"Frank, if you can hear me at all—I'm coming!"

*****

Frankie screamed and screamed, her chest aching with the effort she threw into the noise. But no one was coming.

The chord dragged her to the pavement and scraped her body along the cement as it pulled her toward the water. She shrieked and thrashed until her voice gave out, screamed until not a single noise was left to come out of her.

Now locked in a silent cry for help, the chord pulled her closer and closer to the smiling thing in the pool. Her skin stung from fighting the ground.

Where was everyone? Anyone?

*****

Evan held Not-Frankie down as the spirit thrashed, shrieking in his ear. His mind raced, filtering through possibilities. And trying not to injure her body. Her bleeding arm pooled onto the wood.

He needed salt. And water. He rewound to the day of the Leshy, remembering how she let everyone clean themselves in her bathroom.

She had a huge tub. And he remembered a large jar with a scoop for Epsom salts.

"I got you," he said, hoping his voice could reach her, wherever she was. He picked up her thrashing body and held it over his shoulder as he marched up the stairs.

*****

With one final, horrible tug, Frankie fell again into the pool, feet-first. She sputtered and kicked at the thing, finally finding purchase on its face. It huffed out a cough and gripped her arm, enraged.

There were many frustrations about being a child in an adult's world. One of the hardest things for Frankie had always been her lack of physical strength. Instead, she thrashed against her exhaustion and fought the thing like a cornered bobcat. She used her teeth and her nails.

But somehow, it gripped her neck with one hand and held her up from the pool's surface. She smacked and clawed at its arm as she began to lose consciousness.

*****

Evan straddled Frankie's chest with his legs on the floor of her bathroom and turned the cold water knob to full blast. He couldn't reach the knob for hot, so this was going to be an unpleasant bath. Not bothering with the salt scoop, he grabbed the glass jar and dumped half of its contents into the water.

He looked back down at the spirit, which fought him wildly, black eyes tunneling through him, teeth gnashing. He wrestled it, careful to not bash any part of her against the bathtub. He managed to get it into a light chokehold and pulled it into the tub. He stepped in with it, gripping its back to his chest. He pulled them both down into the cold, gasping at the shock.

*****

Frankie felt the cold of the water cover her up before the lights went out.

Light.

She reached for that sacred light she'd heard so much about on Sundays, imagined sending it out from her form in blinding waves and illuminating the pool.

But nothing came. The thing had disappeared, but she felt it inside of her body, using her eyes. Swimming calmly and looking at her hands.

*****

Frankie's body stopped fighting and began to shake. He turned off the cold water, and changing position with her, switched on the knob for hot. He shivered and held her firm, then switched off the knob before the tub could overflow. He angled her injured arm along the back of the tub, above her heart, to help stop the bleeding.

Relief slowly set into him in warmer water, but she still shook with violent tremors.

"Come on, Frankie. Come back."

*****

A brine washed over her, the water more like an ocean than a pool. Frankie and the thing swam deeper down. She looked at her arms in motion and noticed ink blooming there under her skin. Symbols appeared on her hands. She swam deeper down still, away from the light.

She had always felt safe down here. Cooled. Calmed.

And then she remembered she had escaped this hell before, years ago, and had locked it behind a vault door. Pushing through numb nerve endings, her fingertips on one hand wiggled. She clenched her fist to gain control of her arm and pulled a shadow from the bottom of the pool. It sang back to her, gliding over with ease. Wrapping it around herself, she freed her legs, freed her other arm.

She yanked at the pool's shadows with both hands, wrapped them around her like a blanket, and surfaced.

Moving with intention, she walked into the shallow end with her darkness wrapped around her. She felt the thing clawing inside of her, suffocating under the weight of it.

"Get out. Now."

It hissed and fought, not unlike she had moments ago.

*****

Evan held Frankie until she stopped shaking. The dripping of the faucet felt impossibly loud in the silence after the spirit's shrieking. He sputtered and fought to catch his breath.

She twitched and began to claw at his arms. "Frankie?"

Her head tipped back, teeth bared.

"*I SAID GET THE FUCK OUT!*" She bellowed the phrase in a roar to the ceiling, to the world.

Her shadows flooded the room, blacking out every speck of light. In the dark, Evan was aware of a ghostly form fleeing, the stink of sewer and flowers strong in the room. The smell faded, and the dark receded.

Frankie panted hard against his chest, and he sat up straighter with her. Her panting became sputters. Thick sobs tore from her, echoing off the tile.

Evan moved his arms to wrap around her middle so he wasn't pinning her. He pulled her back into a hug against his chest, placing his chin on her shoulder. After a few moments, he tried to speak.

"What can I do?" His tone was soft. His relief was existential.

She gripped his hand across her stomach.

"Oh, fu—I'm going to be sick." She wrenched away from him, out of the tub, and stumbled into the throne room, barely making it to the toilet in time. Evan eased out of the tub, noting that the bathroom was completely soaked. With careful movements, he came to Frankie's side and held back her mass of hair. Vomit the color of a void exited her for several minutes. Once empty, she slumped on the floor and curled into a fetal position.

Evan rolled her over, lifting her from the ground. He carried her over to the sink and gently sat her on the counter. Her silver eyes were back but unable to look at him, haunted and vacant. Using a washcloth with hot water and soap, he cleaned her face.

Without looking at him, Frankie removed her sweater, leaving on a soaked tank top. He wiped down her arms. He was cautious around the slice on her forearm but tried to get it as clean as possible. It looked like it had already started to clot.

"If I bring you some clothes, can you change out of these?" He tapped her knee.

She nodded, mute. Evan retrieved a soft, clean shirt and cotton shorts from her dresser and entered the bathroom to find Frankie staring in the mirror, her pants already off. He averted his eyes and placed the clothes on the counter.

155

He turned around, listening to the sounds of her changing. She moved slowly. He hadn't seen any cuts, aside from the wound on her inner forearm. He heard her hoist herself back on the counter. Taking her arm as gently as possible, Evan cleaned the wound and wrapped it in a bandage. There were no healing herbs in sight, and he didn't trust himself to dig through her pantry and find the right stuff, so he prayed that her body would heal itself well enough on its own.

Evan brought her a glass of water, which she emptied. "Do you need anything?" he asked. Still avoiding his gaze, she shook her head. Tears began to form along her bottom eyelids and Evan felt his heart rip in half. He didn't understand what the fuck had gone down over the last hour, but she was clearly traumatized.

"Come on," he said and lifted her from the counter. With one arm under her knees, he held her to his chest and tucked her head under his chin, hoping it would feel to Frankie like she was surrounded by safety. Frankie's enormous king-sized bed called out to him, and he spent a minute getting her under the covers. She lay on her side, facing away from him. When he was certain she was as settled as possible, given the circumstances, he stood to go and sleep on the sofa. There was no way he was leaving her alone tonight.

"Evan?" Her voice was so quiet, he nearly missed it. "Don't leave."

Relief filled him up, and he quickly grabbed an oversized pair of sweatpants from her dresser to change into, stripping off his soaked clothes on the bathroom floor. He eased under the covers, giving her plenty of time to feel where he was.

"I'm right here." He placed a light arm over her. She scooted backward into him, so he tightened his hold around her waist. She cried for a while, before slipping into a deep sleep. Only then did Evan let himself drift off.

CHAPTER 32

Soft white light warmed Frankie's swollen eyelids. Her nose detected disinfectant close to her as well as potatoes being pan-fried a little farther away. She felt far away. Far from herself, far from the present. Carefully, she opened her eyes and found Clemmie nestled next to her face on the pillow. With her stirring, Clemmie rolled into a belly-up stretch, a rich purr coming from his chest.

She stroked his tummy and ribs and rolled onto her back to match him, the stars and whorls of her bedroom ceiling calming her muddied brain. Everything rolled back into her in slow waves.

The séance.

The invasion.

She'd kicked it out.

Evan. Evan had taken care of her. And shit, he'd been on the receiving end of whatever happened while she was under. Panic licked through her at the thought. *While she was under.*

She'd been pulled under again. Her heart rate spiked, her skin washed in hot and cold. She held a finger in front of her face and focused on it, then looked beyond at the galaxy she had made up above her. Back and forth, until the chills subsided. She let the previous night move through her and pass like a storm. After years of lost time, she had learned to be patient with herself with what she did and did not remember. She called on that patience now.

Sighing, she went on autopilot and reached to the nightstand for her phone and found it had been placed facedown and plugged in, waiting for her. She pulled up the Sawtooth Baddies thread to see a string of highly alarmed messages from the entire group.

Evan:
SOS SOS 911, whatever the fuck
Séance didn't go well
I think I need help

Evan:
FUCKING SOMEONE
OH MY GOD
WHAT DO I DO
I THINK SHE'S POSSESSED

Jack:
WTF EVAN
Are you serious??
We're not even in town right now!!!

Bex:
WHAT WHAT WHAT WHAT
WHAT IS HAPPENING
We're in fucking Bar Harbor
Will take hours to get back

There was a several-hour gap before Jack sent a selfie of them and Bex on her front porch after three in the morning.

Jack:
Evan wouldn't let us inside
ASSHOLE
Here's proof that we were here

And we love you

Text when you wake up

Frankie's nose burned with her overflow of feelings.

Frankie:
I'm awake
And I love you fucking lunatics

Also sorry I ruined date night

Glancing toward the bathroom, she saw where the disinfectant smell had come from: Evan had cleaned up. Not a trace of salt water or black bile. No wet clothes on the floor.

Since he was still belly-up, Frankie leaned over to Clemmie and gave him a smooch on his tummy. She was ravenous. She was suddenly sure she'd never eaten a single thing in her entire life and crawled out of bed, noting the bandage on her arm. Padding on careful bare feet down the stairs, she braced herself and eased into her bright kitchen. As she entered, her stomach roared audibly. Evan turned from the stovetop with a smile, glancing down at her hand over her tummy.

"Does that mean you have an appetite?" She noted immediately that he was shirtless. And wearing her sweatpants. She could confirm her theory about the size of Evan's shoulders and arms. Muscles on *muscles,* holy shit. Shirtless Evan in her kitchen was an obscene image, and Frankie wondered if it would be possible or acceptable to snap a secret photo when he wasn't paying attention.

"So hungry that the counter looks delicious." Her voice scratched.

She placed herself on a bar stool, and a giant mug of black coffee appeared in front of her. He was still taking care of her. She felt full of the need to cry and shoved against the feeling—her eyelids were already so chapped.

Watching him make breakfast at her stove was bizarre. He moved as if he knew where everything was, like he'd done this a million times. With him preoccupied, she inspected his body for damage she had caused, and eyed his throat with a wave of nausea as she spotted hand-shaped bruises. Her hands. His arms were covered in cuts, some cuts slicing through even more bruising.

"Oh, gods, I did that to you?" Self-loathing chewed at her.

"No. It wasn't you. Hey," he said, catching her eye. "That was not you, Frankie. I'm okay."

She nodded but didn't feel better.

"Thank you," she said, her throat thick. She hoped that the two words encapsulated all of the thank yous she needed to give him from last night.

"That was a sympathy spoon, don't read anything into it," he said with a smirk.

Surprised he remembered her teasing from weeks ago, a hoarse laugh bubbled out of her. "Well, thank you anyway."

He leaned back against the counter, shoulder muscles flexing with the movement, and watched her with warm eyes, accepting those two words for the hundreds they should be. "How do you feel?"

"Like I ripped a demon from my body and then puked black acid for ten straight minutes."

He crossed to the island to be closer. "No pressure, but do you want to talk about it?"

She sighed. "No. But you deserve an explanation. Especially after all of the shit you've seen while hanging around with me."

He nodded and continued to cook in silence, waiting for when she was ready.

She didn't know how or where to begin, so she started with her younger years, her beliefs, and going to church every Sunday. Absorbing the good word and the feelings of safety it promised. She explained how her parents were both in the military and how going to church had been where they found community every time they had to move.

With the stage set, she pivoted to that awful summer break when her loneliness had been suffocating. Frankie had always been a bit of a loner, always struggled to make friends. Despite being empathic and knowing what people needed, she could never connect with her peers in a way that felt authentic. Not good at expressing herself, her brain short-circuiting from anxiety. Instead of struggling through every interaction, she would find herself alone with herself, day after day.

"I have trouble believing that you were awkward," Evan interrupted.

She snorted over her coffee. "Absurdly awkward. I said weird things. I talked to ghosts. I saw spirits and creatures everywhere in the world around me. Imagine two planes of existence happening at the same time on top of each other. It was overwhelming. So much so that it was easier to just be alone."

She hadn't learned to control her third-eye's sight until much later, able to turn it on and off as the situation needed. Until then, stepping into church every week with her sad and broken mind felt like a lie, like blasphemy. She would have panic attacks sitting in the pew, racked with terror that someone in that sanctuary would figure out what she was, haul her to the front of the altar, make her kneel before the old man leading the service. The last thing she would ever see would be the enormous statue of Christ above her, impaled in the hands and feet. Someone even painted blood on them, just in case you didn't think it hurt enough.

"So, that summer, I started going up to the neighborhood pool every day, hoping to meet some friends. But I never could quite get up the courage to talk to the other kids, so I just swam in the deep end all day. I liked how dark it was down there." She took a steadying breath.

"And one day, I swam up from the depths of the pool, and everyone was gone. I remember that it was storming, with big thunder and lightning strikes. I hadn't heard the call over the loudspeaker to come in when I was underwater. I got out of the pool." She swallowed. "And I found myself not alone but in the company of a spirit. It floated perfectly still in the pool's center. It yanked me in. It was violent. I remember drowning, or what felt like drowning. When things started to go dark, I thought of the Holy Spirit and asked it to purge my body of the demon, to make me clean again. But nothing happened." She wiped at tears with her shirt sleeve and glanced up to see Evan had turned off the stovetop and was giving her his complete attention.

"Everything after that is honestly just glimpses or pieces. It lived in me for a long time."

"How long?" The queasy look on his face made her want to cry harder.

"Years. I don't remember much from that time. I'd come to in places I didn't know, not knowing how I'd gotten there or what had happened while I was under. It damaged me, too. The spirit didn't eat enough. I always had strange injuries on my skin." She held up her tattooed arms. "I'm actually covered in scars under these."

"But you were able to break free at some point?"

Frankie nodded and paused, thinking of the best way to phrase it. "You know, on Sundays, they talk about how there is goodness inside of everyone. And I reached for it, and I pleaded for that light so many times during those years. But it never came to me. I felt... wrong. Immoral. Evil. I'd get sick if I stepped inside of a church. It's a weird feeling to be surrounded by people of your faith and be drowning in silence.

"At some point, I realized my body would give out. And I wasn't willing to die for something that wouldn't help me after years of begging for salvation. So instead, I reached out to the darkness inside of me, reached for those shadows that grew every single day under the demon's control."

Her mind drifted to that day when she won her freedom, remembering how she wrapped herself in that darkness and it swept through her battered body, forcing out the intruder with a violence that she welcomed, that she delighted in. This was something she had grown to understand. The shadows came to her eagerly, flooding her system. Devastated by the ease of it, she learned that she didn't have to plead to summon them, no begging required. No offering needed. And she swore it to her young, broken spirit: she would never beg for her power again.

"That's when you started having the shadows?" Evan asked, snapping her out of the memory.

"Yes. They're always with me. They've never asked anything of me. I don't entirely understand them, but I never want to go a day without them."

"So last night, was that the spirit from your childhood?"

Her stomach turned over. "It was."

"Is it gone now?"

"It's gone. It took advantage of the opportunity in the séance. I hate doing them, all sorts of things can go wrong. But this was the worst séance I've ever had. And I'm sorry—" her voice cracked. "I'm sorry things went to hell. I'm sorry you had to take care of me."

Evan looked like she had slapped him across the face. He walked around the island and turned her stool to face him, his hands on either side of her. "Friends take care of each other. There's no payment, no debt. Don't apologize for needing help. I'm glad I was here to give it."

Frankie did cry then, streams pouring down both cheeks, down her chin. Evan stepped between her knees and hugged her. She'd never been much of a hugger. But she wrapped her arms around his middle and welcomed it, her cheek pressed into his warm, bare chest.

Friends take care of each other. She knew she was lying to herself about Evan. Even before he saw her at her worst and took care of her anyway, he already knew her more intimately than anyone, friend or more-than-a-friend. Frankie had long considered her eternally damned heart not to be a flexing muscle in

162

her chest but something made of bone—immovable, part of her construction. The cornerstone of the foundation that kept her standing. To admit that it was actually tender—that it could bleed so easily—destroyed her. A small, bitter part of her hated Evan for how easily he had slipped past her walls.

And another, newer, more scared part of her welcomed the invasion and found relief in him.

This curse that had brought him to her still hung over his life. She couldn't bear the thought of Evan dying, especially in the way that Agatha was deteriorating.

When her breathing was steady again, Evan pulled back and loaded up a heaping amount of food on a plate for her.

Scrambled eggs, three strips of crispy bacon, toast with some of the mixed berry jam she had canned over the summer, and pan-fried potatoes. He topped up her coffee.

"Damn, Lawson." As if the doors containing her hunger had been ripped open, she began to shovel the breakfast into her mouth in enormous bites, looking forward to a chill day ahead of her.

Then, the doorbell gonged.

CHAPTER 33

Frankie let Evan answer the door, and not two seconds later, Bex and Jack were standing in front of her, both talking at once.

"*Dude!* We floored it like ninety miles an hour to get here—"

"—told him to stop being a dick and let us in the fucking house but nooo, mister white fucking knight over there—"

She smiled around her food and waited for them to stop. Eventually, they fell quiet. "Hi, bitches. I'm sorry for worrying you."

Evan entered the kitchen and walked to the fridge. Still shirtless. Bex's eyes lit up with mischief. Shielding her face poorly with her hand, she whispered to Frankie, "*Nice!*"

"*Stop it!*" Frankie mouthed.

Bex's smile grew even wider. She looked towards the couch with a weighted glance, as if looking for evidence that Evan had slept there. Not finding it, Bex did a little silent hop and waved her hands at Frankie.

"*Oh my god, fucking stop!*" Frankie mouthed to her, shooting her a warning look while jabbing in her direction with her fork.

Jack turned a laugh into a cough, unsuccessfully.

Evan, bless him, pretended nothing was happening and rummaged for something in the fridge.

Frankie needed this to end. "So, Evan, how's the city council data going?"

"Oh, right," he said, pulling his phone out of a pocket. "I'm going to share the file with you guys. I've organized everything, given all of the city council decisions a unique identifier for quick reference and then set up some pivot tables to sort it."

Jack's phone pinged. Because they always had the volume up. Because they were *so* busy and important. Frankie pulled out her phone and scrolled through the tables Evan had set up in the file. A few pie charts displayed the people that Agatha butted heads with most often and on what type of legislation. She noted that he had chosen a very visually pleasing color scheme for his pivot charts, all in soft, dark tones of blue and purple.

What a dork.

Who should really put on a shirt.

"Okay, I'm seeing the same handful of names come up a lot." Frankie ran the names through her mind, trying to remember who still lived in town. *Cynthia Brookes, Martin Santos, Howie Anderson, Ruth Everett.*

"Didn't Cynthia Brookes move recently?" She looked at Jack.

They thought for a second. "Last year, I think. She moved to Boston to be near her daughter."

"Okay, so probably not her." Seeking out the other three would be an aggravating exercise. They needed a shortcut. "Evan, is Agatha up for a visit today?"

*****

Having some forward progress after last night's shitshow gave Evan energy and focus, and as Frankie's truck pulled to a stop in front of Nan's cottage, he was determined to push last night out of his mind.

That idea was quickly shattered when they entered the house to find Nan standing in the kitchen, watching Frankie and her grandson come through the front door.

Together.

In the morning.

After he didn't come home last night.

Nan broke into a hacking laugh, her lovely, leathery voice almost in song, eyes twinkling. "Well, well, well. Evan, honey, I'm honestly relieved that you're getting some social time."

Frankie looked like she wanted the ground to swallow her whole. Evan's face, neck, and ears went bright red.

"Jesus Christ, we are *not* having this conversation. Are you up for looking at some graphs?" He snatched his laptop from the counter and stormed out onto the patio.

Frankie leaned back into a patio chair, blocking out the world with enormous sunglasses. Evan pulled his chair up to Nan's side and angled the screen towards her.

"This is a table to show who you butted heads with most often and on what initiatives. A lot of the disagreements are from when you were working on those programs to help with the cost of living. Like when you were outvoted two years ago trying to get a raise to the minimum wage on the ballot."

Nan huffed. "Oh, I remember. I nearly came to blows over that. Right inside city hall."

"For real?" Frankie raised her sunglasses. "I'll love you even more if you got into a fight over that while dressed in a flawless pantsuit."

Nan gave a rich chuckle. "Let's just say things may or may not have happened in the ladies' room. And I have an excellent dry cleaner."

Frankie grinned ear-to-ear.

Unfazed, Evan stayed on track. "I threatened the receptionist at City Hall with a FOIA request, and she sent me over some of the minutes from those meetings. You really didn't get along with Ruth or Howie."

Nan stared off into space, pensive. "I remember Howie was being an ass because he was worried about ride-share companies pulling out of Sawtooth if that initiative passed." She cut Evan a look. "If it made it on the ballot, it would have passed. I'll never forgive him for it." She paused. "He asked me to come by his house this week if I could manage. He must want me to donate some money to one of his causes when I croak."

"Or he wants to poison you," Frankie interjected.

Evan winced at the both of them. "Okay, so Howie is suspect number one. What about Ruth?"

Nan thought again, staring down at the pavement. "Ruth… She was the maddest about the effort to get some mass transportation in town. I was pushing for a bus system, ideally a free one. I don't care if Sawtooth is small, not everyone can just walk everywhere, for god's sake." Her tone started to slip into that of a city councilwoman.

Evan knocked his shoulder against hers. "Preaching to the choir, Nan."

Frankie interrupted again. "Who could get mad about public transportation?"

Nan rolled her eyes. "Ruth is a real piece of work. She didn't want to allocate any of the budget towards a solution. However, she was *very* interested in dumping excess funds into the police department."

"Is Ruth who you got in a fight with?" Frankie asked with a conspiratorial smirk. Nan mimed zipping her lips closed, to Frankie's delight.

Evan turned to Frankie. "Ruth still lives in town, right?"

She drummed her fingernails on the arm of the chair. "Shocker of a lifetime, but she's not a customer of mine. But I have seen her at the farmer's market. I'm pretty sure she lives on the north end of town."

Nan scrolled through her phone. "Start with Howie. I'll tell him that I'm coming by today, but you two should show up instead."

*****

Howie Anderson lived in the only condo village in Sawtooth Bay. Frankie and Evan strolled up to his door in the complex, Frankie frowning at the corny decoration placed on the landing outside—a smiling scarecrow sitting on a hay bale, cradling a pumpkin to its side. Barf.

Evan knocked on the door, then stepped back in line with her. Behind her back, he trailed his knuckles down her spine, causing her to stiffen and arch a bit. She glared at him.

"*Stop that,*" she hissed up into his dumb, handsome, smiling face.

"Stop what, exactly?" He asked innocently.

The door opened, revealing a smiling Howie in an honest-to-goddess apron. *Ready to feed Agatha some poisoned baked goods?* If Frankie had to describe the man in one word, it would be "suspicious." On the taller side, Howie had a shaved head and wore almost exclusively quarter-zip fleeces, khakis, and bright white sneakers. If Suburban Stepford Husbands were a thing, she'd put him in that category. Everything about him was trying too hard.

Howie's face fell upon seeing Evan. "Ah, Evan. I was expecting Agatha." Frankie had a fleeting thought that Howie might have a crush on the older, badass woman.

Evan gave him one of his infuriating, charming smiles. "Yeah, she ended up needing to rest this afternoon, unexpectedly. Afraid you're stuck with me."

Howie glared over at Frankie. "And Ms. Wolfe, it seems." Frankie tried to summon the most cloying, saccharine smile within her capability. But she had a feeling it looked like she was baring her teeth, so she leaned into that.

Howie opened the door and gestured for them to enter. Glancing around the interior, Frankie noted a black-and-shiny-chrome aesthetic. With a lot of black pleather. Which had not aged well, if the patches of rubbed-raw fabric were any indication. Despite Howie being in his late forties, she had a feeling that his bathroom counter had several drug-store aerosol sprays that were successful at being neither cologne nor deodorant.

Howie headed towards the kitchen area while calling over his shoulder, "Go ahead and take a seat, I'll bring in some coffee."

Evan eyed the weathered pleather couch covered in crumbs and shuddered. "I don't want to sit there," he whispered. "You do it."

"Gross, no way!" She gave a light shove to his shoulder and he stepped behind her, locking his arms around her ribs so she couldn't fight back, and pushed her towards the couch. "*Eww! Evan!* Stop!" she whispered through a giggle and pushed back into him.

Evan craned his neck to see if Howie was coming back yet and gave her a devious face before scooping her up. He moved towards the couch like he was going to dump her on the disgusting fabric. She kicked and hissed at him, trying not to laugh, before he pivoted at the last second and placed her gently in a mildly less offensive winged-back chair. Fully flushed and flustered, she smoothed down her wild hair and glared at him. But she was fighting a smile. *Prick.*

Evan sat back in her chair's twin across the coffee table and stared her down. She fought the urge to squirm under his attention. She wasn't sure at what point everything had become a competition with them. *Fine.* Leaning back into the chair like a queen, she crossed her legs and sent a little shadow tendril across the floor towards him. His brow raised in amusement as he watched it slither his way and wrap around his ankle. She rested the side of her head against her pointer finger and thumb, maintaining eye contact as she sent the shadow up his pant leg. His eyes shot to hers as Howie started to make his way back into the room.

Frankie arched an eyebrow, a challenge, the tendril climbing higher still. He gripped the arms of the chair with both hands as she sent it up his upper thigh and wrapped it around the muscle there, tightening and loosening in pulses. Right by his hip. Aggravation and arousal warred on his face. She could have sworn sweat began to bead on his temple. Deciding that she was the victor and that this was an excellent way to torture Evan for the next few minutes, Frankie smiled at Howie as he entered with an actual tray of coffee cups and baked goods.

"Oh, you're a doll, thank you!" She smiled and accepted a cup. Hazelnut syrup—a bold assumption—and cheap coffee grounds attacked her senses. Taking a sip, she clenched her jaw. The coffee was swill, but it was time to sweet talk.

"Please have some cookies! They're made with buckwheat flour, macadamia nuts, and coconut sugar." Howie settled back against his nauseating couch cushions with his coffee and took a long sip. "I'm just distraught over Agatha, Evan, you must know. I've always been so fond of her, she was such a friend on the council."

Huh? In what world? Nibbling on a cookie, Frankie took another sip of liquid garbage to hide her facial expression. The only thing that tasted worse than the coffee were these joyless cookies.

Evan cleared his throat and straightened in his chair, trying to squirm away from the tendril stroking his hip. She couldn't have that.

Pulling a shadow over from the hallway, so as not to alert Howie that the dark arts were happening in his presence, she sent a second tendril up Evan's other pant leg to wrap around his other thigh. He closed his eyes in a long blink, swallowing hard.

Frankie beamed at Howie. "These are delicious!" She held up a cookie. "So, how long did you work with Agatha?"

"We were council colleagues for at least a decade. A good, classy woman. She was always up for a spirited debate." *Barf.*

Frankie seized the opportunity to pivot to their conflict. "Oh? Did you two have different views about anything in particular?" Howie seemed like the type who liked to explain things that were common knowledge.

She was right. "Yes, you see, Agatha had an audacious idea to raise the minimum wage for the town, including the rideshare services. It's a lovely thought, but the companies would have pulled out of the city. We can't compete with Salem's numbers if we don't have rideshare cars on the streets. But, she always was more of a dreamer than a practical person."

Frankie clinked the coffee cup with a slosh down onto his coffee table. Without a coaster. "I see."

Howie continued as if she hadn't spoken. Turning to Evan, he asked, "I'd love to chat with Agatha when she's feeling up for it. I'm in the process of launching a nonprofit and would love to pick her brain about the best way forward to approach investors."

Although torture had been very fun, she decided that mercy was acceptable and shooed the shadows away from his legs. Palpable relief spread over him. "Uh, yeah, I'm sure she'd love that," Evan said in false earnest.

The next few minutes were spent listening to Howie prattle on about his nonprofit idea that sounded like a program to lure tech-inclined bros from Boston to Sawtooth Bay to hopefully kick-start a new tech hub in the northeast. While his mouth ran, Frankie caught Evan's eye and shook her head slightly. No, she didn't think Howie had cursed Agatha, he was just hot for her and hot for her money.

Howie's phone rang from his pocket, and Evan got to his feet, taking the exit. "Well, we've kept you for too long. Thank you for your kindness, Howie. Nan has always spoken so highly of you."

Back in the parking lot, Frankie could sense something radiating from Evan. As they neared the truck, he laced his hand in hers and led her around to the side of the vehicle. Fires burned in both of his eyes as he turned and backed her against the side of the truck. Her toes curled. She was a big fan of whatever was about to happen.

He placed his hands against the truck on either side of her and stared her down. "You are the *devil*."

She wore a bored expression, as if this was the most mundane conversation she'd ever had. "I have no idea what you're talking about."

"*Frankie.*" His tone was both a growl and a warning. A hand moved to her hip and slid up her back, touching her bare skin.

She pulled away from his reach and walked towards the driver's side door. "Come on, we should head out because we have *so many* things to do today."

He glared down at the pavement. "You're going to be the death of me."

CHAPTER 34

It struck Frankie that Ruth Everett's little house had nailed the cottagecore aesthetic with the English cottage garden in the front and exterior painted a classic warm beige. Deciding that Evan was more likable than her, she sent him to knock on the door while she parked a few blocks away. After a few minutes, Evan came back to the truck.

"Nothing. I guess she's not home."

Frankie eyed the house. She felt a pull from the interior.

She glanced around the street, and finding it empty, jogged all the way to the backyard. Evan followed, whispering, "What are you doing?"

She rounded the back of the house and found a full garden with lots of medicinal herbs. "Something's off with this place."

She tried the back door, and to her eternal amusement, it was unlocked. She snorted. "Need a safer town, indeed. Glad she convinced the council to re-route funds to the police department."

Evan laughed. "Wait, are you going inside?"

"Yeah, keep a lookout for me."

He sighed. "Please be quick."

Checking her shoes first for dirt or mud, she entered the kitchen. The interior was also decorated with a cottagecore vibe. Or maybe she would call it "grandma-chic." Lace, florals, patterns everywhere. Clutter on every surface.

Not sure what to snoop for, she started with the fridge and pantry. As the pantry door swung open, she gaped at the rows and rows of dried, jarred herbs.

"Well, well, well." It seemed Ruth had a dirty, witchy secret after all. She trotted back to the back door. Pulling aside a nearby curtain, she smiled at the protective charm swinging from a nail embedded in the wall. *Let's just take care of that.* She snapped her fingers, burning the charm into dust.

Following her nose, Frankie jogged to the den. Her heart rate began to quicken—she needed to speed this up. Ruth's altar was placed on a nearby console table. A jar of mugwort had been spilled everywhere, its funky, musty scent floating up to her. Trying not to disturb too many things, she picked through the mess, looking for summoning salts or anything damning.

Deep in thought, she peeked inside the primary suite, looking for any sign of deity worship. Nothing. Retreating, she turned and collided with a warm human body.

Shit! Too slow.

She jumped back, relieved to find Evan in front of her. "Don't do that!"

"We have to go now, she just pulled up out front."

"*Fuck!*" Frankie trotted back to the den and took a mental picture of the altar to analyze later. Having a photo of it on her phone would be proof of her crime. Ice ran through her as watched the deadbolt turn open on the front door.

"Frankie, *now!*" Evan whispered from the kitchen, and she sprinted towards his voice just as the front door opened. Outside, she whipped around the corner to the side of the house but didn't manage to close the back door in time.

Ruth's keys hit the kitchen counter and Frankie heard her step toward the open back door. She backed up into Evan, and they fell still against the siding, listening to Ruth search her garden. The woman's nasally voice reached them. "Hello?"

Frankie clamped a hand over her nose to mute her panting.

Ruth muttered to herself a few offensive comments about city safety and hurried inside, presumably to find her phone and call her favorite people, the cops. As soon as the back door clicked closed, Evan and Frankie ran for the truck.

*****

Warm, midday light filtered through the sparkling windows of The Black Cat. Preparations in the square were well underway for the Halloween carnival that would take place over the next few days in Sawtooth Bay.

Workers currently lined the area, some on ladders to hang lanterns, others placing carved pumpkins on any available flat surface. Tents would be erected all over the square and downtown area for carnival games and vendors. Bigger attractions, like a Ferris wheel overlooking the bay and a corn maze from the farm closest to the event, would be in use after months of preparation. Festive chaos would ensue.

Frankie had taken advantage of the situation and closed the shop for the day, happy for anyone who came by to think that she was also preparing for the festival. She hid at her counter with a pad of paper, trying to remember the details of Ruth's altar. She had a feeling that Ruth was their villain, but the pieces didn't fit just yet. She sketched out where the assortment of items had been, jotted down any details she could recall, and thought through the different smells and textures. She racked her memory for anything that could suggest a strong bond with a powerful spirit.

But there was nothing of note. It made no sense. To curse Agatha, the practitioner would need to have a bond with or be building a relationship with a powerful spirit or deity. To procure and manage such a relationship would be beyond most beginners' abilities. Ruth's altar had all the markings of a beginner. The tools—her mortar and pestle, mini-caldron for burning things, candlesticks, everything—looked brand new and barely used. There had been a stack of introductory books on the shelf above the altar as well, further proof that Ruth was just kicking off her witchy journey.

She stared off into space, letting her brain tick away, watching the buzz of people pass by her shop out in the square. Sawtooth Bay was a dreamy place to live at any time of the year, but in October, Frankie felt like everyone else had joined her wavelength. Sawtooth was a babe when it was painted up in the season's colors—blacks, purples, rich oranges and reds, splashes of neon green. Starting in just a few hours, she'd be tripping over pumpkins and smelling roasting apples and kettle corn. What a comfy thought.

Her mind drifted, gaze softening into sleepiness as those glorious, Halloweeny colors lulled her under. She snapped her head up after nodding off, grateful for the security barrier that her shop door provided from the seasonal ruckus.

Security barrier. Something clicked and she froze in place.

What was it that her ancestor spirit had told her?

"I see not blood promised but life itself—in exchange for life." Not blood or sacrifice. Life was offered. Her mouth popped open with the realization. Whoever had cursed Agatha had bargained years of their own life in the spirit contract. And based on the severe decline of Agatha's health, there had been a huge price to pay. If the villain had traded some number of their own years, they would need to protect themselves at all times, with wards everywhere, to keep the spirit from collecting on the bargain. A protective door charm would keep out the spirit for now, but not for long. But a beginner wouldn't know that.

Frankie stood and twined a little shadow around her finger like a lock of hair while she paced, willing the pieces together.

That's it.

There was one way to find out if her theory was right. The entire cast of local government would be at the carnival tonight to kick everything off—city council included. It would be a damn shame if she didn't launch her experiment into motion before that happened.

She grabbed her bag and shot Evan a text.

> Frankie:
> *Wanna go to the carnival with
> me tonight for some recon?*

> Evan:
> *Only if you promise to yell at
> me for not wearing black*

> Frankie:
> *Lawson, are you asking
> me to be mean to you?*

> Evan:
> *I'm asking you to do anything
> you want to me*

Frankie was a grown-ass woman, a practitioner of the dark arts. A heathen, a hedonist. She'd been endlessly coated in gore, monster guts, had faced countless unknowable terrors in her role as a witch. Absolutely nothing shocked her.

And yet, Evan's request for her to "do anything she wanted" to him brought a blush to her face. Her mind became static.

She hated him for it.

Frankie:
Then I'll see you at 8
Don't dress discreetly

CHAPTER 35

Evan spent the extra few minutes he had walking to the carnival rather than driving, glad for the clean air in his lungs. The last few days had left his mind in pieces, and although Nan's condition had leveled out for the moment, things could change at any time. She had pushed him out of the house earlier, telling him she needed a night to herself. Which he decided was a lie, given her reaction when he had entered the house with Frankie in tow.

He hadn't slept much over the last few days. He was fucked up from the other night, gutted by Frankie's story and tormented by the memory of that *thing* inside her body. Her shoulders, hung at an angle like her back was broken. The unnatural way it stood and moved. An unhinged madness in its void-like eyes. Every time he closed his eyes, he saw its legs scramble across the floor in jerking, spider-like movements. Felt its hands gripping his throat while he slipped into unconsciousness. She had lived with another being in her body for *years*. That thought alone made him want to vomit. He couldn't fathom the trauma. That night, he'd held her as tight as she would allow, terrified that it would come back and take her away from him.

It made sense now, how she had calmed him down in the back of her truck that day. She would have calmed herself countless times over the years. Despite her confession, Evan believed there were more details and horrors that she had omitted, and that was okay. He'd listen when she was ready to talk about it.

But tonight, no demons, no séances, just a Halloween carnival and some "recon," whatever that meant. Well aware that Frankie enjoyed torturing him at any opportunity, he hoped to be able to repay the favor. Soon.

The night was chilly and brisk, the perfect backdrop for the splashes of colored lights and smells of fried dough. As the gate came into view, Evan's knees nearly gave out when he caught sight of Frankie.

In a very short, blood-red skirt with black knee socks. Could he even call it a skirt? It was practically a belt.

He wasn't going to survive this evening.

Her expression was pure evil as he approached her. "Evening," she said, indifferent.

He wouldn't take the bait. Yet.

"Hey," he said and started walking at her side, weaving through the sea of patrons already crowding the area. "So what are we recon-ing?" She steered him over to the side of a tent selling vintage Halloween masks from the fifties.

"An experiment is underway as we speak. I snuck back into Ruth's backyard this evening."

"You did *what?*" He hissed. "Why?"

"I buried a return-to-sender hex in the yard, and I destroyed her protective wards. If she's been cursing Agatha, the illness should start to swing back around to her. The entire local government will be here tonight. And we're going to keep a close eye on her to see how she's reacting, away from the safety of her home."

"You really think it's her?"

"I think she's new to the practice and making a mess."

Evan nodded. It made a weird kind of sense. "Okay, I'm down. Where to first?"

"First, alcohol."

Retrieving two drinks from a vendor, Evan handed Frankie a canned whiskey cocktail and sipped on a weaksauce beer. He would *not* get as wasted as he did in the cemetery. Disaster might ensue. Or bad decisions might be made.

They wandered the grounds for a bit but saw no sign of the city council members. She looped her arm through his when a gust of wind ripped by, and he wondered if she was regretting her outfit choice. He spoke over the roar of attendees as they passed another shooting game booth. "Want me to win you a giant stuffed pumpkin?"

She giggled, and he was disappointed that the crowd's noise swallowed the sound before it reached him. "Work first, play later."

He strangled the dirty thought trying to materialize in his brain.

Tents striped in shades of black-and-orange or green-and-purple dotted the streets, and the smell of fair food drifted heavy in the air. The crowd began to thicken, making it more difficult to move with any speed. It appeared that Sawtooth had successfully drawn in lots of tourists with the event. Blaring top-forty pop music crackled out of nearby speakers.

With her arm looped through his, Frankie pulled Evan to the sidewalk and out of the current of people. "If the music is playing, they're probably going to kick off the event at the big stage. Let's go grab a spot."

*****

Carved pumpkins of all sizes lined the center stage. Frankie noted about ten people on stage and recognized a few city council members as well as the mayor standing in the shadows.

Turning to face the crowd, Frankie sighed as Mayor Phelps spotted them. He slapped on a photo-worthy smile and approached Evan.

"Evan! So good to see you back in town. I hope you're doing alright, all things considered."

Evan matched the mayor's smile with the same amount of "authenticity." "Thank you, Mr. Phelps, that's really kind of you."

"And how is Agatha doing? I stopped by earlier to see her, but her nurse told me she wasn't taking visitors."

Frankie couldn't stand Mayor Phelps. He was corny, badly dressed, and ineffective in his role as mayor. He'd held the position for a long time, and she prayed every election cycle that literally anyone would run against him. To entertain herself while the mayor fully ignored her, she critiqued his outfit. He wore designer jeans with a button down shirt under a sweater, not a single item of clothing fitting him correctly. His pants were a size too tight, and the sweater-and-shirt combo were a size too big. It appeared that he had begun to die his hair black, but the graying eyebrows that framed his dark eyes tattled on him.

Her eyes fell to a bulge under his shirt. *Oh, good, and now he wears a chain? Why not.* She finally noted his dress shoes, which appeared to be fancy and European and did not match the rest of the look. She sipped her whiskey drink to prevent rolling her eyes.

The mayor finally noticed her with the movement. "Frankie, how's business in the shop? We've been overwhelmed with out-of-towners this season." His awful cologne, possibly a blend of two different bottles, overwhelmed the smell of her cocktail.

For Evan's sake, she put her fangs away. "Thank you, I've been busy."

He gave her a warm smile. "Well, please enjoy your evening off. And thank you for helping keep the supernatural peace during our tourism boom this month."

She waved as Mayor Phelps headed back to the stage. "I fucking hate that guy."

Evan laughed. "At least he knows who you are. I doubt he knows every shop owner in town."

"I mean, I was featured in an Instagram post physically throwing girls out of my store. I'm sure that's the only reason." She trailed off as she spotted Ruth.

With some tissues shoved up her coat sleeve. *Well, well, well.*

She pulled Evan to the other side of the bandstand, giving them a clear view. Mayor Phelps stepped up to the microphone as a pop song that was popular seven years ago decreased in volume. "Welcome, one and all, to our little town's Halloween Festival!"

He droned on, the volume from the speaker directly next to them far too loud. She focused on tuning him out. Ruth's facial features were sharp and birdlike, matching her tall and wiry frame. The tip of Ruth's nose looked pink, but that could also be from the chilly night air. She watched the woman's every breath for signs of her experiment. Ruth's chest rumbled, and she broke into a hard cough that she suppressed into her shoulder.

Excellent.

Evan nudged her and gave a thumbs-up. Time to make sure this shit was locked down.

After an eternity, Mayor Phelps finally bid the crowd a "fun and frightful evening," and the council dispersed behind the back of the stage. Frankie and Evan followed with a bit of distance.

Thankfully, Ruth's tall frame made it easy to keep an eye on her in the stream of bodies. She meandered aimlessly before she sat down at a tarot reader's booth. Frankie hated people enough to not subject herself to doing carnival readings, and she did not envy the poor woman who now shuffled a deck of cards before this vulture. Regardless of whatever reading Ruth had asked for, Frankie hoped to ferret out her true motivations as her cards were revealed. She caught the tail end of Ruth's question.

"—want to know why I can't shake this cold, and how things look for my finances."

As Frankie and Evan scurried into their hiding place behind the tent, Evan snuck the last few drops of his beer from a crouched position. She copied him, downing the rest of her cocktail. Pointing to her ear, Frankie held another finger to her lips to signal that they would be eavesdropping. He grinned, the low lighting running along his jawbone and scruff. Gold danced on the ends of his curls.

Realizing they could use some additional cover, Frankie looked up at the top of the tent and drew down some shadows over them. She delighted in seeing Evan's awed expression as she cloaked him in darkness. The shadows moved around them like ribbons of smoke, giving them some visibility inside the cloud, but blending into the dark landscape and out of view. She realized a little too late that covering him in shadows also meant she could feel him. Everywhere.

She slapped a serene vibe on, not wanting to reveal how difficult it was to concentrate. Frankie pressed her ear to the canvas and strained to hear the tarot reading.

"… we have here the reversed Eight of Wands, which tells us that you've had difficulty or delays in trying to get what you want. Success has taken a long time to arrive to you."

A hacking cough followed this, followed by the sounds of Ruth blowing her nose. Gods, this poor tarot reader.

"Now in the present, we have the Eight of Swords, which encourages you to break out of the prison you may have built around yourself—"

"What's that supposed to mean?" Ruth's already nasally, and now congested voice bit back.

Frankie covered her face as she snorted. *Prison-minded indeed.*

The reader sounded flustered. "Well, the stars encourage you to not play a victim and take responsibility—"

"Just tell me about the future," Ruth snapped.

"And finally, we have The Hanged Man. This card recommends pausing before taking any further action and trying to see things from a different perspective."

"Well, that's useless. What am I supposed to do with that?" Ruth tore into the poor tarot reader and loud bickering ensued.

Although the brief reading had provided her with more information on the woman's motivations, she waited, just in case anything else would be revealed through Ruth's nonexistent nervous system failings. Evan shifted to a seated position, bored with eavesdropping, and began to scoop and hold shadows in his palms, letting them run like water between his fingers.

Shit, shit. Frankie's face burned, tingles running over her from his touch, and she angled her nose toward the ground, straining to focus on Ruth's horrible voice. But because she couldn't fucking stop her stupid horny brain, she glanced up right in time to watch him lazily spindle some shadows around his fingers. A shock of pleasure jolted through her.

She clenched her jaw but it was too late—she was unable to completely stop the squeak that came from her throat.

Dammit.

Evan's head snapped to her in surprise, slow realization dawning in his aggravating features. Mischief radiated from him as he shifted closer to her. This was not going to end well. He was coming for payback for Howie's house, and she knew it.

"Is there something you need to tell me about these?" The volume of his voice was low, but the tone was guttural.

"No."

"Okay. Then tell me to stop." He held her gaze and grasped a ribbon of shadows from the air. With one hand he wound it gently around his fingers. He stroked down it with the other.

She choked on a gasp, snapping her legs together and clamping down on her bottom lip hard enough to make it bleed. His answering grin made her want to immolate him. She'd never set a person on fire before but there was a first time for every—

He stroked down the ribbon again and she clenched her fingers in the grass beneath her. Fibers ripping free from the earth, her face contorted, breathing hard, desperate for no more sounds to escape her throat. Had she been capable of words, she would have sworn at him. Evan chuckled and moved even closer, whispering in her ear, "What's the matter, Frank? Am I distracting you?"

First, she would set his stupid, gorgeous auburn hair on fire and see how those soft, godlike curls looked inside of actual flames. Next, she would pry open that scruffy jaw and those full lips of his and set his tongue on fire so she would never again think about what it would feel like—

Another slow, firm stroke down the ribbon had her grinding her hips against the back of her boots. "Come on, just tell me to stop if you don't like this," he challenged her again. She whimpered. But she didn't want him to stop. And the bastard knew it. Pounding heat built between her legs.

Evan uttered a low, groaning swear, watching her writhe in fascination, not hiding the lust from his eyes. Leaning to her ear again, he growled, "You have no idea how long I've wanted to hear you moan for me. How often I think about it." Pressing his forehead to hers, he gave another stroke.

Thoughts evacuated her. Stardust in her brain, nothing useful. Her legs began to shake.

She dared another look up at Evan, their noses brushing. He pulled back a bit, wrapped the shadow ribbon tight around both fists, and with eyes like burning coals searing into her, ran his tongue along it.

She felt hot, wet desire soak her underwear.

It was official, this man had to die.

She did moan then, the sound inevitable and loud, her back bucking at a mortifying angle. By some mercy, Ruth and the tarot reader's argument had masked her carnal noise. Pupils fully dilated, Evan leaned in again and whispered, "*Goddammit*, Frankie, you make me fucking crazy. What do I have to do to get my mouth on you? I would bury my face between your gorgeous thighs and eat you alive—I wouldn't stop until you were *screaming*."

Or maybe *she* should die. Yes, that would be better. There would be no living down how outrageously aroused this had made her, and she would not be able to exist for the rest of her life knowing that she could feel this way.

Heat overwhelmed her with a singular focus—she wanted him. But not behind a carnival tent their first time. Thankfully, her temper flared, a lightning strike carving through the darkness. Her hand whipped out and gripped his face, about an inch from hers, and she spoke through gritted teeth.

"Evan, I swear to the goddess, if you don't stop doing that, I will hold you down and fuck you senseless behind this filthy carnival tent in front of everyone in Sawtooth."

"Don't threaten me with a good time," he said, without missing a beat.

Damn this man. Damn him for ruining her like this.

Frankie did not trust herself to remain in this cloud with him for a moment longer. The two of them together and alone would always end like this, tucked away in the shadows and barely containing their desire. Or just giving in and dry humping against a mausoleum. Her restraint was threadbare, and if any further shadow shenanigans went down, she would pin him down and sit on his face.

She fled for her life, stalking through the crowd with raging steps, determined not to make a bad decision. Breathing slow gulps of cold autumn air, she willed her heart rate to slow down. There were far too many people around her for having been *that close* to coming, and she needed immediate space from everyone and everything.

Stepping behind a tree on the sidewalk, she cloaked herself in shadows, welcoming the privacy and cooling dark, calming herself down. She pressed her hands against her face, hoping her fingertips would be cool to the touch. But no luck, her body heat pulsed throughout every nerve ending.

Her phone buzzed.

> Evan:
> *Are we playing hide and seek again?*
> *I'm down*

Frankie choked down a sound that would have embarrassed her if the carnival weren't so loud. She had very much enjoyed their cemetery game, hadn't had that much fun in years. But this could not happen. It was a very bad idea.

Her thumbs typed of their own volition.

Frankie:
*Then you'd better come
get me, Lawson*

She included a few corn emojis and sprinted through the night toward the corn maze at the edge of the carnival.

CHAPTER 36

Evan struggled not to run after her as he watched Frankie's shadowed form move towards the corn maze. Seeing her nearly come undone behind that tent would haunt his mind until he died. Already, he concocted future scenarios involving her shadows that made him dizzy with want. All blood had flowed away from his brain, and he nearly combusted when she sent the taunt and corn emojis.

Tonight, he would chase her. He would catch her. And he would not let anyone interrupt them. He paused outside of the maze and leaned against a light post, holding it with his hand, trying to give her enough of a head start to draw the game out even longer. When the buzzing in his head would not subside, he lurched forward and entered the maze.

The maze was mostly empty, and he let the cold air carry her scent to him. He searched for the smell of rosemary and then pushed his way through the rows of cornstalks in that direction.

Yeah, he was cheating.

But it seemed she knew this. More than once, Evan rounded a corner, chasing after a tendril of shadow, to find a dead end. She was taunting him. Somehow, this wound him up even tighter. He stumbled through another few rows of corn and found a long, straight passageway before him. The sounds of the carnival muted more as he worked his way deeper into the maze.

Up ahead at the end of the passageway, Frankie sauntered past with her hands clasped behind her back, as if escaping him was too easy. He broke into a run, feeling feral.

She was gone. He let out a grunt of frustration.

He paused and smelled again, following the trail around another corner, where the festival lights didn't quite reach. Of course she would hide here. She was close—he could feel himself getting sucked into her gravitational pull again. He noticed a familiar, tiny sparkle inside one of the dark corners. He approached as if he would walk by, then jerked forward and grabbed her around the waist.

Frankie shrieked and disappeared again, corn swaying and a giggle flitting to him as she fled. Evan stumbled into another dead end, but this time he discovered a clearing that hosted a pyramid of haystacks next to a demented-looking scarecrow with an upsetting, stitched sack face. She was here, somewhere. Pacing around the area, he picked the darkest corner and slipped into it, following the black, glittery form he knew so well.

Even when invisible, his hands found her waist easily. Her face appeared through wisps of black smoke.

"I got you," Evan said, his voice quiet and a mile away, brain not functioning.

She stepped out into the light and walked away from him backward. He followed, still in predator mode. She stilled, her arms behind her back, her head cocked in his direction. A Venus flytrap.

He would gladly die this way.

He charged forward.

CHAPTER 37

Frankie wished she could stop time for just a moment and forever burn into her memory the way Evan looked at her.

Before he charged toward her like a starving man. One hand slid around her waist and down her hip, the other speared through her hair until he could angle her skull exactly where he wanted it. He paused and ran a slow thumb over her bottom lip. She was breathless, eyes wide.

He shook with restraint. "Can I kiss you?" he asked in a hoarse whisper.

She gripped his face with both hands and brought it down to hers, claiming his mouth.

Holy hells, his mouth. Stars exploded behind her eyelids, and she pulled him as close to her as she could manage. Though surprised for half a moment, Evan met her with force and angled his face over hers to deepen the kiss. His tongue flicked at the seam of her lips, which parted for him. He groaned into her mouth as her tongue slid against his, running his hands all over her waist, hips, her thighs. Anywhere he could reach. His hands immediately disregarded her very short skirt, sliding underneath and gripping both of her ass cheeks, hard.

Her blood roared, and she melted against him. She wove a hand through his hair and gripped near the scalp, her other hand running up the front of his jeans and finding granite waiting for her. This man would be the death of her, she was certain of it.

Evan pushed into Frankie, trying to back her up against something, but they were both so distracted by wandering hands, the taste of the other's mouth, that they instead stumbled back against a not-solid wall of swaying corn stalks.

Nearly losing their balance and collapsing into a pile of limbs, Frankie snorted with laughter that Evan matched. He reached down and cupped her ass under her skirt again, lifting her up. She wrapped her legs around his waist and gave him another deep kiss. He hiked her skirt up higher, to her ribs. She wanted zero space between them. Her fingers tore at his flannel's buttons, sliding across the muscles in his chest, his shoulders.

A wooden beam scraped against her back, and she realized he was pressing her against the creepy scarecrow's post. She wasn't mad about it. He ground his hips against her in time with the strokes of his wicked tongue, and any remaining rational thought left her entirely. Being pinned against a mausoleum had been fantastic, but this—being pinned in a corn maze with his mouth on hers—made her woozy with need. She was still aroused to the point of pleading, throbbing aches from him *licking her fucking shadows*. The visual scorched through her, turning her into something feral, and an animalistic noise grunted out.

Taking his bottom lip between her teeth, she ran her palm under his jeans and gave his shaft a squeeze. He rewarded her with a loud moan, the noise sounding surprised, and pushed into her hand. She decided she would do whatever possible to keep him that vocal.

Breaking away from her mouth and teeth, Evan took Frankie's jaw and tilted it up to access her throat. He pulled her hand out of his pants as he brushed his lips across her neck. "Nuh-uh, me first." And ran his tongue across her pulse point.

She wasn't going to survive this. At no point in her life had she ever been this turned on, and she chased the feeling, afraid she might never have it again.

Completely at his mercy, Frankie rolled her soaked core helplessly against his hips like a cat in heat, moaning loud enough to wake the dead, almost in tears from wanting more friction, while he licked at her throat in slow, lazy strokes. His teeth grazed over the spot before digging in just a bit. Holding her skin with his teeth, his tongue started lapping at her again and her moans became whimpers. She needed more and was willing to do anything—literally anything—to have him touch her. *"Evan,"* she gritted out. *"Hands."*

He took those two thick, lust-ridden words and read her mind, his thumb finally moving under her sweater, his mouth still on her neck. His fingers found the bottom of her bra and yanked down, a breast sliding free. Unable to stop herself, Frankie grabbed the hem of her sweater and started to pull it off, but Evan stopped her hand's movement.

"Fuck," he muttered against her neck. He was panting. "Hold on, hold on,"

he swallowed, pulling back to look at her. Rage and frustration engulfed her, pinned against the nearly collapsed post almost crying with need.

He stepped back from the scarecrow and set her down. Her mouth flew open to lay into him, but Evan had other plans. He threw her over his shoulder as she yelped, gripped her thigh with one hand to hold her in place, and stomped through the corn stalks, away from the carnival and into the darkness. Her ass exposed in the air, Frankie looked upside down and realized he was taking her into the woods.

*****

Absolutely nothing was going to stop Evan from giving Frankie exactly whatever she wanted, and if anyone followed them into the woods or tried to interrupt them, he would tear them limb from limb.

He stormed through the underbrush and into the trees, head roaring, not a bit of human being left in him. The moon was on his side tonight and lit a path through fallen, rust-colored leaves into a small clearing. A large oak tree sat to one side of it.

Fuck yeah.

He lowered her to the ground and pushed her back against the tree softly. "This okay?" He asked, about to fucking lose it.

Hair and eyes wild, she grabbed his waistband and pulled him flush with her, just like she had in the cemetery. He sunk against her with his weight, his hands resuming their wandering, learning every curve, every inch of her. Frankie ran a hand through his hair with her nails grazing his scalp—fuck, he loved that—and pulled his head back with her grip. She wrapped a leg around him and licked up his throat with a hungry noise.

He kissed her hard, fingers grazing her collarbone and thumb brushing over her throat. Her knees buckled. He slipped a hand under her skirt and thumbed the outside of her completely soaked underwear.

"Jesus Christ, Frank." She moaned into his mouth as one of his fingers started to work under the fabric.

He pulled back to watch her face as his finger grazed over her folds. She gasped, head hitting the bark of the tree and swollen lips falling open slightly at the contact. Her pelvis tilted into his hand. Obscene. The things he wanted to do to this woman were obscene. He kissed her instead, determined to pace himself.

Against her mouth, he asked, "I think I've made it clear how badly I want to take you up against something, a tree, a wall, I don't care. Can we please make that happen?"

"Fuck yes," she breathed, seeming to struggle to find a coherent thought.

Evan reached behind her, found the snaps holding her ridiculous excuse for a skirt together, and ripped it off, throwing it on the ground. "This skirt is criminal. You've been driving me insane all night."

A breathy laugh drifted from her lips at his words. "So, my evil plan worked?"

"If your evil plan was to make me want to drag you off somewhere and rip it off of you? Yes, it worked."

Frankie shucked her sweater to the forest floor, revealing her black bra and tiny underwear, before tearing at his flannel. He stripped it off in one move to join her sweater. She ran her hands all over his torso, tracing his muscles, eyes scanning every detail of him, licking her bottom lip.

"Gods, you're so fucking hot."

Frenzy wormed its way through his system as he clawed for the back clasp of her bra. He'd dreamt of this moment, both at night and while conscious. He needed them in his hands, in his mouth. At last, some combination of his nonsensical movements brought the bra down to the ground, and her perfect breasts spilled into his hands. An involuntary groan ripped out of him, his palms being as gentle as he could convince them to be. Immediately, he brought one nipple into his mouth, holding the nub in place with his teeth, and sucked hard.

His free hand moved between her legs again and worked under the underwear. He tested a fingertip, and despite how tight she was, he was easily able to slide his finger all the way in. Frankie's sounds became deeper in tone. "*More*," she demanded. He would deny her nothing, and pulled out before plunging two fingers in deep.

She cried out and arched her back, pushing more of her flesh into his face. She rode his hand, soaking it. He palmed her other breast, spurred on by her moaning and writhing against the tree trunk. His cock strained against a seam in his pants, pained and begging to be freed.

As if reading his mind, Frankie's hands dove into his pants. The button and zipper opened, and before he realized what was happening, she held his length with one hand, stroking, while the other squeezed his balls. His jeans and underwear had been pushed down to his thighs.

"*Shit, shit,*" he grumbled while she squeezed him, working him in long, tight strokes. No, no, no, she could touch him later all she wanted, but right now he needed her falling apart for him over and over and over again.

He snatched her wrists. She met his eyes. Pushing her back to the tree with a hand on her collarbone, he brought his soaked hand to his mouth. He sucked on those two fingers, letting them drag out slowly. "Let me do this first."

He dropped to his knees.

*****

The sight of Evan on his knees before her nearly sent Frankie over the edge she was already sprinting towards. His chest rose and fell in hard breaths. "I need you in my mouth."

She nodded and he pulled down her ruined, absolutely useless panties, and tucked them in his back pocket. Before doing anything else, his eyes roamed all over her. She was approaching a level of madness that frightened her, and if he didn't do something to her soon, she would have to beg and then punish him for making her beg.

He must have seen the threat in her eyes because he hooked one of her legs over his shoulder and gave her a long lick that destroyed her. She swore a garbled curse and braced her hands against the tree trunk to remain upright when he gave her clit a brief, featherlight brush of his tongue.

"God, you taste so fucking *good.*" He barely got the last word out before his tongue found her again. His voice was muffled against her, but she heard it clearly—she would hear him saying that phrase in her mind forever.

She looked down at him and found his eyes glued to hers. He panted as he sucked and lapped at her clit, eyes blazing. The sounds that came from her throat were inhuman and *loud,* but out here in the woods, away from it all, the only thing that existed was his mouth. Taking his dick in his hand, she heard Evan grunt while he pumped himself in slow strokes.

His tongue's movements stopped abruptly as he smiled up at her with a wet face. She nearly wept. "Evan, I am about to strangle you, *don't stop.*"

He laughed and kissed the inside of her thigh, taking her hand and placing it on top of his head.

"Ride my face."

Hecate spare me. "Wha—seriously?"

He nodded. "Do it."

Threading her fingers from one hand carefully into his curly locks, she leaned back into the tree and waited for him to resume his worshipping. She throttled the basest part of herself that very much wanted to do this. She might not be a lady, but she was certainly not an animal.

Evan growled against her folds and licked hard across her slit, pulling her clit into his mouth.

"Oh *fuck!*" Beyond her control, her pelvis pushed into his face. Her tattooed fingers gripped his scalp harder than she intended, but the guttural, needy noise he made kept her from loosening them. He lapped at her, her cries echoing through the dark trees. She struggled to find lucidity around the sensation, fighting through the fog of heat coursing through her.

Evan added a finger, matching the pulses with his tongue. The scruff on his face rubbed anything that wasn't reached by his jabs. She was going to pass out.

"Evan?" She had no idea what she was asking. What she needed. Thoughts didn't exist here. Words tried to form but fell into blathering. Damn his wicked mouth. Damn him.

He came up for air briefly. "It's okay, Frank, take what you need."

Take what you need.

What did she need?

For the entirety of Frankie's adult life, she had been in complete control. She found joy in controlling her wild profession, wrangling spirits, and driving out monsters. In every case she worked, even when she ran for her life, she was in control. It had been the only thing she wanted, and she wanted it every day while she clawed her way back to sanity after she exorcised a demon from her body. The control gave her power—power over her person, her situations, her destiny. And she wouldn't give it up for any reason.

With no warning, he added a second finger, and his other hand squeezed her thigh, giving her permission. Evan grunted, determination set in his brow. Even now, they were fighting for dominance. He curled his fingers inside her, dragging down her inner wall, and lapped at her with no mercy. Her legs gave out, and to keep from collapsing into the dirt, she seized his scalp with both hands, gripped his hair and rode his face, hard.

She was flung over the cliff, wind roaring in her ears, and she was sobbing, or swearing, or screaming, or all of them at the same time as release ripped her in half. Evan wrung every pulse of pleasure from her body until she was a whimpering mess of a woman, slumped against a tree in the forest.

Frankie braced her hands on his shoulders until her head stopped spinning. Coming back into awareness, she looked down at him. The look of raw hunger on Evan's face nearly sent her over the cliff a second time. He stood, slowly, something predatory now in place.

He leaned in and gave her a deep kiss, his tongue—that same aggravating, wicked tongue that had nearly killed her—slid into her greedy mouth, the taste of herself everywhere. "Goddamn, that was the hottest thing I've ever seen," he said into her ear, pulling the lobe with his teeth.

"Pants off, *now*." She would wait no longer.

He stumbled and kicked them away, now down to just his socks to match Frankie down to her knee socks and boots.

He came at her but paused and glanced down at his pants. "Wait, let me get—"

She made a frustrated sound and pulled him towards her. "I can't get pregnant."

"Me neither." She laughed. He scooped her up as she wrapped her legs around him. No more waiting. No more dancing around this unbearable tension. Now, now, now, *now, now.*

Evan devastated her with another kiss and nudged himself into her entrance, then stilled. "You okay?"

She considered murdering him in this moment, stuck in a purgatory of not being fully joined. "All the way in, *now*," she snarled.

194

"I'll give you whatever you want." He sheathed himself completely with one thrust. Her back scraped against the tree trunk and Frankie clawed at his back and hair, crying out.

They paused, breathing hard. Staring at one another while she adjusted. Evan clenched his jaw, expression strained. "Gimme a second here." He closed his eyes. His muscles twitched.

Thrilled by his reaction to being inside of her and determined to win this power struggle, she rolled her hips against him, causing his eyes to pop open, for him to meet her movements. He growled, the sound coming from deep in his throat, and glared at her. "God, you're so mean to me." He rolled into her with slow, deep thrusts.

"Faster, Evan." She glared back at him.

"No way. I've been thinking about this for a long—fucking—time," he said, punctuating the words with his thrusts. "I'm taking my time with you."

We'll see about that.

His hands were busy holding up her weight, but with a free mouth, he closed it around her nipple and worked it with his tongue. She moaned and leaned back, giving him more access. "Gods, your *mouth.*"

He seemed to like that, to drink up her praise, and his pace increased. She grabbed the back of his neck with a gentle hand and brought his throat to her lips. She licked up the skin there, loving the taste of him. She scraped her teeth across a vein, something she'd been longing to do for weeks. Slamming home again, Evan let out a desperate, deep groan. Holy fuck—he filled her up *perfectly.* His hands gripped her thighs and ass in a way that would bruise.

Almost where I need him.

"Fuck, Frank, I've wanted this for so long. You've—you have no idea," he interrupted himself with a small whimper against her shoulder. "No idea what you do to me. All the depraved things I want to do to you."

"Tell me." In as much detail as possible, she preferred.

"I want you to straddle me in the back of your truck. I want to spread you open on your kitchen counter and feast until you're dripping down onto the floor." He paused, catching his breath. "Fuck, I want to hike your skirt up, bend you over your shop counter and slam into you. I want to take you back to that mausoleum wall and fuck you hard enough that I have to carry you out of there."

She liked the sound of all of this. And while fucking like two animals against a tree was easily the hottest experience of her life, she would not be satisfied until she completely destroyed this man. Her fingers dug through his hair and pulled him up to meet her mouth. She baited him with a sweet kiss before taking his bottom lip between her teeth and biting down, her fingers pulling his hair, hard. She clenched her inner muscles.

Evan's eyes went wide before his brow furrowed, shadows elongated by the bright moonlight. He snapped and pounded into her, grunts becoming loud moans that she devoured with tongue and teeth. He began to twitch inside of her, and her own moans morphed into something primal and aggressive, her hair tangling on the tree's bark.

Concentration lined his brow as he reached down to where they were joined and thumbed her clit. "God, you're squeezing the life out of me." She gasped and knew release was barreling toward her. "You're gonna come with me, Frank. Hard. Are you gonna scream for me?"

She nodded, far beyond words, and clenched around him. He gulped, then shouted, *"Fuck!"* The pace of their rutting didn't falter when she felt liquid warmth pump into her. And she did scream for him—she didn't care how wild she sounded, she let her body make whatever noise it needed to as Evan wrung another orgasm from her, waves rolling for longer than she thought possible until her shouts became small cries against his neck and she collapsed into him.

They remained there, breaths slowing back down, and a cool autumn wind floating through the clearing, scattering leaves. Evan cradled her close to him like she was precious and ran his hand down her back. Nocturnal sounds began to awaken in the area now that they had both stopped screaming.

Dazed, Frankie sat up a bit and found Evan watching her with something unreadable on his face. Not quite concern or awe, but the intensity of it nearly brought her to tears.

"Fuck. Frankie, just—fuck." He shook his head. "You've ruined me. I'm ruined. For the rest of my life."

She couldn't stop the smile that broke across her face.

"Are you okay?" He put her down carefully, helping her steady herself.

Somewhere in the distance, an owl sounded. Tracing her fingers over his chest and collarbone, she felt heat start to pulse through her again. "Come back to my place so we don't traumatize these animals any more than we already have."

CHAPTER 38

Evan might as well have died on the car ride back to Frankie's creepy house. There was no returning to normal, no business as usual, no way in hell that he would slip back into daily life after being altered so completely.

The cab of the trunk stirred in darkness, and Evan realized the shadows on the floor of the vehicle whirled around his feet. Glancing up at Frankie, he found her deep in thought with her eyes on the road. The way her shadows writhed indicated where her mind was, and he reached across the space between them and traced a circle on the inside of her leg.

Her breath hitched. "Are you trying to make me crash this truck?"

Fingers moving up her leg on their own, he said, "No, I just want to hear you scream like that a few more times before the sun comes up."

Her cheeks went red, her eyes two silver moons in the truck's dark. "Only if you scream with me."

"You seem to have that effect on me." He leaned over, and moving the sea of her hair out of the way, began to kiss her neck. He pulled the collar of her sweater down over her shoulder.

"Where is my underwear?" Her tone was tense, trying again to deny him the satisfaction of making her moan.

"In my pocket. They belong to me now." He gripped her collarbone with his teeth.

She took a sharp breath and leaned back into her seat, giving him better

198

access. His fingers grazed the apex between her thighs and found it newly soaked.

"Please drive faster."

He wasn't sure who started the footrace when they pulled up in her driveway, but both of them sprinted towards the front door. Frankie fumbled with her keys, bumping him out of the way with her hip, so Evan made it worse by stepping up behind her and pushing her against the door, one hand rubbing between her legs, the other winding up her sweater. She somehow managed to get the door open and yanked him inside by his shirt.

Evan kicked the front door closed as Frankie leaped onto his waist. He turned them, pinning her against it. He switched the deadbolt before he said against her mouth, "Because people in this town have a tendency to interrupt us."

She giggled—he loved that sound—and writhed against him. He carried her through the hall and into the library. He heard her fingers snap and felt the blast of heat against his side as the fireplace lit.

"Oh, I see how it is," she said with a smirk. "You don't want to fuck me, you want to fuck my *library*. You *nerd*."

"No, I'm *going* to fuck you *in* this library. Perfect setting." He brought her to the floor and settled over her. "Perfect mouth," he kissed her. His hand drifted between her legs to part her. "Perfect pussy."

She groaned. "Damn you." Her legs tightened around him.

Evan wasted no time this round, ripping off her skirt and sweater, pulling off her bra without bothering to unhook it. He paused when she clawed at his buttons and removed the flannel again. She yanked his pants and underwear down to his knees. Using the flat of his palm on her stomach, he pushed her back against the floor and gave her torturous, slow kisses down her chest, down the soft of her belly, further south. Then started from the inside of her knee, moving upward.

"I'm running out of patience, Lawson."

"Too bad," he said, mouth still working.

She snarled in frustration and sat up on her elbows. The way she glared at him made his balls tighten. He moved back up to her face.

199

"Tell me what you want, Frankie. What do you like?" He worked on her neck, a hand stroking between her legs.

"Do you want me to show you?"

"Fuck yes."

He felt that familiar tingle of her shadows wrap around them, and then he was flipped. Frankie straddled him, black, glittering tentacles sinking back into her. His face went slack.

"Oh, *shit*." His head spun, blood pouring away from his brain and down to his hips.

"Are you ready for me?" she asked, a bit breathless.

"I might die if you don't mount me right now," he replied honestly, praying he didn't blow his load immediately.

She held his gaze and lowered herself slowly, so horribly, cruelly slowly, just a tiny movement each time. He gritted his teeth, willing his hips not to rise up and meet her yet. With no warning, she fell down the remaining length and he cried out to the ceiling.

"God*fucking*dammit." He wasn't going to live past the sunrise. And he was fine with it. His hands gripped her hips.

"You okay?" she asked with an innocent smile, echoing his teasing from earlier.

"I will beg you if you don't start moving." Shame was long gone—it had no place here. She could torture him with her tight, wet heat as much as she wanted.

"I'd like to hear that." She gave a roll with her hips and threw her head back. She rode him in slow, deep movements, both of them moaning. Something about her made him want to be loud in moments of pleasure, go full carnivore. His eyes rolled into the back of his head. She felt perfect, fucking perfect. He fucking loved this.

But she was moving too slowly. He sat up until her bare breasts grazed his chest, hooked an arm on her shoulder, and pulled her down while he thrust up. She whined, shadows dancing from her hair.

"Naughty boy." She threw him back down to the hardwood and held his chest in place with her lovely, inked hands, fingernails digging into his skin as she held still.

Shocked, he nearly lost it, and conjured up anything mundane to take the edge off: sitting in traffic, the chill of the dairy section at the supermarket, changing a lightbulb. But it was useless. He was a goner.

"Oh god—fuck, *please,* Frankie, *please, please, please.*" She remained still. His hips writhed up into her of their own accord, but she didn't budge. He didn't recognize the panicked sounds of his own voice. Had no idea what he was begging her to do.

"Please what?" Her voice was cold, which he found very, very hot.

"Anything! Please do anything you want to me, holy *shit.*"

She showed him all of her teeth and began to ride him again, harder. Delirium pooled in his mind. He grunted and pistoned his hips with her rhythm. Part of him hoped his heart would give out so this would be his final memory as he fell into the afterlife.

Frankie craned down and ran her tongue up the center of his chest, his chest hair dragging along her mouth. His thoughts melted into a string of swear words. Or maybe he was saying them out loud?

She took his hands off her hips and brought them to her chest. He took the silent instruction and worked eager thumbs over both nipples, then kneaded them. She let out another loud moan, rising up and dropping down on him. She did it again.

He hissed and focused on his breathing. He never wanted this to end.

Their sounds drowned out any crackling logs in the fireplace. The house could have burned down around them and he wouldn't have noticed.

Frankie's control was slipping. He watched some battle move across her face and knew it was the perfect time to break her. He reached around with both hands and gripped her ass firmly. She yelped. Step one.

Step two: he felt through the ends of the black hair that fell to her hips, sorted through the strands until he found two tingly shadows, and wrapped them around his fingers. He pulled down.

"Mother fuck!" Frankie's shocked expression dissolved into feral pants and she rode him in aggressive thrusts, taking what was entirely hers. Her insides clenched as she sprinted towards release.

"Can I sit up?" he asked.

"Come here," she said, helping him up to bring their chests together. The new angle sent them into a frenzy and Evan came hard with deep thrusts, her ass cheeks squeezed in both of his hands, spilling inside her clamping muscles. He groaned into her neck while she gripped his hair and screamed, riding out her release.

They collapsed back down to the floor. Frankie placed her head on his chest and slumped, exhaustion setting in.

A log cracked in half in the fireplace, falling into pieces.

That pretty much sums it up.

He stared up at the ceiling in a haze, running a hand down her hair as they listened to the fire snap and pop.

She didn't move her head or look at him, but after a while said, "Mmff. Carry me upstairs."

He laughed. "Carry *me* upstairs."

She giggled. "I'm not sure I can even walk right now."

He stroked down her hair again. "Then let's stay here for a few minutes."

She extracted herself from his hips and fell onto her side, placing her cheek on his chest.

"I know I said I wanted to hear you scream a few more times before morning, but I'm about to pass out and sleep for three straight days after that."

"Same," she said, voice slurring in sleep. "So come up to bed with me."

Heart thudding and feeling full of a warm goo, Evan nodded.

Breaking through his afterglow, thunder rolled in the night sky. A curtain of rain pounded against the roof as the power flickered and went out.

"Oof, I think that's our cue." Evan started to sit up, joints popping, and helped Frankie onto her knees, then into a standing position. They stumbled up the stairs, illuminated by the fireplace's glow.

He flashed back to the other night, after Frankie's possession. He hadn't been able to enjoy her luxurious bed, terrified out of his mind that something else would come for her in sleep.

Tonight, he fully intended to sink into those silky sheets and sleep until the sun woke him. He almost dove into them, welcoming oblivion with a hunger. Frankie fell onto the mattress and wiggled under the sheets. Without giving her a chance to move away from him, he settled in behind her and spooned her, just like she had when she took care of him in the back of her truck. Just like he had the other night when he'd thought he lost her.

Sleep claimed him the moment his head hit the pillow.

CHAPTER 39

Evan felt thunder vibrate through the house and cracked open an eyelid. In his wooziness, one thought stirred him fully from sleep: yes, it had happened. Finally. And he was still in her bed.

He shifted, realizing a lock of Frankie's hair was draped over his face. He breathed in her rosemary scent deeply before moving the lock of hair back into place. Damn, this bed was comfy. Super silky sheets.

Basking in the room's calming aesthetic, Evan looked around and let himself slowly wake up, something that never happened at Nan's. It felt like a sinful luxury. Normally, he'd be staggering out of bed to get her coffee or tea going before she started to stir. He felt a pang of guilt that he wasn't at home with her now.

The ceiling over the bed had been hand-painted in a celestial dream—rich blues and purples, gold stars and cloud-like whorls. Rain still fell hard against the roof, bringing him back down to Earth. Clemmie dozed in a heated bed-hut in the corner of the room, belly up, with his front two paws stretched out of the entrance.

Same, bro.

Frankie turned in her sleep and nestled against the pillow near his shoulder. He turned to face her. Black curls everywhere, her lips slightly parted, and her delicate nose looked even more precious. Her brow was furrowed, even deep in sleep. She still looked far too serious, but she didn't have that haunted look that he'd seen so many times. Frankie was around his age, but Evan had noted more than once that her eyes carried the weight of several lifetimes. Some kind of ancient, spiritual exhaustion hung over her features during waking hours, but she seemed free of it in sleep. She looked younger. Shadows twined all around them in the bed, and feeling a tingle, he looked under the sheets to find one of her shadows wrapped around his calf.

He sighed and sank back down. He'd said as much to her last night, but it was true. He was in deep shit. Completely ruined. She held his fucking soul in her hands.

Scrunching her face up, Frankie groaned and flipped to be more facedown on the pillow.

"You awake?" Evan whispered and ran a hand down her spine.

"Mmm. No."

He traced a finger down her left shoulder. He'd seen glimpses of her tattoos throughout the last few weeks, but he'd been too distracted last night to take in any of the details. He was dying to see everything now, even in this low light.

"You're not going to let me go back to sleep, are you?" Her voice was muffled under the weight of her hair.

He laughed. "No."

She rolled to face him with a grunt, eyes thick with a glazed, sleepy expression. She scrubbed at them with her tattooed knuckles. "Hi."

"Hi. You're cute in the morning." He tapped the end of her nose. "Less teeth."

Her groggy expression shifted to something predatory. "Oh really? Seemed like you liked my teeth last night." She draped a leg over his.

Memories from last night swept over him. They had gone a little crazy. An image flashed in his mind of the two of them in front of the fireplace, clawing at each other, fucking like animals. "Did you like last night?"

She grinned. "Duh. Did you?" She nudged her leg higher against his.

How could he say exactly what he was feeling without scaring her off? *You may as well bury me in your backyard because death itself wouldn't keep me from crawling back to your feet.*

Instead, he said, "Absolutely."

He ran a hand over her thigh and pulled her closer. His hand then cupped her chin as he brought his mouth to hers. The kiss was sweet and slow, their tongues brushing briefly. She made a small noise that had him immediately hard and ready, and before he let things go too far, he sat up a bit. Frankie grunted in disappointment. "Where are you going?"

"Nowhere, I just was hoping to see these, if that's alright?" he tapped the black ink that covered her right arm.

She rolled her eyes. "If you must." Flipping on her back, she sighed, folded her hands together across her belly and waited.

Evan started with her arms. She let him position her to get a better view of the detailed work. Her right arm was one piece, a scene of a ship getting taken under the waves by a kraken, he assumed. The broken ship stretched across the deltoid and bicep area, and those tentacles he'd spotted when she shucked oysters wrapped up around the top of her shoulder, pulling it under. The skin of her forearm was heavily inked out in areas to indicate dark seas, using gaps in the pigment to highlight the tops of waves. And under the surface of the water, more horrors of the deep—on one side, an angler fish with a light around its face. On the other, a human skull with seaweed growing through the eye sockets. He realized all of her tattoos were without color, and she seemed to favor designs with bold lines and high contrast, with big areas completely blacked out. Any space between designs was filled with different florals.

"Are they all done by the same artist?"

"Yeah, I've got a girl in town. I don't like strange men touching me," she provided, tone a bit defensive.

Moving to stretch out her left arm, he noted that it was covered in singular tattoos, probably done at different times. She rolled onto her right side so he could see the bird skull on her left shoulder, a vine growing through it. Evan racked his brain trying to name it.

She spared him. "It's a moonflower," she yawned. Her left bicep held a raven with its wings spread wide. Her forearm was wrapped in a large bundle of herbs, not unlike the ones she sold at the shop or used in her work.

He moved her to lie on her back and noticed a handful of scars that weren't covered by ink on her belly. He ran a soft touch over her ribs: a lunar moth on one side with crescent moons on its wings, and on the other, Evan could see a huge giant squid that wrapped up her side and hip, continuing up her back, done in heavy black ink. Tentacles everywhere.

"Tentacles. Like these?" he asked, plucking at a ribbon of shadow lying next to her.

"Yep."

"You're definitely scarier than a giant squid."

He trailed along them, admiring the details. His fingers stilled as he found some ridges and raised areas, not entirely disguised by tattoo ink. Scars, he remembered. Her eyes shone with vulnerability. She looked away.

"You said you had scars under these." He touched a tentacle on her rib.

She gnawed on her lip and nodded at the ceiling. "When I was under— under the demon's control—I mean," she cleared her throat, stalling. "There was a lot of damage done to my skin. I wanted my body back." Thunder battered the walls again.

Evan understood completely. She had covered herself in images of her power, reclaiming her body for herself, all with things found in dark places. Something powerful and mythical with huge dark tentacles. Something to be feared. Something to run from for your life. For a moment, he could see her as a child, covered in fresh wounds. His heart crunched in on itself, and he leaned down to plant a kiss on the squid's head. She ran a soft hand through his hair.

Glancing down to her hips, he shifted the sheets to look at her legs. Her left thigh featured a hand clutching a rose, with drops of blood leaking down to her knee. Her right thigh held a wolf, sprinting up with an arched back, teeth bared. He chuckled. That certainly fit.

In the shadows under the bedding, he couldn't quite make anything else out. "Is that all of them?"

She rolled onto her belly and moved her hair. On her back, the squid's tentacles wrapped around most of her back and one shoulder. On the other, he found three jellyfish with long tendrils that draped down almost to her waist. While he ran his fingers over the detail, Frankie popped her legs up and kicked her feet absentmindedly. He caught a blur of more ink.

"Wait, what was that?" He lurched and grabbed her foot. She squealed and tried to pull it away. He threw a leg over her butt to pin her down and snatched it. Across the top of her foot was a perfect, anatomically correct overlay of a skeleton foot.

"Uh, it's badass, but why?"

She gave him a serious look. "I've always got one foot in the grave in my line of work."

That's dark. He examined her face. Did she really feel that way? And would that change now that things had changed between them? Or did she not feel the same?

The moment stretched a bit too long. A rumble from underneath her broke the tension. Not thunder. She clutched her stomach. "Fucking hell, I'm starving."

Evan did not want to leave this bed but swallowed a lump of disappointment, groaned, and stretched his arms like a cat. "Let's go get some food. Although, I think the power is still out."

Frankie sat up and crawled to the edge of the bed. "The stove is gas, it might still work."

*****

Frankie tried again to flip the circuit breaker. Nothing. "Damn."

Something was off, but she couldn't quite place it. Drumming her nails on the counter, she tried to tease it out. Something about this storm. It wasn't right.

Wearing just his underwear, Evan entered the kitchen clutching his phone. "Shit, my phone's dead and I need to check in with Nan's nurse."

Frankie pointed to the hall. "I think there's a portable rechargeable block in the closet. It might still have some charge." She paced to the windows overlooking the front porch and listened to Evan rummage.

"Got it." Still looking out the window, she followed the sounds of him retreating to the kitchen to plug his phone in. He came up behind her. "Is it still raining?"

She shook her head. "No. But something's weird. We don't normally get storms this strong in the autumn." She opened the front door and stepped out. Cool humidity slapped her face, and gusts of wind ripped by her house.

The smell hit her first. The rain that had gathered on the walkway smelled like stagnant water or low tide. Or a lake. Not the fresh, cleansing scent that accompanies a nice shower. Particles in the air felt especially charged, like each ion carried its own storm.

She turned to Evan, finding him masking his nose with his hand. "Something's really wrong. I have a terrible feeling." She yanked her phone from the shorts she'd put on and texted the Sawtooth Baddies thread.

Frankie:
Yo! You two busy? This storm is weird

Bex pinged back immediately.

Bex:
Right? What is that smell? Our
power is out

Frankie:
Mine too

Can you come over? We
have updates on Agatha's case

Bex:
For sure

Be there in a few

Evan tried his phone and found it still too dead to access. He sighed.

"Bex and Jack are coming over to chat Agatha."

"In that case, as much as I enjoy Bex objectifying me, I should put a shirt and some pants on." He snapped the band of his underwear before trotting upstairs.

Frankie tried to take her mind off of the weird weather event and tidied up the library from the previous night. She snapped her fingers to get a fire going and stared at the flames in fogged thought. Eventually, she went upstairs to change and found Evan wearing more of her oversized clothing options. This time, he wore a pair of her baggy joggers and a huge shirt from a metal show she had gone to with Jack.

He yawned. "You want some coffee?"

"Yes!" She headed to the dresser. Evan's footsteps came up behind her, and he leaned down to her ear, his hands wrapping around her hips.

"Or maybe coffee can wait a few minutes?"

"I'm going to need caffeine before we go another round, Lawson."

She bumped him with her hip, and he laughed, retreating to the doorway with a last glance that indicated he would happily participate in her changing. She smiled to herself.

Shit. She'd been so busy on Agatha's case that she hadn't done laundry yet this week, and her options were limited. With a sigh, she snatched up a black miniskirt and a crewneck sweatshirt that read, *"If you've got it haunt it."* Her mind ticked away while she changed. Why did the rain smell so bad? And where had the storm come from? Realizing she was freezing without the heat running, she grabbed some socks and tugged them on, pulling them up as high as they would go.

Frankie walked downstairs and smelled the coffee brewing in the French press. *Coffee, coffee, coffee, coffee.* A sacred chant in her mind. Last night had been… earth-shattering. Reality-altering. Physically exhausting. Her muscles burned in the best way. Frankie hated most people and did not date much as a result. She was unsure if she could call what she and Evan were doing "dating," but they hadn't been "just friends" for a while now. She turned the corner into the kitchen and almost crashed into Evan. He placed his hands on her hips to steady them both and froze. He looked down at her skirt.

"Jesus Christ. Choosing violence today, huh?" His expression was dark and intense.

Confused, she looked down and understood: she was once again wearing a stupidly short skirt and knee socks. Sure, she could have been honest and said it was an accident, that she just needed to do laundry, but where was the fun in that?

"No clue what you mean," she said, false innocence on her face.

His hand wove behind her head to her nape, his other hand sliding up her waist. "What exactly are you trying to do me?"

She ran a finger along his jaw and cocked her head. "Ruin your life, of course."

He sighed down at her. "You've succeeded." He gripped her face with both hands and kissed her soundly.

Yes, yes, yes! All thoughts of coffee gone, her body responded with urgency, and she pushed into him, nerves pounding between her legs. Evan's hands slid down under her skirt and over her butt, giving it a squeeze. He made a hungry noise and scooped her up and carried her out of the kitchen, down the hall, and once again into the library.

"Is this a rematch, Lawson?"

He smiled and brought her to the floor with a nip to her earlobe. She moved his face in front of hers and held his head in place to keep him right where she wanted him. This man could *kiss*. Flipping between long and sweet, or hard and demanding, his tongue dancing with hers. Her head spun—she loved the feeling. Positioning himself over her, he ran a light hand up under her sweatshirt and found her breast and freed it from her bra. He worked it with his fingertips, pulling a deep moan from her throat. "I love these," he said, in between kisses.

Already, her head was fluff, and when Evan pushed her skirt up to her waist, she wrapped her legs around him, tugging him down on top of her. Evan made a little noise that sounded like a question. She loosened her legs, and he sat up slightly, a faint blush on his cheeks.

"Um, Frankie?"

"Yeeeees?"

He just stared down at her. Her smile faded. "What's up? You okay?" She ran a tattooed hand through his curls.

"No, yeah. I'm—I'm good. Um."

He stalled again.

"Use your words, Evan, I'm about five seconds away from pinning you down."

"That's actually… Last night. You…"

She softened her expression. "Kind of… topped you?"

He honestly looked mortified. "Yes." Now his face was a deep red, as were his ears.

"Did… you like that?" she asked.

He froze, not breathing, and his blush deepened to something close to purple.

"Yes," he whispered.

The vulnerability on his face cracked her horrible, frozen, stupid heart wide open. "Do you want me to do it again?" She asked softly.

He swallowed hard. "Y-yes." Relief filled his face. "Fuck yes."

Mouths colliding again, Evan ran his hands to grip her hips and started to roll them over.

The front door opened. Because Frankie forgot to lock it back. Jack and Bex stood inside with gaping expressions at what they saw—Evan and Frankie, with her pale white ass cheek fully exposed and being gripped by Evan's hand, and her teeth around his bottom lip.

"*YES!*" Bex screamed and jumped up and down. Jack turned her shoulders and started to push her back outside. They spoke at the same time.

Jack said, "We'll come back in ten minutes."

Bex said, "I told you the skirt and high socks would work!"

The door closed again.

Still locked with Evan, Frankie looked up at him. "Please tell me I'm dead and this is hell."

Evan laughed. "I mean, they said ten minutes," he murmured against her neck, giving it a small bite, causing her to grind up against him again, a movement he mimicked with his hips.

The muffled sound of Jack's voice came from the porch. "*Actually, it's freezing and wet out here. Can you please make yourselves decent?*"

CHAPTER 40

Frankie sipped coffee at the counter, watching Evan pour cups for Bex and Jack. Seeing him in her kitchen—in her clothing with tussled morning hair that *she* messed up—and not being able to do a single fucking thing about it was an act of violence on level with armed robbery. She would never forgive them for interrupting this morning.

Jack leaned in, whispering so only she could hear, "Can you please stop eye-fucking each other? I already need a shower." Frankie punched their arm.

"Dick."

Jack laughed, a low, warm sound that she always liked to hear.

Frankie cleared her throat. "Right. So, updates. At the carnival last night, we followed Ruth to a tarot reader's tent." She paused to banish, strangle, murder, and dump over a bridge the memory of Evan's tongue on her shadows. Evan caught her eye over the ridge of his mug, eyes glittering.

Prick.

She continued, well aware of Bex grinning from ear to ear and Jack rolling their eyes. "The reading was interesting. She's got conniving intentions. At the very least, she's been scheming *something* in her life against someone else. But even more interesting than that: I buried a return-to-sender hex on her property, and last night, she was sick with a mysterious illness—one that she seemed to think was supernatural."

Bex made a noise over her sip of coffee. "That's pretty damning." She looked at Evan. "How has Agatha's health been over the last twenty-four hours?"

He crossed his arms in front of him and leaned down on the countertop. "Weirdly stable yesterday. I'm hesitant to say improvement, but it's not nothing."

Jack nodded. "Yeah, I think you're onto something. What's next?"

Frankie drained her mug but held it to warm her hands. "I still need to figure out who she bargained with. I'm going to try to scry next."

Jack frowned. "We'll be joining you for that. No more nasty surprise texts in the middle of the night about you being possessed, okay?"

On the counter, Evan's phone pinged with several notifications. He blanched and snatched it, scrolling as fast as he could. His face paled.

"Oh shit." His eyes scanned the screen, frantic. "Nan took a turn for the worse early this morning—she's been hospitalized. I got to race home and get to Boston." He chugged his coffee down, wincing at the burn.

"Do you need a ride?" Frankie asked, leaping to her feet.

"I don't know what's going on, but you can probably do more here by working on the case." He trotted to the door, Frankie following closely behind. "The cottage isn't a far run from here, less than ten minutes. They said she's stable for the moment, so I should be fine." He looked out the window. "Besides, there might be road debris on my side of town. Better on foot."

He stuffed his feet into his sneakers and straightened, looking at her with emotional eyes. A combination of fear and sadness. They should have had a relaxed morning together. He and Agatha should have had years more together. Everything was happening too fast. This couldn't be it for Agatha. It was too soon. Frankie took his hand with both of hers.

"I will break the time and space barrier apart to crack this if I have to."

"I know." He kissed one hand, then the other. "Please don't do anything dangerous. I'll see you soon." He gave her an all-to-brief kiss and bolted out the door.

Numb, Frankie found herself in the kitchen again. She heard the chirp of Clemmie jumping onto the counter and felt the brush of his bony tail on her arm to try and comfort her, the iridescent shimmer of his eyes flipping from a green marble to an amber lens. Bex pulled her into a hug. "Hey, everything's going to be okay."

Frankie wiped at the water lining her eyelids. She wasn't solving this thing fast enough. Logically, she knew this had never been about saving Agatha from her fate. She couldn't stop Agatha from dying, but she could still save Evan.

Bex held both of her cheeks and tilted Frankie's head up to meet her gaze. There was no more teasing to be found in her rich brown eyes. "We aren't going anywhere. What do you need?"

Frankie sniffed and gave herself a mental shake to focus, scrubbing a hand in her hair to stir her shadows up.

"Alright, the power's still down, might be for the day. We need to brew some stuff for a scrying session. Even if it's still cloudy, there's a waxing moon in place tonight, and it'll be a good time to scry."

Jack stood and adjusted their glasses. "What are we brewing?"

"A tea for spirit communication." She yanked open a drawer, heart pounding now that she had something to focus on. "I'm going to make a list for you both. Bex, can you help me gather stuff from the garden? And Jack, can you go to The Black Cat and get the things on your list? You can take my truck in case any of the roads are flooded."

Frankie spent the next few minutes muttering to herself, deep in thought, pen scribbling on paper.

Pansies from the autumn pots displayed on the porch. Valerian.
Moonflower from the garden post… nope scratch that. Toxic.
Mugwort. Cedar branches. Goldenrod. Dandelion root.
Oh! Cinnamon.

She grimaced. This would taste nasty as hell. But she would drink an entire keg if it made any difference. She handed Jack a list, then snatched some kitchen scissors and handed them to Bex.

"Alright, my dudes. Let's begin our dark work."

CHAPTER 41

Evan's head pounded as he eased back into the uncomfortable rocking recliner that always accompanied hospital beds. He was well-acquainted with them by this point. Nan dozed, a nosepiece in her nostrils to feed her oxygen. Despite only being a half hour away from Sawtooth, Boston had not been hit with a freak storm, and the hospital had power.

Guilt burned a hole through him. He should have gone home last night. He didn't regret a single thing that had happened with him and Frankie, but fuck. Terrible timing. It made him feel better to blame himself, so that's what he did.

When he'd raced home and entered Nan's room to grab her favorite blanket, he'd found an awful, bloody scene that made him gag with dread. The carpet was soaked with a large blood stain. His brain had frozen, then collapsed in on itself, and then burst into flames, panic reeling in all of his limbs. He'd had an absurd thought at that moment: *maybe I can give her my lungs.*

Nan's nurse, Kathy, had found her on the floor around four in the morning, hacking up blood on the carpet. A bronchoscopy procedure this morning confirmed that her lungs had somehow deteriorated significantly in a matter of a couple of days. It should have been impossible. At the start of October, Evan would never have believed this illness to be supernatural in nature. Just awful luck and genetics. It would have been perfectly horrific for death to come for her as an act of nature.

But now, he knew better. As he watched Nan's chest rise and fall with an unmistakable rattle, Evan was blinded with fury. One thought tumbled around his mind, refusing to be silenced.

He would harm the person who did this. He would make them suffer.

The doctor who performed the bronchoscopy let Evan know that Nan wished to go home as soon as she recovered from the sedatives, and while he didn't at all recommend it, she wouldn't take no for an answer. She'd be sent home with an oxygen tank, but he knew that was a Band-Aid.

A horrible realization sat in the room with him, its presence like an unwelcome stranger. This was likely *it*. It could all be over in the next few days. But no relief came with this knowledge, he would live in this health purgatory forever if it meant she stayed around for just a little bit longer.

Elbows braced on his knees, he heaved through sobs, let them rip out of him. With no one else here to witness it, he couldn't hold them back any longer, and they came and came.

The motion triggered a muscle memory, a reaction he had felt for weeks when trying to go home, to the old, Victorian house that he and Nan had shared. He let the panic attack hit him in full force. What did it matter? He let it consume him, burn through him, his inability to breathe mocking him, an echo of Nan's symptoms.

In his cold hand, his phone buzzed.

Frankie had texted him.

> Frankie:
> *Hey, just got hit with a big*
> *feeling and thought it might be you*
>
> *No need to reply, just letting you*
> *know that I'm here, and hustling*
>
> *And I am out for blood.*

She sent a line of black heart emojis. His breathing's staccato rhythm eased, the text a reminder that he was not alone, that he would not be afterward. He had a pack of lunatics holding him upright.

He eased back into the chair and held a finger in front of his face. He looked at it, then looked out the window at the gray autumn sky. He did this for a long time, long past the point that he needed to.

His brain quieted except for one chant:

They wouldn't fail.

CHAPTER 42

Frankie's clothes were soaked with stinking rainwater as she and Bex rooted around the wild, end-of-summer garden for what she needed. Bex had been unusually quiet and focused, a sign of the gravity of their task. As the day turned to dusk, Frankie's house remained dim. There was still no power anywhere in town.

Deciding that the smell of her scrying tea would be too gross to steep indoors, she fired up the grill. So much of this situation was out of her control, and to soothe herself, she allowed her hands to cut the herbs into precise sizes with sharp, perfect cuts, arranging them in the cast iron skillet in a sigil pattern. The brutal lines of the sigil shape had been intentional—it was meant to look severe, to carry the weight of her focus and rage.

As the cold, useless sun dipped behind the trees and the town of Sawtooth fell into a dense darkness for a second night, Frankie poured water into the skillet and placed it on her grill on the deck. She stood still in the grim darkness, watching the flames lick up the side of the iron. She poured some of her shadows into the water to steep with the herbs. The effect was immediate—the sounds of the forest around them amplified, the groan of wandering spirits within a few miles of her house an endless chatter in her ears. Mind splintering into several planes, she breathed through the discomfort, reminding herself that she had survived hell before, and it would not claim her tonight.

Jack and Bex stayed in the doorway, waiting. When the tea was steeped enough, Frankie removed the skillet from the grill and took it into the kitchen.

She ladled out a mug of the disgusting beverage. Bex fetched herself a mug.

"Gimme some."

Unable to laugh, Frankie gave her a weak smile. "You don't need to drink it with me, it's super nasty."

Jack also grabbed a mug. "Me too."

"Guys, it serves no purpose for you to ingest this."

Bex glared at her. "Don't be a bitchbag. We're in this with you, we do it together."

Frankie blinked away raw emotion and wordlessly ladled them both a mug.

"Cheers, I guess." They clinked and drank. All of them gagged after the first sip. "Told you it was nasty." The trio giggled, the sound feeling like a rebellion in the face of the night's horrors, of the curse's unfairness.

With no word yet from Evan, Frankie drew runes on her face and set up her library's pentagram for the evening's circle. She snapped her fingers, igniting the fireplace and every candle. Multiple flickers played along the walls, painting an infernal backdrop. So, she stored away her humanity, and let the shadows in her hair form into huge horns framing her face.

So mote it be, motherfucker.

Jack and Bex moved around the space with purpose, placing in front of her a mirror that Jack had fetched from the shop, a knife, and a bucket of salt water. As part of her preparation, Frankie had dug through her closets and pantry, locating an example of each kind of element for potential offerings. She placed the elements behind her for quick access. She wasn't sure who would answer but wanted to be prepared.

Frankie looked up at them both from her seat on the floor. "I'm going to call for an elemental spirit. My ancestors couldn't guard me last time. And goddess knows I've got better relationships with wild spirits."

Jack sat behind her on one side of the circle, Bex on the other, all three facing the mirror. The black glass swirled with a smoked surface.

"Are we ready?" She looked between their reflections in front of her. "I don't know what we'll see. It might be freaky."

"We'll be fine, Frankie. Hit it," Jack said.

Frankie raised a hand and poured shadows into the mirror. She felt her eyes blacken with her call to power. The voices of spirits outside quieted to a faint whispering and then into silence. Their own reflections dimmed as a fog bank rolled into view.

An outline of something appeared in the glass, tucked away in the mist.

"I ask you to please step forward, spirit."

The figure's form straightened and moved toward the glass. They spoke, their voice like two overlapping sounds: a deep, low pitch as well as a quiet whisper.

"And who calls me forth?"

"Frankie Wolfe." Giving her first and last name was a sign of deep respect in the spirit world. If a spirit had these as well as her middle name, she'd be in serious danger.

The light from her side of the veil illuminated its features through the glass as it stepped closer. She heard Bex shudder out a breath. Jack didn't seem to be breathing at all.

Beautiful and terrifying, with pebbled skin the color of a cloud heavy with rain, the spirit's form was nude and genderless. Small streams of blue lightning danced across the surface of their skin. The spirit's hair resembled gray jellyfish tentacles floating on an invisible current, and Frankie realized that those tendrils were what sent lightning skittering across the rest of the spirit's body. Their face was the color of a pale cloud with childlike features and small, feathered wings across the cheekbones, brow, and jaw. In place of eyes, the elemental had two oversized lenses, like iridescent marbles with no pupils.

"Spirit, I will not ask your name," Frankie had planned to include this line to ensure that whoever answered did not feel threatened. *"But may I ask what kind of element we are in the presence of?"*

Two horizontal eyelids closed briefly in a blink. *"Storm."*

Frankie paused, about to go off-script. Because something had been bothering her about the storm all day, and now might be her only chance.

"Spirit, did you call this storm in from the Bay?"

Their face twisted into something ugly that would have made her knees shake had she been standing.

"No, witch. I arrived to feast when it was summoned."

Summoned? Frankie's mind whirled, sorting through clues. The storm had arrived out of nowhere in the night, after previously clear skies.

And Agatha had fallen ill in the night, after previously stabilizing.

The spirit continued. *"This storm has a bad taste. You have called me forth, mortal. Have you an offering for me to feed on?"*

Frankie thanked the goddess for her chronic over-preparation and reached behind to grab a Mason jar of stormwater. *"I may have something satisfactory."* She held up the jar so the spirit could see. *"This is from a summer storm in early August."*

They sniffed the mirror's glass. *"How strong?"*

"Tornado warnings, fallen trees, flooded streets."

A forked tongue dragged across its bottom lip. *"Satisfactory."* The jar disappeared from Frankie's hand, and she watched the mirror as the spirit drained the water in huge gulps.

Lightning strikes spiked from their hair into the surrounding fog clouds. They hissed in pleasure.

"Mortal, why have you called me forth?" Water ran down their chin and was absorbed into the skin.

Here goes nothing. She sat up a little straighter. *"If it pleases you, spirit, I ask if you can see a bargain that was struck to curse Agatha Lawson of Sawtooth Bay? Perhaps what spirit it was made with?"*

The spirit turned their head into the fog and stared for a few minutes. Frankie watched the jellyfish tentacles float and tried to slow her heart rate.

"Ah, there." The elemental pointed into the fog. Frankie's heart pounded anew. *"I see a deal made with life promised in exchange for death."* Okay, they already knew that part. *"And I see a signature on the agreement from not one of my own kind, but something more ancient."*

"If it pleases you, spirit, what is older than you?"

222

The elemental snapped their head back to Frankie, features contorted in rage. *"Do not ask me to speak its name, witch."*

Shit, shit, shit. *"I meant no offense, spirit."*

Horizontal eyelids blinked again, the elemental staring into her. *"I see you carry an element of your own, mortal. I suggest you guard it before trying to reach out to this being. This is a spirit only a fool would summon. Yet I suspect you plan to do just that."*

"This curse must be broken, spirit. I will do what I have to."

They tilted their head at her, considering. *"Your offering pleases me, mortal, so I give you this advice: do your research."*

And then the mirror went black. Frankie stared at their reflections in the glass once more. Thoroughly rattled and confused, the trio sat in stunned silence for a moment, before a large, heavy book fell off one of the library's shelves.

"Motherfucker!" Jack exclaimed as the book landed right next to their knee.

Frankie waved a hand to break the circle and picked up the book.

"A book of maps?"

The front door opened, and Evan stepped inside. A small noise came from Frankie's throat, and she sprinted to him, crashing against his chest and wrapping her arms around him.

"How's Agatha? How are you? What's going on?"

Evan made a choking sound. "Frank, you're stabbing me in the throat with your horns."

"Oh! Sorry." She dissolved them in two puffs of black smoke.

Evan rubbed his esophagus and beamed down at her. "I'm really glad to see you," he said quietly. "But I have bad news. Nan's lungs are barely functioning. She's home on an oxygen tank, but she…" His sentence choked off. He tried again, "I think this might be it, is what I mean."

Frankie's eyes burned. A high-pitched tone throbbed in her ears.

"How's it going here?"

"We have some progress. An elemental spirit dropped a book of maps from the shelf."

"No idea what that means. Please continue." He draped an arm over her shoulder and led her back towards the library.

"I don't either, but I have an idea." She pulled the chain holding Agatha's ring from her pocket. "I'm going to use this as a pendulum and try to narrow the possibilities down to a location in the world."

Jack and Bex moved the coffee table back in place while Frankie thumbed through the book for a spread of the entire world. She placed it on the table and perched on the edge of the sofa, letting the pendulum swing down, and waited for it to still. Always self-conscious when performing a spell in front of people, she whispered to herself. *"Ruby red, please lead us to the ancient being we seek."*

The necklace swung in circles and Frankie tried to read the pattern, holding it over South America. Maybe Africa? Nope. North America? Also no. She grunted in frustration. She glanced up at Evan, with his auburn curls and pale skin. The same hair and skin that Agatha had.

"Any chance Agatha has Irish heritage?" She snapped her attention back to the map and centered over the United Kingdom. The pendulum fell still.

Hell yeah.

She flipped through the pages to find a map of just the United Kingdom, and started the pendulum again, starting from the south of Britain and moving it up towards Ireland. It paused over the land there. Frankie felt a smile form on her face.

The chain broke, and the ring fell perfectly in the center of the Irish Sea.

"Whoah," Bex mumbled from her perch on the loveseat. "So it's what, a sea monster?"

Frankie stood and paced the floor, one hand gripping her hip, the other clutching a thick lock of hair, tugging. Little shadows cast out to the ground with the movement. She mumbled to herself.

"It's got to be something from the deep, something deep at the bottom, something that was gone, something ancient…'

She stopped abruptly and let out a small gasp.

Evan crossed his arms. "Please tell me you have good news."

She faced him. "I can't."

CHAPTER 43

"It's a Fomoire. And it's ancient. I'm talking early human era ancient. Before recorded Celtic history ancient. Like, primordial-level ancient. Like we will be in serious-danger-level ancient."

Jack leaned back against the loveseat cushion next to Bex. "Ruth summoned an ancient Celtic demigod and made a deal with it?"

Frankie tapped her foot, mind still working. "Her altar wasn't set up in a way that a seasoned practitioner would do it, and she had no understanding of the tarot cards that got pulled for her." She stopped tapping her foot. "I have a feeling she might be in over her head. If she managed to find some old text that would summon a Fomoire on the internet or something, she'd be indebted to the spirit, and it would be trying to come for her and collect on the bargain.

The elemental confirmed that she offered years of life as payment for the curse. She did have protective charms by the front and back doors, but it would eventually start to hunt her down in public. Which could be why she was so anxious and pissy at the carnival and seeking answers from the tarot reader."

"Does this have something to do with the storm?" Jack asked.

"I think so. It smelled wrong, more like pond water than fresh rain. I think the spirit was summoned last night to escalate Agatha's illness, and this gross storm that smells like muck followed the Fomoire up from the Bay as it arrived."

Evan stared at the map in thought. "If Ruth summoned it again last night, why didn't it just take her years then?"

Frankie considered this. "I don't know. She might have some way of protecting herself that I'm not aware of. It'd be tricky to do and difficult to maintain, but it's possible for the short term. That Fomoire is going to be hungry and furious, especially if she's cranking up the terms of her contract with more attacks on Agatha. That's a positive for us—we might not need to offer it something better, we could just offer it what it already wants. It needs to feed on the years of life she offered. It will be permanently weakened if it can't claim them. That's a huge insult to a deity."

"What's our next move?" Evan crossed his arms, ready for battle. Frankie gave him a devilish smile.

"Now we fuck her up."

*****

Sawtooth Bay's spooky season tourists had not left town with the power outages, and many wandered through the streets shouting or singing, drinks in hand. Like it was fucking Mardi Gras. Citizens had begun to place carved pumpkins on their porches and along streets to offer a small bit of light in the dark, and most hid in their houses, waiting for the power to come back on.

The Sawtooth Baddies, minus Frankie, walked towards Nan's cottage in the dark. Bex held the bag with herbs and materials, and Jack carried a bucket filled with stormwater gathered from a drainage ditch. Evan walked with one hand on a flashlight to carve through the night's mist, the other hand clutching storm-downed branches to form Frankie's pentagram at Nan's.

Before they had departed Frankie's house, she had pulled him into the kitchen and pressed something into his chest. He looked down and saw he was holding a sheathed sword.

She had given him a sword.

"I don't know how to use this," he said, sheepish.

"I'm pretty sure there's only one sharp end." She gave him a long, slow kiss, and said, "Let's raise hell."

The sword strapped across his back gave him comfort as he walked. He'd examined the hilt by her fireplace—and it was fucking gorgeous. The grip was a soft black leather, and the crossguard formed into severe, almost evil-looking points. It was the kind of sword that would terrify a traveler if they stumbled upon it in a cave.

He knew she'd be coming along to join them after she prepped, but he still wished Frankie was there to walk with them through the dark. She'd know if anything stalked them, maybe even rip it apart with her bare hands.

Evan reached inside for his focus but found only anger as he watched the dark forms of chaotic tourists collide with each other in the gloom. Everyone was acting odd, especially the visiting revelers. It gave him the panicked feeling of a world about to end, and everyone who was still alive was dancing instead of running for their lives.

Upon entering the cottage, Bex and Jack moved the den furniture out of the way for their ritual. Evan stepped into Nan's room and found her awake, sitting up in bed. A row of candles on a nearby credenza flickered across her tired face. He'd thrown a towel down over the bloodstain when they came home. There was no time to try and clean it, and he knew they both hated the omen that mocked them from the ground.

Nan gave him a weak smile with rattled breaths. "Sit with me."

He eased into the chair and placed his sword against the side of it. "Hey. We're going to do a ritual in the den."

She sighed, the exhale ending in a cough. "We knew this was coming for us at some point, honey." She took his hand. "You're going to be okay, I promise you."

Tears streamed down his face. "No, I really won't."

Feeling like an absolute child again, he buried his face in her blanket and cried. She ran a hand in his hair. "I'm sorry," he choked out. "You shouldn't be comforting me right now."

"Evan, look at me." He wiped his nose on his shirt and found her watching him. "You have family in that room there." She pointed in the direction of the den with her chin. "I am so, so proud of everything you've done in your life, especially over this last month. You're my world." She took his face in her hands. "And spiritually, you're my son. You know this."

He nodded.

"So please listen to your parent when I tell you this: if you have learned nothing else from the last few weeks, remember that you are never, ever alone. In the land of the living, you have people who will lift you up. And when it's

228

my time, I'll always be around you on the other side."

It hit him then, why she'd been pushing him toward Frankie and the Gang at every chance. Being in their circle meant exposing himself to death, to the unknown. She'd been trying to teach him one last lesson.

"Please stop saying goodbye." His chest was hollowing out, he could feel it.

"I'm not going anywhere until I know who did this to me, so I can torment them from the afterlife." Her sharp, take-no-shit tone had returned. A fire in her eyes. Evan laughed.

"Then we'd better get started."

Evan walked back outside, sword strapped to his back, hoping to see Frankie arrive. He shivered in the cold for a while, watching shapes stumble by. He tried to will the town's power to come back on with his brain, as ridiculous and futile as the effort was.

Out of the dark gloom, the mist parted, and Frankie's features emerged into view.

Different though. Frightening. Her normally contrasting coloring was pronounced to the point of something monstrous. Her black, fitted clothes and hair fully were camouflaged by the darkness, casting an illusion of her face floating on its own. Eyes and cheeks hollowed out by black, lips colored black, face in stark white, even brighter when surrounded by shadows. A black sigil on her forehead, looking like a crescent moon with a few letters stacked on top of it. A few on her cheeks. Her face resembled a skull bare of skin, and covered in powerful symbols. Paint, Evan realized—she'd arrived painted up in full Spirit Face.

His throat tightened at the vision approaching him. Here she was, a goddess of death who would save or damn him. That was it, how he felt. Frankie was terrifying. He'd known this before, but not why. It settled in him now, that she was terrifying for everything that she meant to him. For what she might be able to do for his family, for his life, and for what might happen to her if she succeeded.

She stood before him, and they stared at each other in weighted silence, too many words surging under the surface, too much to try and verbalize. Without realizing it, Evan had become very intimately acquainted with death over the last few weeks. By walking next to Frankie, he walked hand-in-hand with the spirit world. Death was petrifying, existential, unknown. But it felt less awful with Frankie standing in front of him. He swallowed his fear, took her hand, and turned to face death at her side.

CHAPTER 44

Agatha's little cottage felt smaller in the dark. On entering, Frankie willed away some of the shadows, sending them to hide behind furniture or curtains. They would need a tiny bit of visibility.

Jack and Bex had come through with the storm branches and formed the pentagram and circle, as requested. "Is it pointing west?"

Bex rolled her eyes. "Yes, mother."

Frankie stepped into Agatha's room. Agatha gave her a hoarse chuckle. "Well, you look scary as hell."

"Enough to scare off whatever spirit cursed you?"

Agatha nodded. "It doesn't stand a chance."

She sat next to Agatha's bed. "It's going to have a physical form when I summon it, so I'm going to have Evan guard your door. I'll trap it in a circle and convince it to follow us out of the house and over to Ruth's."

"So it was Ruth?"

Frankie nodded. "She's about to have a bad night."

Agatha gave her hand a squeeze. "Thank you."

"Don't thank me until the job is done." Franke smiled, which probably ruined the effect of the makeup.

The hour chimed. Midnight had arrived.

Frankie positioned herself in the pentagram and poured shadows from both hands to flood the floor. Evan stood in front of Agatha's door with his sword in hand, and Jack and Bex once again positioned themselves behind Frankie, outside of her circle.

The spirit communication tea from earlier was still in effect, and Frankie worked to dim the whispers of spirits outside of the house. Stepping near the trap circle, she pulled the bucket of mucky stormwater into it.

"Alright, here we go." She dipped a hand in the disgusting mixture and stirred it clockwise.

"As above, so below: I call now to a god of the deep, of murk, of chaos and illness. Breaker of ships, I beseech thee—answer our call."

She stepped back and dove for the safety of the pentagram. Remembering the elemental's warning from earlier, she tucked her shadows away, nice and tight. The bucket began to rattle before it fell over and spilled onto the floor. Frankie gagged. The smell was overwhelming, like a lakebed that had been fully drained.

Brown water rose into the air, forming a humanoid shape. The Fomoire's skin was slick and shiny in the dim light of the candles, the color shifting at all times, somewhere between a dark blue and a brownish purple. Gills lined its thick neck and ran entirely down its torso, stopping at its waist. The form was male with no hair. Black, glossy orbs speared through her instead of eyes. Its almost-human mouth gaped open and closed, the way a fish's mouth would out of water. It was just south of seven feet tall.

Eww, eww, eww. The monster spoke. Frankie could only describe its voice like someone talking through an inhalation, and also a stream of bubbles.

"Twice in a day I've been summoned to this little town. But I don't know you, mortal." The "r" and "t" of the final word sounded like someone being pulled under the waves.

Unable to flood her system with her lake of power and risk exposing herself, Frankie spoke with a clear and commanding voice, free of her shadow's influence.

"No, spirit. I am Frankie Wolfe."

"Frankie Wolfe." The being rolled her name around in its mouth as if tasting it from all angles. Her stomach turned over.

"Spirit, I summon you to speak about a bargain you made with someone in town."

The Fomoire hissed. *"There is only one."*

"I won't ask you for specific details," she added, to show respect to this entity. "But I ask: am I correct that this person has not settled their bill?"

It hummed in agreement, the sound like a torrent of bubbles. *"A debt must be paid. Are you offering to pay it, witch?"* It ran a finger around the barrier of the circle, testing it for a weakness. The Fomoire froze and a winding tongue snaked out of its mouth to wipe the air in front of it. *"What's this I smell? Do you hide something from me?"*

She refused to let her voice shake. "Nothing to worry about," she said, carefully choosing her words. The spirit eyed her, suspicious.

"Then let me out of this snare so I may collect on the debt. I will break free eventually."

"I have a solution that might suit us both. I will let you out, but only if you agree to go after your original summoner."

The Fomoire considered the agreement. *"What do you gain from this, mortal? Why bother?"*

Time to sweet-talk. "I summon you for vengeance. To ruin. I want this person to face consequences."

"And what do I get in return?"

"Dinner?"

It huffed a bubbly laugh. *"Not enough. If I agree to this, I need something from you."*

Fucking hell balls. Frankie schooled her face into one of calm. Sure, just going to make a deal with a devil, what could go wrong?

"In exchange, I want information. You will answer one question of my choosing, and if you lie, I can claim something else from your life."

She felt the blood drain from her face and was grateful she had painted it white.

"Frankie…" Evan warned quietly.

She flipped the agreement over in her head. It couldn't be as simple as the spirit was making it out to be. This was a trap.

"Those terms don't benefit me, spirit."

Rage contorted the Fomoire's face. *"You are lucky I don't try to break out now and claim you all."*

So that was that. She didn't have a choice.

"Very well." She heard her friends all shift, dread heavy in the room. She stood and walked to the trap circle. "And you will stop harming Agatha Lawson. And not hurt anyone else present."

The Fomoire smiled, rows of shark teeth. *"Deal."*

"What can I call you, spirit? Do you have a nickname?" She knew it would never give her its full name, but even a syllable would be helpful.

"You may call me Lir."

Certain she was about to projectile vomit, she held her palm to the wall of the circle, and the Fomoire met hers with its… webbed extremity. A jolt of lightning struck them both, knocking them apart. The walls fell.

Bex and Jack scurried over to stand with Evan. This delighted Lir. *"You are right to fear me, mortals. But I am a god of my word. Now, take me to my dinner."*

CHAPTER 45

Walking next to a seven-foot-tall ancient god-predator in complete darkness was next-level stupid. Evan walked behind the creature with his sword out, ready to strike. He was furious with Frankie for making that deal and was waiting for the world to fall apart.

Frankie was silent and stoic. Now that he knew her better, he could recognize her tells. The tightness in her shoulders. The way she strummed her thumb along her other fingertips. She was scared out of her mind. His instincts screamed at him to throw her over his shoulder and sprint back to safety. But this was her battle and her decision. So, he would stand at her side with sword in hand.

As they approached Ruth's house, Evan felt panic try to skitter in. He squashed it. Not now. Not tonight.

Frankie held a finger in front of her mouth, asking the Fomoire to keep quiet. It grinned at her with its shark teeth. The absurdity of the visual almost brought a laugh out of him. In the backyard, she whispered to the group.

"It feels like she put up new wards near the back door. I'm going to destroy them, then we should be able to enter." She faced the door and snapped her fingers. A small orange glow brightened through a window and fell dark again.

Lir placed a hand on the door, and Evan heard it unlock. Fuck, that was creepy. It opened the door and casually stepped inside—like it was human— and held the door for everyone else. The action did not read as helpful, but threatening, and the spirit flashed those sharp teeth at Evan as he entered the house, confirming his dread.

The spirit's tongue poked out and licked the air, confusion on its face. It whispered, or as close to a whisper as it could manage, *"I don't smell my charge. Are you lying to me witch?"*

Alarmed, Frankie faced it and whisper-hissed, "She lives in this house! She's just in the other room. Go, feast!"

The Fomoire invaded her personal space, looming over her. Frankie held her ground with narrowed eyes, baring her teeth. Lir snarled in her face. Evan's vision went white with protective rage, and he found himself in front of her with his sword on the spirit's chest.

"Back the *fuck* up!"

Oops, that had been loud. Ruth appeared in the doorway to the kitchen in a set of flannel pajamas.

She screamed as she beheld the monster in her kitchen. "What is—oh god, oh god, oh god!" She fled for the front of the house.

Frankie pointed after her, seething. "Is that not your contractee?"

Lir made a sound like a jet stream. *"Not a her, a* him.*"*

A him? Evan mentally scrambled through his data, accessing the other male council members. A him? What had they missed?

*****

Frankie's brain felt like a black hole. This was bad. If she didn't find Lir's actual meal, she was well and truly fucked. She walked back outside in a daze. They had missed something. *She* had missed something. The Fomoire followed her out, spewing out angry, aquatic noises.

"My patience wears thin, witch." It stood in front of her, mouth gaping open and closed. *"You know how this works, I cannot speak on the terms or parties involved, and I cannot see him while he guards himself. You must take me to him. Or I will claim you instead."*

Fuck, fuck, fucking fuck. "Okay, okay, just give me a second to think." She glanced to the road and saw Ruth sprinting away, screaming bloody murder. "I think we need to do something about that."

Lir held a hand towards her fleeing silhouette and pulled the air. Ruth came flying back into view and floated a few inches above the grass in her front yard.

"Sleep, shrieking woman, and do not remember us."

Ruth fell to the ground in a heap. Bex leaned over and checked for a pulse. She gave a thumbs up. "Yeah, feels like she's got a fever, but she's fine."

"What the fuck did we miss?" Frankie paced and tore at her hair. "Who else could it possibly be?"

Evan placed his hands on top of his head and let out a stressed sigh. "I mean, I know Nan was certain, but what if it's not someone on the council?"

"But everything points to *this* dumb bitch!" Frankie gestured towards Ruth's sleeping form. "Her house looks like the Sanderson Sisters threw up in there." She started to pace again. "And she got sick after I buried the return-to-sender in her yard."

Jack chimed in, trying to rationalize the high emotions. "But she also sucks, right? It might just be some karma from being an awful person."

Frankie paused her pacing. "Wait." The answers to two questions were braiding together in her mind. A scene from the past few weeks flickered to her.

A return-to-sender hex that she buried in a yard. *Teresa's* yard. Teresa worked at the farmer's market, which Ruth visited weekly.

"Holy shit, Ruth hexed *Teresa!*" She turned to Evan. "*She* was the one who hexed Teresa. When I buried the return-to-sender hex in Teresa's yard, she must have felt the effects, then hung those shitty protective charms. And when I burned those off before the festival and buried another return-to-sender, the illness hit her."

Jack shook their head. "Okay, but back to Agatha. If it's not someone from the city council, then why did Agatha also get voted out of office? Who else could have had bad blood with her?"

Frankie tugged at her hair. Something was trying to surface in her memory. Small details scratched at the inside of her skull. "Oh, fuck!"

"What?" Bex asked.

"Mayor Phelps."

"*What?*" Bex exclaimed.

Frankie listed off her rationale on her fingers. "The over-interest in visiting Agatha to check on her condition, the suspicious nice guy vibe. But also, at the carnival, he had a bulge under his shirt. That was probably some kind of huge protective charm to keep him invisible in case Lir came calling. Even his smell—I thought it was bad cologne, but it was probably some kind of protective herb mixture. He asked Evan how Agatha was doing last night." She turned to face the Fomoire. "And I'll bet he summoned you to try and take her out of the picture completely."

The spirit rumbled. *"Shall we, then?"*

CHAPTER 46

Mayor Phelps lived in the small mayoral manor just off the square in town. Protected from view by the large stone wall surrounding the property, the crew tucked in close together. Lir unlocked the front door for them, then hissed at its sizzling hand against the wood. *"Remove the wards first."*

As the group approached his front door, Frankie faced them, hiking her bag of materials higher up her shoulder.

"Jack, Bex. You two should leave us here. We've already committed crimes, but we're about to commit several felonies. You two are respectable people with proper jobs and responsibilities. You do not have to come in with us."

Jack glared at her, then snatched the bag from her arm. "Bitch, do not make me fight you."

Bex gave Frankie's shoulder a squeeze. "As promised, I'm on lookout duty. I'll text if there's trouble."

Lir stood in front of Frankie, blocking her path.

"I wish to collect on my end of the bargain, mortal."

"Seriously? Right now?" She already knew what it would ask, and clenched her fists at her side, hoping for the best.

The spirit leaned down, its tongue jutting out and wiping the air in front of her face. She stifled a disgusted shudder.

"You smell of something. Something lives in you. It smells like the old world. What is

it?"

The nocturnal sounds of the manor's garden and passing drunks flitted around them while Frankie took a moment to compose herself. A tiny part of her wondered what would happen if she lied. What Lir would take from her. An image of Clemmie cat-loafing in front of the fire entered her mind. She wouldn't let that happen.

"They belong to me," she stated, a declaration. A warning. "They are mine, and you cannot take them from me."

Lir smiled in her face, unease growing in her with every tooth revealed. *"Then show me, and I will collect my charge and leave you."*

Just as she had revealed them in the quiet of her library to Evan, or when she summoned the storm elemental, Frankie allowed two shadow horns to form out of her hair. She made them large, curving around her head, and positioned them in a way that suggested that they were always present, just under the surface. She held her shoulders back and tried to become as big as possible in front of this giant spirit.

Lor shivered, as if in pleasure. *"Oh, yessss. I see."* It reached out a webbed appendage toward a horn, and Frankie heard Evan shift into position beside her.

"Touch me and I will hurt you." She let the threat sit in the air, in the single inch of space Lir had given her. A simple warning, a clear one.

"No need to threaten, mortal, I'll give you no trouble tonight." It took a step back. *Tonight.* Frankie knew enough about spirits to capture the full meaning of Lir's wording. But she had paid her end of the bargain for *tonight,* so she pointed at the front door.

Frankie heard Lir's voice in her head as it watched her for another moment. *"You can't hide your nature from me, you unholy, terrible thing. Don't worry, godkiller, your secret is safe."*

What? There was only one "secret" that she kept. Did Lir somehow know about the Leshy heart in her basement? Alarmed, she said nothing to its grinning face and wore a mask of calm. That seemed like a problem for a different evening.

With that, they entered the hall. Frankie snatched the protective spell bag hanging visible to the right of the front door and burned it in her hand. Lir entered the manor to join them, licking the air.

"He must have other wards in place. I can't yet sense him."

Jack jerked their chin upwards, whispering, "Primary suite is probably upstairs."

The manor's carpet was plush and ornate and absorbed the sounds of their footfalls. In the dark of the upstairs hall, Frankie could make out antique Victorian furniture spilling out of almost every available space. Walking next to Lir's enormous frame in the crowded interior felt like getting stuffed into a wardrobe. They followed the sounds of a podcast on low volume—good, he was home.

Jack reached the door first and began to ease it open before Frankie stopped them.

"Wait, wait. Let's put on a little show."

*****

Mayor Phelps lay asleep in his bed in his overcrowded bedroom. Frankie still considered the volume of antiques to be borderline hoarding, even if someone would call it "collected" or "intentional." It had taken a few minutes of silent miming and getting into position around creaking floorboards, but Frankie knew it would be worth it for the reveal. She nodded to Evan, who tapped the mayor's phone and turned the podcast off. She nodded to Jack who snatched the protective charm from around the mayor's neck and then slapped him hard across his face.

He sputtered awake, sitting upright, terrified. "Wha—what is this? What do you want? Wait, Evan? Wolfe?"

He looked between them and flinched when he beheld Frankie in her Spirit Face and magnificent horns. The color drained from his face. *Busted, motherfucker.*

"Now wait, I'm sure we can work something out. There's nothing permanent done yet—"

Evan stepped forward and gripped the footboard of the bed. "Yes, there fucking is. Her lungs are destroyed. *You* are responsible." He glared down at the mayor, the air around Evan's body thrumming with fury.

It made her blood sing. Frankie clasped her hands behind her back and let Evan have at him for a few more moments. Jack leaned against the wall by the door in nonchalance, placing their hands in their pockets.

"She has suffered over the last ten months more than you'll ever know. You have destroyed my only living family member. We should have had *years* more together!" He was shouting now, the wood creaking beneath his fingers, Mayor Phelps flinching at every other word. "But beyond me, she's a force for good in this town. She has only ever wanted to help people in her position." Evan stepped closer to the mayor and grabbed his chin, pulling the mayor's face towards his. His pupils lit from the flame of a nearby candle, giving his rage a physical, burning form in each eye.

"Now tell me why you did this. Tell me the reason."

He did not step back, did not release his chin. Mayor Phelps heaved through breaths and sputtered.

"I—look, it's not like that—"

"Not like *murder?*" Evan roared. "Not like *killing her slowly?*"

Tears streamed down the mayor's face. Gods, this was satisfying.

Phelps closed his eyes and tried to steady his breathing, trying to get some words out. "Look, Agatha has been on a warpath. She would have done anything to drive away the tech companies trying to set up here. We could be the next Austin, Evan! Think about that! Sawtooth would explode under Howie Anderson's plan." His voice cracked on the last word.

Explode is right, Frankie thought.

Evan nodded, the gesture slight, and released the mayor's face. He turned and walked back towards her.

She tilted up into Evan's ear and whispered, "Are you sure about this? It's permanent, no going back." She looked up at his exhausted face and banished any judgment from her voice and expression. This was Evan's decision. She would honor whatever he chose, even if he chose mercy.

"I know," he said quietly. "I want this to happen." He turned back to face the mayor. "I'm not going to hurt you." Phelps' face slid into relief. "But I am going to make sure you pay."

A dark, delicious thrill ran through Frankie. She gave the mayor a full, toothy smile, shadows filling her eyes to black them out, and stepped forward. If watching the man weep and plead for mercy was satisfying, what was coming next would be like a slice of dark chocolate cake after a good meal.

She unclasped her hands and held them in front of her, each holding a few protective spell bags from around the primary suite. Phelps let out an embarrassing noise and scrambled out of the covers, getting on all fours and holding out his hand toward her.

"No, no, no, no, no, please! *Please!*" He looked between the trio as if a savior existed, hidden amongst them.

It did not. Frankie began walking towards Phelps and set the spell bags aflame in her palms, shadow tentacles lurching out from her back to keep him from fleeing. When the charms were nothing but dust, Frankie allowed the light to dim even further in the room and then brighten for the big reveal.

Lir filled the doorway and stepped inside, its overwhelming aura one of promised violence. All teeth on display. The mayor's pajama pants darkened as he pissed himself.

"Okay, okay—fine, I surrender. Take them, take the twenty years, as promised. They're all yours!"

He'd given Agatha a death sentence for twenty years of his own life? Un-fucking-believable.

Lir grabbed the mayor by his throat and hoisted him into the air, feet flailing above the mattress.

"If you had set me free last night after attacking your victim, I would have collected on those terms. But you never planned to uphold your end of the deal, did you?"

Gasping, unable to answer in the spirit's clutch, Phelps slapped in vain at Lir's arm.

Lir rumbled as if in thought. *"Yes, you shall learn."* It dropped him on the mattress and turned around to leave the room.

Frankie opened her mouth to protest, but a reeking rope of kelp shot from Lir's wrist and wrapped around the mayor's entire body, wrapped snugly around his face, and pulled him off the bed and into the hallway.

The Fomoire dragged his thrashing body as it thunked painfully down each stair and through the front hall. His muffled screams filled the manor. Bex stumbled to the side of the front steps in surprise as she watched the monster drag away its prize through the front garden. Shrieks rang as he was dragged through the open gate and into the square, drunken bystanders staring or fleeing in fear. Frankie and Evan followed closely.

Lir led the group down to the edge of the water, probably right to where he had been summoned from the previous night. It looked down at the mayor in indifference. *"You will live for twenty more years, mortal. Underneath. With my brethren and me. I think we will feast on you slowly. But don't worry, we won't let you drown."*

Screams burst in the air as more tourists fled the scene. Without saying another word, the Fomoire raised its free hand, opening a swampy portal with awful, stagnant water whirling. Lir dragged the mayor through, his head thrown back in one last plea towards the two of them on the shore, and was gone.

The golden radiance of Sawtooth's lights eased back into full brightness as the town's power returned, causing the fog around them to glow in gilded orbs.

Frankie sighed. "If it weren't for so many people screaming, it would be a nice night."

CHAPTER 47

The last week of October passed in a glorious, slow, cozy blur for Evan. Agatha's condition slightly improved, and although her lungs were too far gone for a miracle, something in her had brightened. She and Evan moved back into their Victorian house for a few days and spent them as they always had—in the garden, on the sun porch, or reading in her study. Agatha was wheelchair-bound but spent the week with a permanent smile, laughing and chatting with her grandson.

Frankie had given Evan space during this time. She knew this was it, and made sure Evan knew that she was just a text away, sending a line of black heart emojis every morning and checking in with him every night. The Sawtooth Baddies each took turns dropping off food so that the pair could enjoy every single second that they had together.

And three days before Halloween, on an unseasonably warm and sunny morning, Agatha asked Evan to help her lay down in the garden, like they had when he was young. They dozed together for a few hours, a few happy words said here or there to each other in between dreams. Evan took Agatha's hand and felt her pass, comfortably, in her favorite place with her favorite person.

The work and administration that accompanies death awaited him, but he called Frankie over to sit with him and Agatha for a few minutes.

"This was the best and worst week of my life," he said, through tears of joy and mourning. "I have no idea how this happened, but this was as perfect of a passing as I could give her, after everything."

Frankie held him tight and smiled in silence at his wonder. He didn't need to know what she had done. How she sliced her hand open and once again

245

extended the life of someone very important for just a bit longer. Even if she did not know what it would cost her.

The two of them spent an extra hour together in the garden, dressing Agatha in her favorite flowers.

EPILOGUE:
NIGHT OF SAMHAIN

Halloween night arrived in Sawtooth Bay, and the town sank into it like a comfy chair. The streets and town square were packed with enough visitors to rival Salem. A fuzzy video shot by someone's phone had gone viral, and now visitors asked any local they could corner about a sea monster dragging off a screaming man through the square.

Sawtooth buzzed with too much life tonight, and Frankie was grateful for the quiet of her dark street. Although her street didn't have any surrounding houses near her creepy Victorian home, she dressed it up anyway. Evan had helped her carve at least twelve pumpkins for the porch steps and had spent half an hour debating with her over where to place them for maximum effect. An enormous plastic caldron bowl overflowed with the good candy on the top step—no generic bullshit or old-lady-purse-treasures would be found on this porch. The last few days had been awful, and Frankie was determined to enjoy the holiday with her family.

But first, an experiment.

Frankie positioned herself with Evan inside of the pentagram of her library. The sun had begun to tip over, the sky cast in a thick dusk of blues and indigos, and the spirits were already noisy in her mind as the glorious evening rose.

Frankie and Evan had spent the afternoon carving pumpkins until their hands ached, then ate her plates of cookies until their stomachs hurt. She eyed him now, as he sat across from her. Perhaps the worst part of those early, raw days of grieving was the administration and lists of things to get done when all he'd wanted to do was sit in silence out in Agatha's garden. His shitty parents were nowhere to be found, so she'd taken the lead on pushing through some

247

of the "arrangements," or whatever the fuck people called the socially-correct garbage you have to do when someone passes. The worst was still ahead of them with Agatha's estate and fortune needing to be settled and the funeral scheduled to take place in a few days. Tonight, they deserved a break. Some spooky goodness. Laughs. Warmth.

But now, Evan looked nervous. She caught his eye. "You okay?"

He shifted, folding his legs in the opposite direction, trying to get more comfortable. "What if nothing comes through?"

She melted a bit, her heart a throbbing ache. "That might happen, and it's okay. We'll just send a signal out and see who's around, okay?"

He nodded, looking boyish and vulnerable. He took the ghost radio in his hands and hit the channel "scan" button.

Frankie poured shadows into the pentagram and took his hands.

"We call out to any passing human spirits who may know us. We wish you a blessed evening on this Sabbath and ask for any messages from across the veil. Does anyone wish to speak?"

The radio flipped through channels, some chunks of radio host dialogue here, a few notes of a Rob Zombie song there, and back to static. They listened to the jabber, music, and white noise, the rest of the house quiet, waiting. Clemmie perched by the fire with his eyes closed, a loud purr escaping his bony chest.

The sky outside grew dark, and the house fell into darkness with it. Frankie had not left any lights on when they began their séance and now regretted that decision. The room lit by only firelight felt empty and lonely against the crackle of radio channels. She kicked herself for not getting the vibes right for this.

Evan glanced at her with sad eyes. After a long time, he said, "It's okay, we can turn it off." He turned the volume down.

"We can try again soon. Any time you want to."

He nodded.

Frankie reached for the radio to turn it off but heard a small voice and paused. "What? What was that?"

She arched a brow and turned up the volume dial, placing it against her ear. Warm static greeted her. A loud pop stabbed into her eardrum, and she dropped the device on the ground, startled.

"Evan? Are you seriously trying to reach me already? It hasn't even been a week."

Evan let out a loud bark of a laugh, shocked, elated, all of it. "I just thought I'd give it a try!" He laughed again, shaking his head at the radio.

"Let me phrase it this way. I have not seen your grandfather in almost thirty years. We need alone time."

Evan wrinkled his nose. "Uh, yeah, yep, okay, great. Um, what's ghost phone etiquette? Talk to you soon?" Agatha's leathery laugh sounded through the speaker.

"Take a few months, honey. I'm going to give you a bit of time to adjust. You need it. And remember what I said?"

"I remember." His voice barely audible.

"Love you."

Then, she was gone.

Frankie and Evan stared at each other for a while, listening to the fireplace. She threaded her fingers through his and wished she could vacuum out all of his pain and burn it alive. Listen to it scream. Make it suffer the way it made him suffer.

He read this on her face and wiped at his eyes. "I'm okay, Frank. Let's try to enjoy the holiday."

Their phones buzzed.

Bex:
Knock, knock

*We're standing on the porch
but I can see the fireplace going
in the library*

*Are you boning? Should we come
back later?*

Or actually can I watch?

Frankie cackled and shouted toward the front door, breaking the circle. "You should be so lucky! We're decent, come on in." Bex burst inside wearing a Snow White costume. Frankie fell over laughing, rolling on her side. "Holy shit, that's perfection."

Bex entered the hall and twirled, a gold tiara glinting on her head, and some gold shimmer on her shoulders and collarbones, casting her deep brown skin in a godlike glow. It was frankly obnoxious how gorgeous Bex was.

Jack stepped in behind her dressed as the Goblin King, complete with an athletic sock stuffed in the crotch of their pants. Instead of wearing the full mega-mullet wig, Jack had styled their hair in a messy but intentional way. They looked hot as hell.

Frankie laughed, screaming, "No! Oh gods, I can't handle it! You didn't have to dress up!"

Bex put her hands on her hips. "Don't tell me I can't be a princess, you monster."

Evan helped Frankie stand. With a smile to Jack, he said, "You know, I've never been attracted to David Bowie before, but you're making me rethink that."

Frankie looked down at her sweater. "Shit, I'm still covered in pumpkin guts. You guys go ahead and set up, I'll be right there."

She trotted upstairs as fast as her legs could move and slid on her socks across the hardwood to her dresser. Humming "This is Halloween," she thumbed through her crewnecks. She grabbed the sweatshirt with a Ouija board motif and tugged her pumpkin guts sweater off. As her pulled-back hair breached the bottom, she felt Evan's arms wrap around her bare middle.

"Did you come up here for a reason, Lawson?"

He pulled her hips back against him and leaned down, pressing a kiss on her shoulder. "Yes, there was something very important for me to come in here and get." She felt him grow hard against her backside, and ground back into him, her hand lacing through his hair while he kissed her again. He made a small hissing noise, his hands starting to wander, fingers inching towards the waistband of her leggings.

"Really? Something you had to *get*, huh?"

He groaned. "I'm going to go tell them that we're actually both sick and they need to leave right now so I can ravage you."

Frankie faced him and grabbed his chin, glaring. "If you intend to deny me baked goods and horror movies during Samhain, I will make you pay for it."

He grinned, cheeks pushing against her grip. Taking her other hand, he held it to his pants so she could feel him get even harder. "Please use this tone later, *fuck.*"

She kissed him, using that hand to palm him through his jeans. He groaned. "*Frankie.*" Pulling back, she patted his cheek and trotted out of the bedroom before he could grab her.

The Sawtooth Baddies retired to the den, a virtual stack of horror flicks and baked goods awaiting them. Frankie nestled into Evan's side with her drink, cramming next to costumed Bex and Jack on the sectional. "You two are taking up twice as much space in costume."

Jack stretched their long legs out and propped their feet on the coffee table. "Hey, I went wigless for your comfort, so I don't want to hear it." They took a long sip of their whiskey.

Clemmie approached the group and stood on his hind legs, trying to locate an empty space. Not finding it, he yowled loudly. Frankie patted her lap, and he leaped up, already purring, the final piece now in place.

Frankie knew that November would be a weird, liminal month. October always felt like approaching a strange door. She never knew what was behind it but loved the excitement, the danger, the possibilities. But November felt like her front door had been blown wide open, and a stranger was already inside her house. This year especially filled her with dread of what might come for her. But tonight, it was still October. Tonight, she was crammed onto her sectional with her favorite people, who were starting up the first *Scream* movie. Outside of her creepy Victorian house, the dark stirred with invisible, watching things. And she would worry about them tomorrow.

THE SAWTOOTH BADDIES WILL RETURN IN BOOK 2 OF THE BLACK CAT SERIES

Follow @kendallmckenzieauthor on Instagram for updates.

ACKNOWLEDGMENTS

Putting together an Acknowledgments page for a novel I wrote is surreal to a level I can't comprehend. A Taste For Hell lived inside of me for months before I had to exorcise it and get it on paper. It kept me awake at night, noisy in my brain, invading my dreams. I wrote the bulk of the first draft when I was grieving and also recovering from a hysterectomy. I wasn't able to use my normal outlet to process the tough stuff (weightlifting), so I had to find another way. It was uncomfortable and hard. I turned my brain inside out trying to articulate it.

The two events are intertwined in my mind, and during this season of discomfort and grief, I leaned on so many people while this story was haunting me and absorbing my focus. Thank you to everyone who sent us flowers, food, and virtual hugs during that time.

First and foremost, to my partner, Matt: thank you for giving me the space and capacity to take on an insane project at a hard time in our lives, and for understanding my ADHD brain's hyperfixation while I was working on it. Thank you for listening to me rant and question myself, and for going on walks with me when my hands ached from typing. Thank you for believing in me. Thank you for always making me laugh on the hard days, which we had plenty of over the last year. I love you, I love you.

Sarbs, thank you for being an endless fountain of industry knowledge, suggestions, encouragement, and for always having the answer. I'm so lucky to have you as a friend.

Melia, Amanda, and Shaunna—thank y'all for always asking me how the process was going, being my champions, and cheering me on. You have no idea how much I needed that during this process. It fueled me on the tough days.

Mom, Dad, Cam—can y'all believe this weird ass idea has come this far? I cannot. Thank you for being so supportive and interested in the process while I was learning and working through it. Mom, thank you for reading those early pages and your kind words. You were the first to read anything, and having your notes encouraged me to keep going when I had doubts. Thank you for also taking a risk on reading something that might give you nightmares.

A huge, huge thank you to my reader and copyeditor, Kimberly Dyer (@thekimberlydyer). I'm sorry for my dyslexic brain and so grateful to you for your labor on this story. Your brilliant notes improved the manuscript tenfold.

Another huge, huge thank you to Damian Modena (@demilustraciones) for creating a cover design that made me actually cry. What a badass way to introduce this series to world.

I have to thank my Familiar here, who was with me on my desk when I first unearthed the idea for this series, and whose passing opened the door to let it flow out. She always found her way into my spelling circles and screamed at my feet when I did fire magic. I love you, Pumpkin. I wrote Clemmie just for you. And although I couldn't sell a piece of myself to keep you around for a bit longer, you know I would have. I'll see you again someday, and in the meantime, I'll see you in my dreams.

And thank you, reader. I hope you enjoyed it. If you are also grieving, I hope the story's processing of death spoke some truth to you. If you are healing or about to start the process, I believe in you. If Frankie can do it, so can you. May you all have a found family like the Sawtooth Baddies.

Y'all come back now, ya'hear?

ABOUT THE AUTHOR

Kendall McKenzie is a displaced Southerner living in Minnesota, and a poet and author of spooky stories. She holds an M.F.A. from Queens University of Charlotte, and has published poetry in places like BlazeVOX, Permafrost, and Bayou Magazine.

A perfect weekend day entails weightlifting for two hours, eating her weight in barbeque, and then typing away on her new book on the couch with a glass of whiskey while her partner watches Philadelphia sports. She has two cats, who are destructive, adorable, goofy assh*les. They're lucky they're so cute.

Kendall is a practicing witch and pagan. When she isn't writing, she can be found watching horror movies, getting stuck in an enormous DIY project, or gardening.

Made in the USA
Columbia, SC
14 September 2024

744013f0-c433-41d8-8939-a88aa4e143a6R01